Her face was ~~buried betwee~~ y
buried betwee t.
She wore a shirt and o o
mid-thigh.

Something about this body struck me like a warning blow to the chest. I thought I knew it. If I was right, my hand had been in love with this body, had caressed it. As I bent to find out, my gut clenched.

A river of dried blood flowed from the slashed neck; a carotid artery had doubtless been severed, maybe both. I had to lean across the body and move the bed skirt for a glimpse of the face. But by then I knew.

ARTIST'S PROOF

GORDON COTLER

WORLDWIDE.

TORONTO • NEW YORK • LONDON
AMSTERDAM • PARIS • SYDNEY • HAMBURG
STOCKHOLM • ATHENS • TOKYO • MILAN
MADRID • WARSAW • BUDAPEST • AUCKLAND

ARTIST'S PROOF

A Worldwide Mystery/February 1999

First published by St. Martin's Press, Incorporated.

ISBN 0-373-26300-7

Copyright © 1997 by Gordon Cotler.
All rights reserved. No part of this book may be reproduced or transmitted in any form or by any means, electronic or mechanical, including photocopying, recording or by any information storage and retrieval system, without permission in writing from the publisher. For information, contact:
St. Martin's Press, Incorporated, 175 Fifth Avenue,
New York, NY 10010-7848 U.S.A.

All characters in this book are fictitious, and any resemblance to actual persons, living or dead, is purely coincidental.

® and TM are trademarks of Harlequin Enterprises Limited. Trademarks indicated with ® are registered in the United States Patent and Trademark Office, the Canadian Trade Marks Office and in other countries.

Printed in U.S.A.

For
Amy, Joanna, and Ellen
with love

1

A LONG FRIDAY...

ONE

THE MORNING OF THE DAY I was accused of murdering a sixteen-year-old girl I happened to open my eyes at daybreak, an hour or more before my usual time. I had every intention of shutting them instantly. No such luck. I found myself looking up at that offending hand, the grotesque hand that had begun to bug me yesterday. That did it; I knew I wouldn't get back to sleep. Not until I'd fixed the damn thing.

I once read somewhere that Beethoven's family would get him out of bed in the morning (was it Beethoven or was it Haydn?) by playing an unfinished phrase on the piano (or was it the harpsichord?) The poor composer would have to drag himself to the instrument and hit that last note to get some relief. The principle seems to work for painters. For this one, anyway.

I knew that hand wasn't right from the moment I painted it. The way the thumb met the palm wasn't abstract, or expressionist, or surreal, it was just unhuman—more like a saguaro cactus that had been hit by a truck. I couldn't stand looking at it that way another minute, especially as it was about twice the size of a normal hand. It would have to be fixed, and now.

I was working large. Really large. The back wall of my studio/home was higher than it was wide. I had twelve feet of canvas nailed across it, and the canvas fell fourteen feet, to about waist height. To reach that miserable hand I had to scramble to the top of my rolling aluminum scaffold clutching a can of brushes, naked as a blue-assed baboon. I had a week's supply of acrylics plus a couple of rollers stashed on the platform.

I put in a concentrated twenty minutes on the hand before I finally felt the sense of relief Beethoven, or whoever, must have gotten from playing that final note. By this time there was no way I would get back to sleep, so I figured I'd put in an hour with a sketch pad somewhere down the beach.

It had been at least a year since I'd gone out to draw with the morning sun still almost touching the ocean and the beach houses flooded with that low, straight-on light. My drawing doesn't have much to do with my painting, but I have to draw every day—people, houses, beach junk, anything my eye falls on. Call it a compulsion, but drawing is a use-it-or-lose-it proposition. A violinist who doesn't practice every day is a fiddler whose hat sits upside down on the sidewalk. I pulled on sneakers, jeans, work shirt, and heavy windbreaker. At the beginning of May, the east end of Long Island can still get a chill breeze off the ocean in the early morning. I scooped up my drawing kit and a giant pad.

My house has two doors, one to a footpath through the dunes to the beach, the other facing the gravel automobile road that is scratched across what was once a potato field. I went out the beach door.

I've mentioned "the east end of Long Island" and "my house," and I may have conjured up an image of some post-modern bleached-wood architect's conceit in the Hamptons costing in the neighborhood of a million. I was not in that neighborhood. In actual fact, my place was not much more than a shack that could have been cast ashore on a high tide and might go out again on the next. Nor was it located in one of the cutting-edge, frantic, celebrity-intensive Hamptons. Not nearly.

When I was on the NYPD—I had been off the cops about a year at this time—word circulated that Sid Shale had this beach house out on the South Fork. On a lieutenant's salary. Internal Affairs fell over itself launching an investigation.

Two IA guys actually shlepped out here on the Long Island Expressway on a Friday afternoon in July, a journey I support as a harsh alternative to capital punishment. When the guys reached my place, hot, sweaty, irritable—ready, I suspect, to file charges if they found so much as a deposit bottle I couldn't account for—they took one look and collapsed in each other's arms, dissolved in laughter. I happened to be in residence at the time (I was taking a vacation week to paint), and I witnessed the scene through a window, including Cop A's gasped, "That's a *house?*"

Since then, the beach house had become my principal residence—in fact my only residence—and I had done some work on the place. I insulated and heated it for year-round use. I cut a window on the beach side in the shape of either a swordfish or a blowfish, take your pick. I raised my bed on a platform, so I could store paints and stretched canvases underneath. I painted the outside walls in three not nearly complementary colors and constructed a huge found-object sculpture outside each exterior door and named them *Flotsam* and *Jetsam.* Most important, I lifted one wall eight feet because I wanted the added painting surface. That made for a shed roof, and I installed a skylight in it.

Despite what I had spent on winterizing, the structural changes made the place nearly unheatable in months with an *R* in them; I consoled myself during those months by eating oysters whenever I could afford them. I took further comfort in the thought that my abode was probably as warm as Buckingham Palace; if the queen could take it, so could I. And with the added height I could work big. Really big.

THE DIRTY SAND was strewn with assorted junk and the remains of marine life—most prominently, the nearly black lengths of stringy seaweed I think of as the discarded hair of mermaids who come ashore in the night for a cut, bleach, and set. A few more weeks would pass before the village would begin raking the beach to tempt sunbathers. I would more than likely make a find this morning for either *Flotsam* or *Jetsam.* These were, and always would be, "works in progress."

I decided to head west. I had drawn the houses in that direction many times—the nearest was nearly a quarter of a mile distant—but the unfamiliar early light made them seem almost a new challenge. The low sun barely warmed the left side of my face as I picked my way over the minigorges and temporary rivulets created by winter storms.

I walked a few hundred yards without seeing a soul. But then, as soon as I found a likely spot to settle down for a first sketch—an overview of sand, sky, and houses—a gaunt figure rose over the dunes some distance ahead: Don Quixote with lance. He came from the road, made for the high-water mark, and then ambled along it in my direction. When he got close I saw that his pantaloons were actually baggy jeans tucked into high rubber boots, and the lance was a fishing rod. He wore a floppy hat and a torn T-shirt, and a creel was slung over a shoulder.

He was a surf caster out after bluefish. If these guys ever haul one in, I've never seen it. I'm willing to believe they're all following doctor's orders to do an exercise designed to strengthen a weak wrist.

I hoped this one would take his stand before he reached me, so I could put some foreground interest in my sketch. But on an otherwise deserted beach the man of La Mancha didn't stop walking until he was abreast of me. By this time I was sitting on a west-facing perch on the high-water shelf, pad on my knees, pencils, pens, and charcoals stuck points up in the sand, water jar, paints, and brush beside them.

The fisherman eyed me resentfully. Since I had picked this spot, it must be a good one; never mind that I wasn't equipped for fishing.

"You planning to stay here?" he asked stupidly.

"Maybe twenty minutes."

He thought for a moment. "Well...you was here first." Fair was fair. He turned and continued on down the beach.

"Hook the queen of the bluefish," I called after him. I was glad to see him disappear. After ten minutes of futile casting he would have put down his rod, taken up a position at my back, and advised me that I wasn't getting it quite right. Bad enough I had to take criticism from the seagulls that sometimes waddled up and quickly waddled away, unimpressed.

I faced up the beach and began drawing. Pencil to virgin

paper, I started as I always do, in the lower right-hand corner and working my way up and across. No blocking, no erasures, no hesitation in my long unbroken lines. No conscious thought, actually; my eye signals my hand without the message passing through my brain. Total commitment to the moment. Drawing is the purest, truest, most naked form of art, the keenest challenge to the artist. It brings my senses alive, it makes my blood pound. As almost always, I had a hell of a good time.

BACK HOME AGAIN I was surprised to find the answering machine blinking at this early hour. I punched Play, recognized Leona Morgenstern's voice, and started making coffee. I knew it would be ground, dripped, and possibly half drunk before Lonnie signed off. She was in her shrill mode:

"Sid…? Are you there…? For God's sake, pick up.... *Hello-o-o-o…?* Where the hell are you at seven-forty-one in the a.m., passed out? Have you taken up serious drinking? Sid, you can't drink like Jackson Pollock until you *sell* like Jackson Pollock. Which brings me to my point. I've got hold of a live one. Remember the Texan I told you about who came in on Tuesday asking to see your work? Rich Texans are harder to sniff out since they got out of oil, but this one gave off a heady aroma. Computer software? Rocket components? Something.

"Sid, he wants to meet you. Six p.m. sharp at the gallery. To*day*. This is a command performance, don't fail me. Show up on time and make nice for a change. And Sid, need I remind you, your daughter is not in community college, she's at *Bennington* College. For ten dollars less she could live at the Waldorf. With room service. Sid, you can paint, but can you sell? The jury is still out.

"Oh! I forgot to ask the other day. Are you still on that 'I'm working big, really big' kick? Because the buyers for corporate board rooms aren't buying these days, and if they were they wouldn't buy a larger-than-life expressionist painting that shows the final collapse of the greedy class on the beaches of eastern Long Island—your cry of conscience that

I think of as the *Guernica* of the Hamptons, and who needs
it? So, Sid, will you please—''

I shut the thing off and climbed to the top of my extruded
aluminum scaffold with my coffee mug and went back to
attacking the canvas. Lonnie was wrong, of course. No way
was this work an homage to Picasso. If it had been, I would
have admitted it. Many good paintings have been inspired by
other paintings. And *expressionist?* Not by a long shot, but
Lonnie felt more secure when she had a handle to hang on
to.

I hate having my work dropped in a slot, assigned a style,
a school, a fashion. I don't have any theories about painting
and I don't want to be put in a school. I never did like school.
I paint, take it or leave it. And if Lonnie saw a moral statement here, the baggage was hers. I called the piece *Large*,
and that was as much as I had to say about it.

Large II, actually; I had destroyed a failed *Large I*. The
Roman numerals were to mark the work as an event, like
those attached to the Super Bowl. I needed the attention because I needed a sale, and Roman numerals are emotion neutral; they don't tell you how to think about the work.

But Lonnie could not be dismissed out of hand. She was
a shrewd judge of the market, and she had more than an art
dealer's interest in the salability of my work. I did have a
daughter at Bennington. Lonnie and I split the tuition, the
dentist, the works, as Sarah was daughter to us both. We had
been divorced eight years, but Lonnie was a staunch promoter of my work, and the Leona Morgenstern Gallery had
been the force behind whatever success I'd had as a painter.

She and I met at the Art Students League in 1977, when
I had been on the cops about a year and was taking a couple
of evening classes. All I had really wanted to do since I was
six was make pictures, but I knew early on it was unlikely
I'd make a living at art. My father had said, "Get a job with
the city. Teach school. The pension will allow you to paint
till your ass falls off."

A pension looked good to my father, who would never
have one. Pop was a cab driver—one of a fading breed of

true professionals who knew the city block by block, from Kingsbridge to Coney Island. He and my uncle Carl were paying down the cost of a taxi medallion, and they each drove twelve hours a day, six days a week. Two guys leased the cab from them on Sundays. When Pop was shot to death a few years ago, it was in a cab bearing the medallion he was still four years short of co-owning.

I had piled up sixty credits at Brooklyn College when my father gave me his career advice. Rather than wait the additional years I would need, with the added financial pressure, to get a teaching license, I looked around for another job with the city. I could become a policeman in a fraction of the time it would take to become a teacher; the Police Academy, I was told, was easier to get into than Shea Stadium. And the police pension would also let me paint till my ass fell off, and I could start collecting after twenty years. So I went on the cops.

That nearly killed my mother, but she survived—anyway, until Pop was murdered. That knocked the stuffing out of her and she joined him a few months later. It was the day I made sergeant. Ever since, the word *sergeant* has carried negative vibes for me.

I HAD BEEN on a white hot painting streak all week, determined to pull the top third of *Large* into a cohesive whole. My brush hand flew, guided by no more than a vague notion of where I was headed. The salesman who kept me in acrylics—he did a circuit of the professionals in the area once a month—had been around the day before, and he left a happy man. He must have thought I had a commission to paint a barn. A three-inch brush was the smallest I wielded on this big top-size canvas, and I was using that sparingly. Mostly I laid on with rollers and quality house painter's brushes.

That morning, the morning of Cassie Brennan's murder, it was working high on the wall at the top of my scaffold that triggered my troubles. What happened was this: After an hour or so of painting I laid down my brush to get some perspective on what I had done. I could have climbed down from the scaffold and backed off to the east wall of the shack to survey the work, but that would have wasted precious minutes at a time when I was on a streak. Instead, I did something dumb.

My scaffold was a lightweight construct with wheels, and it had a brake I could control from the platform. I released the brake and pushed off from the painting to roll the scaffold tower back to a six-by-six beam that ran from side wall to side wall, parallel to the painting and about eight feet away from it. The roof used to sit on this beam, but since I had lifted it into a shed there was enough air above the beam to allow me to crouch or lie on it and contemplate my work. An awkward arrangement, but did Michelangelo have it any better in the Sistine Chapel?

The trouble was, I was so intent on seeing what I had wrought that I forgot to reset the brake. When I hopped from scaffold to beam, one of my departing feet sent the tower rolling back to the painting wall, well beyond safe reach. The work I had done looked good—it looked *very* good—but there now arose the problem of how to get safely back to it.

A daring leap might have put me back on the scaffold. Or it might have deposited me on the floor. I didn't like the odds, nor those of the alternative, purposely dropping straight from the beam to the floor. My right ankle had been broken years earlier in a foolish jump from a fire escape while I was on a stakeout that unraveled. During weather changes the ankle still reminded me of that day.

What had been my all-fired hurry to get off that tenement fire escape? My showboating hadn't resulted in a collar. And what was my hurry now? I had no immediate place to go, and—I consulted my watch—I was expecting my model, Gayle Hennessy, in about ten minutes. Gayle would rescue me.

So I stretched out on the beam and admired my work. It pulsed with life. It held together. The colors worked. It was good. It was damn good.

And then, because I had all the time in the world to contemplate it, I did start to see things I could fix. Little things, but there they were. Par for the course. I don't fiddle with my drawings, but my paint can pile up on canvas like butter cream on a birthday cake. It would happen here.

The minutes crept by. I had thought maybe Gayle might be early; she wasn't. I wasn't in pain up there on that beam, but neither was I having much fun. And the longer I looked at the damn painting—there wasn't anything else to do—the more things I saw wrong with it. There would be damage control tomorrow. Severe damage control. Working large, really large, carried penalties.

The phone rang. My outgoing message is brief, some say abrupt. Preferable to cute. "Sid Shale here. Please leave your name and number, the purpose of your call, and the time. Thank you." I figure if I keep it short, they'll keep it short.

I knew the voice before he said his name: Chuck Scully, a likeable youngster who was acting chief of the small village police force. "Hello...? Lieutenant Shale, you there...?"

I had told him more than once please not to call me lieutenant. "I guess you're not there," he went on. "This is Chuck Scully down at the police station? Could you give me a call when you get in? Something's come up I want to talk to you about. No hurry, it's not that important. Well, sooner's better than later. Oh, it's—let's see—nine-thirty-two. In the morning. 'Bye,"

Looking back many hours later, I knew I should have risked a broken ankle to pick up the damn phone.

My immediate problem was solved a few minutes later. Gayle walked in, radiant as always. She looked around, called, "Sid? You here, or what?"

I grunted, and she looked up, startled. Then she grinned. "You devil," she said. "Are we going to work today, or are we going to play hide and seek?"

TWO

I REFERRED TO Gayle Hennessy as my model. She would have called me her planning consultant. We were on a barter system. When Gayle moved out from the city to open a small shop in the village to sell beachwear of her own design, I helped her lay out the place, paint the interior, and make a sign to go above the door that would attract the summer people without violating the village signage code.

Gayle and I had crossed paths a few times in New York. The first was many years ago when she was seventeen, a skinny high school junior who had just started picking up change after school by running errands for a small-time north Harlem drug middleman. I was the one who nailed her, only I never made it a collar, never took her in for booking. I did make a point of cuffing her, and the hard reality of cold metal against wristbones scared the daylights out of her. She swore through a gallon of tears that if I let her go she would never get in trouble again.

I had heard that song often enough before, but—I don't know why—this was the first time I believed it; certainly the first time I acted on it. Maybe in part because she wasn't a user, mostly because she seemed smart enough to be able to take hold of her life.

She lived with a grandmother who obviously couldn't handle her, but she had an aunt in South Carolina. I told her she could go down there and finish school; or, if she preferred, I would run her in. I put her on the bus myself the next day. My partner didn't approve—he didn't approve of blacks in general—but I didn't approve of everything he was up to, and our code was to keep our mouths shut about what the other one did.

The next time Gayle and I met, years later, she was the

live-in girlfriend of a painter I knew and earning a decent living as a dress model on Seventh Avenue. I wouldn't have recognized her but she remembered me, "the Jewish cop with a heart of chopped liver." She whooped a greeting and hugged me tightly. In addition to a certain savvy she had gained a shitload of confidence. She knew who she was.

We kept vaguely in touch, mostly through her boyfriend. When she eventually dumped him she decided to strike out on a path that would give her a measure of freedom from both employers and men. She had evolved into a no-hips, long-waisted stunner with legs to her belly button, velvety brown skin, enormous eyes, and auburn hair out of left field. She dressed mostly in clothes of her own design, and friends had been urging her to turn the talent to money.

Was it a talent? Gayle would have drawn applause dressed in twin pillowcases. The question was, Could she do for women who ground their teeth in jealousy when she sashayed by what she had done for herself? Probably yes, but it would take another season or two before they trusted her.

In advance of the tourist season she was paying off her barter debt by giving me two mornings a week—helping me organize the place and sitting for an easel portrait. I hated doing academic painting; fortunately, I could never be truly academic. But I knew as well as Lonnie Morgenstern that I was unlikely to sell *Large*. Gayle in a green caftan against a bare wood wall might be marketable—especially since, for insurance, one of her long, perfectly shaped legs was exposed, like a smooth-flowing river, all the way to its source. I was calling the thing *Green and Brown Morning*. A working title.

Months before, when we first got together on our two projects, I had hopes that the same thought would enter Gayle's head that had crept into mine: Wouldn't it be lovely to hop in the sack with this person? I sensed that the needle on her sex-awareness meter did jump once or twice in response to me before it settled down at zero.

By then, so had mine. The choice was between a brief, passionate fling that might come to a sour end, and a long friendship. I valued the possibilities in the friendship. Maybe she had gone through the same reasoning. It had been more than a year since there had been a woman in my life, but I told myself that was by choice; it allowed me to focus on my work.

GAYLE AND I put in a productive couple of hours on *Green and Brown Morning*. The canvas was turning out even slicker than I had intended. Sometimes you have to bend with the prevailing winds—in this case the monstrous college tuition bill that loomed before me.

It wasn't until Gayle left at about noon that I remembered the message from Chuck Scully on my answering machine. I called the police station in the village hall and got the civilian clerk who doubled at the switchboard, a retired school-teacher I knew only as Helen. She said, "Yes, Mr. Shale, Chief Scully did want to talk to you, but he's not here." She sounded distraught. "He went out. I'm really sorry."

"Okay, no problem. Just tell him I'm returning his call."

"I'll tell him when I see him, but I have no idea when that will be. Really no idea at all."

She was breathless; something was up. There had been a rash of bicycle thefts in the area (at least four); maybe Chuck was following a hot lead.

"Is he out on a case?" I asked.

"I'm not authorized to talk about anything," she said. "Anything at all."

Authorized was too big a word for everyday use in a nine-man police force; something was definitely up. I said, "Thank you, Helen." And then, as an afterthought, "Do you know what he wanted me for?"

"Oh, that. I... He..." She made a decision. "He'd better tell you himself." A second mystery. Heavy.

No sooner had I hung up than Gayle charged back into the house, her big eyes even bigger. "Sid," she gasped, "there's been a murder. Right up the beach."

So that answered question number one. "Where?"

"About a quarter of a mile. The big white house? Actually, it's the next place west. You know those people?"

"Name of Sharanov. I've never met anyone there, but I'm not surprised. Who got killed?"

"I don't know. I was driving by and there were two police cars out front. I've never seen two police cars together in this town except at Mel's." Mel's Deep Sea was the diner favored by locals. "A cop was posted in the driveway and I asked him what was up. He said someone had been killed inside. That was all he would say, except that Chief Scully was in the house."

Chuck Scully was really only acting chief; the chief, a much older man, had been on extended sick leave for over a year. The paperwork on a homicide was going to overwhelm poor Chuck; he was barely up to the challenge of the bicycle thief. I said, "Maybe I'll take a run over. Just to see what's going on."

Gayle and I left together.

I LIKED SKETCHING the Sharanov house, but I found it otherwise to be a rude intrusion on my low-key east end skyline, way over scale in size and cost. It was only two stories high, but an especially tall cathedral ceiling on the ocean side pointed a "screw you" finger at the sky. Of course that was a subjective judgment, but from what I knew about the owner, he was a "screw you" kind of guy.

Mikhael "Misha" Sharanov was a Russian immigrant, one of the earliest settlers in the vast Russian, mostly Jewish community in Brooklyn centered in Brighton Beach. He had come from the Soviet Union in the first wave of emigration the Soviets permitted Jews after decades of hassling them while at the same time denying them the option of leaving the country.

Most of those who came out were a cross section of ground-down Soviet citizens, but the commissars didn't miss a chance to stick it to America. They dipped into the prisons and shipped us a choice assortment of hardened criminals, establishing an MO Fidel Castro gleefully followed in Cuba with the famous boat exodus from Mariel.

The engineers, doctors, musicians, and other professionals among the Russian immigrants mostly struggled for years before they got a toehold here. The criminals went right to work in their chosen field, and many of them flourished. When I first learned Sharanov was my neighbor in Quincacogue I looked him up in confidential police reports.

As a young punk, not much over twenty, he had formed a small gang that shook down Russian merchants in the busy shops under the el in Brighton Beach, a craft he learned by studying Chinese gangs in lower Manhattan and Italian gangs on the Brooklyn waterfront. America proved to be the land of opportunity, and he moved on to fancier stuff—insurance ripoffs, smuggling, and, most profitably, a complicated scam that robbed the federal government of millions in cigarette taxes, his "thank you" for having been given sanctuary here. Several murders were laid at his door but, unfortunately, none *inside* that door; he had been arrested a few times, but no charge had ever stuck.

As he passed forty, he had gone almost mainstream. His designer beach house (too upscale for the neighborhood) was only one sign of his new gentility. The most important was the huge restaurant/nightclub he owned in farthest Brooklyn, the Tundra, the kind of place that otherwise exists only in movies made in the 1930s.

The Tundra was well beyond what was then my bailiwick, Midtown South in Manhattan, but a year or so before I retired I did go there one evening on a tip that a witness who had been dodging me for weeks had made a reservation for that night. When I walked through the door my jaw dropped to my belt.

In a vast space lit by countless fairy lights (this had once been a warehouse, but you'd never know it), waiters and captains in tuxes hovered attentively over the patrons, many hundreds of them, almost every one a Russian, dressed to the nines. Plates of hors d'oeuvres—herrings, meats, dumplings,

God knows what—covered the tables in such abundance they had to be piled two and sometimes three high.

The revelers danced to an orchestra of twenty-six musicians, my count. And serious revelers they were, juiced to the scalp. Drinks were by the bottle, and the bottles, all vodka, were being carried off empty by busboys almost as fast as glasses might be in a lesser nightspot. It looked like New Year's Eve, but this was a nothing-special rainy Saturday night in November.

My witness was expected, I was told, but had not yet arrived. While I waited I hoped to get a glimpse of the famous Misha Sharanov—I had seen a surveillance picture of him—but he was nowhere in evidence. The place was in the hands of minions, four or five of whom formed a loose cordon around my partner and myself when we identified ourselves.

They gave us a range of attitudes. Two or three were big, with faces that had been carved, badly, from yams; they glowered and pressed close, but they knew enough not to make physical contact. The others were smaller, more social, actually polite. All were in starched dickeys. The scene was right off a cable TV rerun of a Warner Brothers movie starring a snarling Edward G. Robinson and a dapper George Raft.

When my witness showed, we took him into the cloakroom and scared what we needed out of him. Then I sent him to join his party, and I took one more look around the big room, still hoping to spot Sharanov. No such luck. I was reminded of the unseen menace in horror movies; once it's shown the terror dissipates.

As I turned to leave, one of the politer minions smiled expansively. In an accent you couldn't cut with a chain saw he said, "Enchoy your eef-ning, Lieutenant."

I said, "I'll do that. And please thank Mr. Sharanov for his hospitality."

The minion looked as if I had socked him in the nose, and those behind him twitched. He called after me, "What Mr. Sharanov? Dere is no Mr. Sharanov." In the Soviet Union of old you admitted nothing to the police, not even that you might have taken a bath that day.

A yam head was holding open the door for me, a huge man, antsy for me to leave. I looked up at him and said, "Boris, do you check to make sure that every party in the room has a designated driver?"

He didn't have the least idea what I was talking about, but for a fleeting instant he looked worried. I patted him reassuringly on the shoulder and left.

So I never did get a glimpse of Sharanov. Not even as his neighbor at the beach.

GAYLE DROVE ON toward the village and her shop, Gayle's Provocativo; preseason, she didn't open until one o'clock. I was right behind her in my aging Chevy pickup, but I peeled off at the long Sharanov driveway.

The front elevation of the aggressively modern Sharanov house was an affront to the eye, with more angles than an origami. It was now partially blocked by the two police cars Gayle had spotted, plus a large maroon Cadillac I had seen parked there before. I recognized the tubby cop on duty out front when I pulled up. He tipped his hat in deference to a former big-city detective.

"Afternoon, Lieutenant."

"It's Sid, Walter. What's going on?"

He looked up the road before he answered, an unnecessary caution; there wasn't a chance anyone was close enough to eavesdrop, as none of the houses immediately beyond, all strictly summer places, had been opened for the season. When he confirmed that we were alone he ventured, "There's been a murder. How about that? Someone got killed in there."

"Who?" If someone had to be dead I hoped it was Sharanov or one of his thugs.

The cop leaned his moon face in my open window. "I suppose it's all right to tell you. The girl who cleans up. Housekeeper, maid, whatever you want to call her. How about that?"

That came as a surprise. "Okay if I go in?"

"I guess. The chief's inside. Sure, Chuck'll be glad to see you."

I climbed out of the cab. "He call for a Crime Scene Unit from County?" I asked.

"Supposed to be one on the way."

That was a start. I turned toward the house, walked a few yards, then stopped and turned back again at the sound of an approaching vehicle. A tow truck was roaring toward us from the west at a speed the road wasn't prepared for; gravel flew. The truck spun into the driveway and headed for the Cadillac's rear end, seemingly prepared to climb in its roomy trunk. It stopped on a dime, inches away, and a dark, good-looking young guy in coveralls leaped out and started toward the house. His bushy brows were knitted in pain or anger, maybe both.

The tubby cop grabbed him around the waist and held him. It wasn't easy. "No you don't, Paulie."

Paulie's dark face grew darker. "For Chrissakes, Walter, that's my girl in there."

The cop's arms were short, but he held on. "There's nothing you can do for her. We even sent her mom away. I got orders not to let anyone in. You wouldn't *want* to go in. You understand?"

"The hell I do," Paulie exploded. He broke Walter's grip with an elbow to his gut and a sharp chop to a restraining arm with the side of his hand. Then he took a couple of long strides toward the house.

The cop was hurting, and he didn't follow. His contribution to securing the crime scene was to gasp through his pain, "You get the hell back here, Malatesta!"

Paulie Malatesta. I had heard the name somewhere. I stepped in front of him. We were chest to chest, roughly the same height. "Easy, Paulie," I said. "Didn't you hear the officer?"

"Who the fuck are you?"

"A neighbor. Why don't you do what Walter says, Paulie? Go back to work. Better yet, go home." I figured that a few sentences delivered in a reasonable voice would help steady him. "When the time is right, they'll tell you everything you need to know. I'm sure they know how to find you." I had read the logo on his truck, HUGGINS SERVICE STA.

"Screw you," Paulie said. He jerked his head toward the Caddy. "That's Sharanov's car. You with him? One of his goons? The creep did it, didn't he? I'll kill him, so help me." His rage was still building, and it was making him a little crazy. "Get the fuck out of my way."

When I didn't, he raised both hands to my chest and pushed. Fat Walter was letting me handle this—in deference to my previous rank, I supposed. I gave with the push, dissipating its force. Then I grabbed one of Paulie's outstretched arms with my two and bent it behind him and up. I had done something like this often enough, but not in years. My body responded grudgingly; I was forty-one, Paulie twenty-three or -four. But the move still worked well enough, and I managed to get him down on his knees. Almost by reflex I reached for the cuffs I didn't have.

Paulie gasped, cried "Hey!" and then *"Hey!"* He had acted tough, but he was mostly bluff. I eased up a bit.

Now Walter came lumbering up, breathing hard, his service revolver half out of its holster. "Okay, Paulie, back in your truck. Out of here. Now."

The fight had drained entirely from the kid. He stumbled to the tow truck, biting his lip, holding back tears. "That bastard. I'll kill him. I'll kill him."

He suddenly bent down, scooped up a handful of bluestone pebbles from the driveway, and hurled them at the Cadillac. But the action, like the threat, came more from despair than anger, and the pebbles bounced harmlessly off a wheel cover. He climbed into his truck, turned the motor on, and poked his head out the window toward Walter and me.

"She was sixteen years old," he called through his tears. The motor roared, and he backed out and drove off as recklessly as he had come.

IT WAS ONE of those upside down houses—bedrooms below, common areas upstairs. The living room had been placed on

the upper floor to give it a dramatic perch above the ocean
and to allow for the cathedral ceiling that reached for the
moon. An exterior ramp, curled like a wood shaving, led
directly to the main entrance on this second level.

The door was open, and I walked in. From just inside I
could hear voices rising from the bedroom floor, but I was
alone on this level. I took half a minute to soak in the room.

"For the rich they sing," my father used to say as he
wiped the bird droppings from the windshield of his taxi.
And for Misha Sharanov, who was rich enough, the ocean
looked bluer, grander, more dramatic through the huge windows of his floor-through postmodern living room than it did
through the smaller, salt-crusted windows of my shed. Scully
hadn't put up crime scene tape, nor had he posted a cop up
here, so he must have assumed the bedroom floor was all
that counted for purposes of his investigation. A possibly
foolish assumption.

It was a minimalist room—unfussy designer furniture in
lacquer finishes and pastel fabrics, with plenty of space between the pieces. Nothing dark or lumpily Russian; Sharanov's taste, or his decorator's, was cutting-edge American.
Except for some dirty drinking glasses, crumpled cocktail
napkins, and half-filled ashtrays, the room looked in order.
In an adjoining open kitchen I glimpsed dirty dishes piled
next to a sink. I made sure not to touch anything, and I
crossed the bare, hardwood floor on tiptoe.

Like most painters, when I walk into a house the first thing
I look at is whatever is on the walls. I used to catch myself
doing that when I entered a crime scene as a cop on duty. I
don't know why I hadn't done it here. When I did get around
to these walls, after about fifteen seconds on the view and
the furniture, my eye locked instantly on the single piece
hanging there. It startled me.

Because it was mine, an ink drawing, with wash, of Covenant Street in the village. This was the wrong room for it,
and it was on the wrong wall, but after the initial surprise it
gave me a surge of remembered pleasure, like running into

an old friend I thought had gone away forever. And then I had a further reaction—a flash of uneasiness, as though the ground had shifted slightly under me.

I had donated this drawing to the volunteer fire department months before, to be auctioned at their annual fund-raiser. The chief had sent me a grateful note a few weeks ago letting me know that it had been bought, at a nice price, "by a collector who wants to remain anonymous."

A good drawing. My eye traced its lines, and I was carried back to the bench in front of the ice cream shop where I sat and drew it on a raw fall afternoon and knew almost from the first few lines that it would go well. So this was where it had ended up. As the tubby cop out front might have said, How about that?

An interior ramp substituted for stairs. I took it down to the first floor, where I had heard the voices, and followed a hallway past a closed door with a single length of crime scene tape angled across it, like the seal of approval on a motel toilet seat. Chuck Scully was standing just inside an open doorway farther along. He was closing his cellular phone and his greeting to me was a nervous half-smile. I doubt Scully had ever been to a homicide scene before, and the gravity of the occasion had dampened his usual high spirits. But I could tell he was not unhappy to see me.

Chuck was a narrow-faced man with a prominent nose, and he might one day mature into everyone's image of Sherlock Holmes. Not yet. He was smart, but he was green. Several village cops had more seniority than he; Chuck had been anointed acting chief because he was the only college graduate on the force, and he had minored in criminology.

"Lieutenant Shale," he breathed, almost in relief.

"Afternoon, Chief."

He waved the phone. "Walter filled me in on your help out front. Thanks."

He didn't ask what had brought me to the murder scene, and I didn't correct the "Lieutenant" salutation; maybe he needed the weight here an older authority figure would lend him. Behind him in this good-size bedroom in addition to a uniformed cop standing at ease near the windows were two other men.

I recognized Sharanov at once—wide, fleshy face, silvering hair combed straight back from the broad brow, stocky body. The fuzzy surveillance photo hadn't done justice to the impenetrable blue eyes, dead as slate. He had been sprawled across a chaise, dressed in a business suit, but he sprang to his feet when I walked in the room, a jungle cat come suddenly alert. The stocky body didn't appear to be soft.

The other man I recognized as the *shtarke* who held the door for me when I left the Tundra the night I was there. His tux had been replaced by a chauffeur's uniform. He was like something out of a paper doll kit: a parade of costumes could be attached to the same huge body and distinctive yam head. I doubt he recognized me—it had been over two years—but he moved to interpose himself between me and the boss.

"This is the man you spoke of, Chief?" Sharanov murmured. "Can we now move this business along?" Unlike his restaurant employees, he had almost no accent. His voice was mellow, almost soothing.

Chuck said, "No, Mr. Sharanov, we're waiting for Detective Docherty, from County. He should be along any minute." Proudly, he added, "This is Detective Lieutenant Shale, NYPD."

"Ex," I said, my eyes locked on Sharanov's; a closer look told me he was either hung over or had had a sleepless night, maybe both. "Mr. Sharanov, that's my drawing of the village in your living room." I was looking for a reaction.

Sharanov's dead eyes narrowed; something had registered. He said, "Is it?" He considered. "Very good. So you're what they call a Sunday painter?"

"No, I paint all week." I looked to Chuck; if he needed my support until County showed up, I wanted him to know he had it. "I'm a Sunday detective."

Sharanov had no interest in my wordplay. He murmured smoothly, "Either way, if you have some authority here, would you explain to Chief Scully there is no reason for me to remain? This is a tragedy—a young girl, and I believe a good person—but I have told the chief what little I know of what went on here. I intend to go back to the city.''

I said, ''To answer your question, no, I have no authority here. I stopped by in answer to a phone call from the chief.''

I had jogged Chuck's memory. ''Oh,'' he said, ''that was about something else. I wanted to ask…''

He trailed off and shifted gears. ''Mr. Sharanov is the owner of the house. He came out from the city about an hour ago and found the body.''

''Correction,'' Sharanov said mildly. ''Nikki discovered the body. I didn't come in the house. When we arrived, Nikki unloaded the car and I drove it into the village. When I came back Nikki had already called the police. He was of course distressed by what he saw.''

I tried to picture Nikki distressed. Couldn't do it.

Scully had chimed in. ''Helen, the woman on our switchboard, had a time trying to figure out what he was saying.''

Sharanov was humming like a high-performance car engine. ''What more could I tell you? Nothing. If the young lady was the victim of a robbery''—*victim* came out *wictim*, virtually the only clue that he was a foreigner—''it has nothing to do with me.''

Chuck said, ''There's no sign of a break in.''

''So, then,'' Sharanov continued. ''The young lady is local, your neighbor. If she had enemies, and I can't imagine why she would, they would be known to you, not to me.''

Sharanov wanted out of there, but he kept a tight rein on his impatience. ''All I know of her is that she was employed by my wife to come in every Friday from nine to two to prepare the house for the weekend. Nikki walked in the door at a little after eleven, when we arrived from the city. There was no sign of the young lady.''

''I don't hear nobuddy clinning,'' Nikki volunteered. ''Nussing.'' I could see where Helen, at the other end of the 911 line, might have had a problem.

''He came down to this floor,'' Sharanov went on, ''and he found the body in the master bedroom. He touched nothing. He could see at once that the young lady was dead." I had no doubt Nikki knew dead when he saw it.

"Mr. Sharanov, save your breath," Chuck said. "I'm afraid you're going to have to stay and tell it all to County. I'm sorry."

Sharanov's serene face took on a dangerous color. It quickly faded—through an act of will, it seemed—and, serene again, he looked to me for support. When he saw none, he sank back down on his chaise. He was not a man to spend his energy foolishly. But he was not happy.

With Sharanov more or less settled, Chuck asked would I please take a minute and come look at the body? He excused himself to the Russians, and we left the cop with them and walked down the corridor.

I said, "You have a medical examiner on the way?"

"I asked for one, sure."

At the master bedroom Chuck unstuck the single band of crime scene tape and opened the door. This was a much larger room than the one we had been in, and the wall I faced when I entered was decorated. An arc of dried blood swooped gracefully toward the ceiling. Nature imitating art.

To my left, double-hung windows faced the ocean across a stretch of beach. After that sight of sea and sky I took notice of the king-size bed against the bare wall opposite; it was lugubriously cheery. The lacquered headboard was piled high with oversize throw pillows, most of which matched the bedspread in a riot of bright beach colors. There were two chests of drawers, a single chair, and doors to closets and a bathroom.

"She's on the other side of the bed," Chuck said quietly; he could have been directing me to a seat in church.

I slipped off my shoes and walked around the bed. My head was filling with images of the rooms I'd entered to eyeball bodies. The last one was nearly two years ago, and I had lost the ability to distance myself from the sight. Paulie Malatesta had said this victim was sixteen. The young are the hardest to take; they inhabit your dreams for years. I felt my muscles tighten.

Chuck had stayed back at the door; he wasn't going to look at this sight again until he had to.

The girl was sprawled on the floor parallel to the bed—a slim, long-waisted girl with a slight curve to her hips, and chestnut hair that splashed across her face. Her face was turned in toward the bed, effectively buried between the cascading hair and the bed skirt. She wore a shirt and a thin cotton skirt that came to midthigh.

Something about this body struck me like a warning blow to the chest. I thought I knew it. If I was right, my hand had been in love with this body, had caressed it. As I bent to find out, my gut clenched.

A river of dried blood flowed from the slashed neck; a carotid artery had doubtless been severed, maybe both. I had to lean across the body and move the bed skirt for a glimpse of the face. But by then I knew.

My dread was instantly confirmed. Inside the thin cotton skirt and blouse was Cassie Brennan. I recoiled in shock and stood up. Maybe too quickly, because I went light-headed for an instant and had to touch the headboard to steady myself.

Chuck said, "You okay, Lieutenant?"

I don't know how many times I had told him not to call me lieutenant.

I said, "I'm okay."

THREE

THE PREVIOUS SEPTEMBER, when the summer people were mostly gone, poor fools (the east end of Long Island is in its full glory in the fall), I went on a nearly nonstop outdoor drawing kick. By the last Sunday in the month I was just about drawn out, and it was then, as if to kick start my motor, that a minor miracle bathed in a nimbus of coconut oil wandered along the beach path at my back door.

I had my giant sketch pad under one arm, and my drawing tools in the opposite hand, and I was trying to get the swollen door open when a young female voice behind me said, "Are you an artist or something?"

The drawing session had gone lousy and I was in a sour mood. "I paint," I said, "but someone else will have to tell you whether I'm an artist."

By then I had turned around to face a girl in a hot pink bikini and a towel draped across her shoulders. "Well, la-de-da," she said. "Maybe what you are is a stuffed shirt."

It was probably the answer I deserved. "I hope not," I said. I had the door open by now. "But you may be a better judge of that than me. Nice talking to you."

I was halfway into the house when her voice came floating after me. "Do you hire models?"

"Not often." I turned around and took a good look. "I can't really afford models."

That last was a negotiating ploy: I wanted to draw her. I wanted to draw her real bad. She had a pixie twinkle and a way of moving that was at the same time coltish and graceful. She straddled the line between girl and woman—a flat-as-a-breadboard tummy, smooth legs and arms just past the coltish stage, proud breasts. In a couple of years she would be all woman; prettier, maybe, but more conventional to draw.

She said, "Well, what *can* you afford?" She was also in a negotiating mode.

"Have you ever modeled?"

She shook her head slowly.

"You'd find it boring."

"Everything I get hired for is boring."

I kept her dangling for a few seconds. "Okay. This is a one-shot proposition, two hours next Saturday, three to five p.m." I told her what I would pay, somewhat above the local going rate for baby-sitters; I could see in her face that it was more than she made at anything else she did.

"Deal," she said, stifling her elation, "but could you make it four to six? I've got a mother's helper job until three on Saturdays."

"Four to six'll be fine."

"What should I wear?"

"It doesn't matter."

"Because I'll be naked?" Absolutely deadpan.

"No," I said firmly. "Because whatever you decide to wear will be fine to draw you in. There's no naked in this deal. How old are you, anyway?"

"Sixteen."

"As of when?"

"Last Thursday."

At least she was honest. "Bring me a note from your father stating—"

She laughed; it was light, musical. "Sure. If you find him, let me know."

"Your mother, then. You live at home?"

"Yes."

"Stating it's okay for you to pose fully clothed for an artist named Sid Shale. *S-h-a-l-e*."

"So you do call yourself an artist."

She had caught me. "It's a kind of shorthand."

"Uh-huh. See you Saturday." She skip-hopped down the beach, the triumphant teenager; then, in a conscious effort, she switched to a hip-swaying sashay, although there were hardly hips enough to make the point.

HER NAME WAS Cassie Brennan, and she was a natural; I almost never had to instruct her. She fell into poses without giving them any more thought than she would have to flopping down on a blanket to sunbathe. And it didn't seem to matter to her whether I asked her to hold the pose two minutes, ten minutes, or longer. She held it.

The Saturday session went to a second, a third, a fifth, an eighth; some indoors, some out. Many of the poses were tough. I sometimes thought she was challenging me: handle *this*, Mr. Smart-Ass Artist. I took the challenges. My pencil, my pen, my charcoal, were smitten. They caressed her in jeans, in pedal pushers, in shorts, in a skirt—foreshortened, pretzel-shaped, with the light source behind, low to the side, straight above. It mattered not.

She held the poses, but she did move one thing: her mouth. With nothing to do but stay still, she free-associated teenage profundities, and they poured from her as from an open hydrant. She was only a couple of years younger than Sarah, but Sarah was a barely dripping faucet these days, at least with her old man. I paid attention to Cassie's chatter because I thought it might help inform me as a parent.

And because, since my mind is not engaged when I draw, her monologues gave it something to do. Cassie was ignorant, but she was smart, and she did know when to keep her mouth shut. I was working on *Large I* back then, basically twelve square yards of broken clam and oyster shells, and every time her eye fell on the canvas—how could she avoid it?—her face filled with loathing. But she never said a word.

Some of what she did have to say was entertaining, some touching. She definitely believed in God, she let me know, so long as He saw things her way. Maybe if her mother wasn't so strict about churchgoing, made her *hate* church so much, she'd be willing to listen to some opposing arguments from on high. But then again, maybe if her father wasn't such a no-good runaway drunk, her mother wouldn't be so strict about church and about everything else. She loved her mother—"She's definitely my role model"—but did she have to be so darn *strict?*

"Cassie," I interrupted, "she wasn't strict about letting you sit for me."

"Believe me, she asked around. She found out you were a genuine artist, not some, you know, pervert."

"I'm relieved. Thanks."

"That's okay. The fire chief—Jack Beltrano?—assured her you had morals." That must have been Beltrano's thank you for the drawing I had just promised to the next volunteer fire department auction.

Early in our second session she announced she was a virgin.

"Did I ask?"

"I thought I ought to let you know."

"Why?"

"I just thought I should."

"Noted."

But she didn't let it rest there. "Being a virgin's got nothing to do with morals, it's just that my mother would kill me if she found out I wasn't one. Can you believe her? Anyway, she's got nothing to worry about."

"Because you're afraid of disease?"

"Disease is not even in the picture. Disease is what happens to other people. Older people."

"Foolish thinking, Cassie." I managed to let a few seconds go by. "All right, I'll bite. Why doesn't your mother have anything to worry about?"

"Because of high school boys. Ugh. They are thoroughly disgusting, totally unsexy creatures. Tolerable to be with in class, but repulsive when you think of them *that way*. Can you imagine doing it with a high school boy?"

"I honestly can't. How about college boys?"

"Around here? Where? Please."

That ended that discussion. At our next session Cassie revealed her life plan. She had been accelerating her schoolwork for years, and by January she'd have all the credits she needed to graduate—a year and a half earlier than the kids with whom she entered kindergarten. That would leave her free until next September to earn enough money to get a leg up on college tuition. She already had a tidy sum in the bank. She was eager to "get out of this town, once and for good" and make something of herself.

"What's your hurry, Cassie?"

"Time is too precious to waste on teen stuff." Her face clouded over. "When you have a sister die when she's five years old it brings home how every day counts, every hour. I intend to use them." Her face brightened; she didn't like to dwell on the dark side. "This pose okay?"

"Couldn't be better. How does your mother feel about your cutting out so young?"

"It so happens she doesn't really object. She's a workaholic herself; she thinks it's work that keeps me on my feet, if you know what I mean. Three girls in my class are pregnant this year—pregnant enough so they're going to have the babies. I'm not talking about the ones who had abortions. My mother thinks the high school is a hotbed of sin. 'Cauldron of sin' was the way she put it. Isn't that a big pot? Hotbed says it better, if you follow my drift."

"I believe I do. Cassie, you sound like you're all jobs and schoolwork. My advice is, slow down enough to smell the roses."

"Everybody's got a different clock ticking inside. Right now mine says earn some money and get out of here. Next year, or the year after it may say smell the roses."

When we broke for the day she would ask to look at the drawings I had done. She never commented on them, but I could tell she liked what she saw. One time she said, "I wish you'd paint me. Why don't you paint me?"

"I'm not much into that kind of painting."

"You never do portraits?"

"I have, of people I'm close to. My ex-wife, my children. Like that. Mostly for the record."

"You have kids?" She seemed surprised.

"Even painters have kids."

"Do you have a girlfriend?"

"Not at the moment."

"I *do* wish you'd paint me."

"Why?"

"I don't know." I had made her think about her request. "Painting's permanent." She rattled a drawing. "Not like this."

"You looking to be immortalized? Drawings are permanent too. We have Da Vinci's drawings. Michelangelo's."

"Sure, Michelangelo." Meaning I was no Michelangelo. "I'd like to hang in a gallery," she went on. "Even a shop window. People wondering, 'Who *is* that girl?' And someone saying, 'Probably the artist's mistress. It's always the artist's mistress.' What a giggle."

"Not if your mother walked by."

She made a face. "Definitely not." She lit up. "Or they'd say, 'Might be the artist's daughter.'"

"That she'd like?"

"Uh-huh. So will you paint me?"

"Nope."

In the middle of our eighth session she had to go to the bathroom. I used the break to reshape my pencils; it takes time to bring them to the beveled point that allows me to do a fine line or a broad one with the same implement. When I looked up, Cassie was back at her chair and taking a pose— stark naked. The gravity-defying breasts floated serenely above the flat tummy and the tiny dark V where the long, tubular legs met. I felt a rush of blood to my face; it was as though I had never seen a nude model before.

"Cassie!" I barked. "Get back in there and put your clothes on."

She was calm; she had decided she was going to do this. "Why?" she said. "You've seen nude models before." She could have read my mind and was now debating it.

"This was not in our deal." My voice was tight. "Get dressed."

"I will. I promise. As soon as you do a couple of five-minute sketches." She was determined.

What the hell, the damage was done. I did her in charcoal, and then, in another pose, in pen, with wash. And once I started drawing, the shock quickly dissipated. I was at work, and the motor responses took over. She seemed to jump off the paper. The drawing went well. So well I did a third.

As she was taking the third pose I said, "Why are you doing this?"

"I owe you. Really. This is the way models pose."

I sensed there was more. "That's it?"

"There's another reason."

"Which is…?"

"I wanted to see what it would be like to be naked in front of a man."

Did she mean a nonthreatening older man? Or a man who could be provoked into making a pass? Her manner had never been boldly flirty, but she was not unlike many teenage girls who sharpen their courting implements on their girlfriends' fathers. One of Sarah's friends had practiced harmlessly on me.

I said, "This is the last sketch. Now you know what it's like."

"Oh, I knew. I didn't say this would be the first time a man saw me naked. I just didn't want the second time to be disgusting." She bit her lip to keep from saying more. And I decided not to pry.

Fifteen minutes later she was dressed, and I paid her. I told her I would be busy the next few Saturdays but I would call her when I was ready to use her again. I said she was a hell of a model and a hell of a person, and that whatever path she took in life, she had the will and the resources to succeed.

The session had knocked me off center. Cassie hadn't been the world's first sixteen-year-old nude model, probably not even the first that day. But she had gone too far with me, and she knew it and that I might not call her again. And I was possibly sorrier about that than she was.

I WAS SURPRISED when she called in December. "How're you doing?" she asked, and I said, "Good enough, how about you?"

She said she was busy with a batch of part-time jobs; not

bad, she said, when you consider that "nothing much happens around here in the winter."

I said I was glad she was booked because I was on a still-life kick these days and wasn't doing any figurative work.

She chirped for a minute or two and got off, graceful but disappointed. She had been testing the waters.

ON A BLUSTERY day a few weeks later I spotted her in the village wearing a too-thin windbreaker, her cheeks pink from the cold. In three or four short months she had moved rapidly—too rapidly—from girl-woman to almost woman. When she saw me she ran up and kissed me on the cheek.

"You're looking older and wiser," I said. "I like it." I did and I didn't.

"It's being out in the world," she said. "If you can call this the world. It's school that keeps you a kid. I'm finished with it."

We didn't talk long; it was cold, and she was on her way to some job. She had given up on me, and the words no longer gushed from her in a torrent. I missed that. And when she disappeared around a corner I realized that I missed her.

Gayle Hennessy stuck her head out the door of her shop. "That the girl you been doing Saturday afternoons?" she asked.

"Not doing, Gayle. Sketching."

"Right. She's something." And she ducked back out of the cold into the shop.

By then I had abandoned *Large I* and started several smaller canvases, none of which I was crazy about. I was moving back and forth among them, waiting for one to catch fire. The afternoon I ran into Cassie I went home and pulled out the sketches I had done of her. They were good. I taped the best of them—a dozen or so—in two rows to the wall that had held *Large*, and stepped back for an overall objective look. Yes, they were very good.

Within an hour I had started a canvas based on the sketches. The work went like a steak knife through Jell-O, and I finished the painting in a week. I had dismembered her like a bucket of Kentucky Fried Chicken in a way someone would doubtless stamp as marginally cubist—an arm here, a torso there and also here, a head tilted high and in the same space low, a leg, and another leg, and then, from a new angle, still another leg. And so forth. But there was no mistaking her for anyone else. It was Cassie.

And I may have made a mistake by including among my reference sketches two of her nude.

"WHAT DO YOU THINK?" Chuck Scully asked.

I had rejoined him in the bedroom doorway, and we walked back into the corridor. I was still shaky. "She's been dead at least a couple of hours." My voice sounded as if it had arrived from somewhere else and was directing the comment at me.

"Looks that way," Scully said. "Where the hell's the ME? He might pinpoint it."

"Possibly not, but it doesn't matter."

"What do you mean? Of course it—"

I cut him off. "She was due at work at nine?" My body and voice were reconnecting.

"Every Friday. So the place would be ready for the Sharanovs' arrival. Sharanov says so, and the girl's mother verified it. The girl had her own key."

"My guess is she was killed within minutes of coming in the house. Before nine-thirty."

"Minutes? How do you figure that?"

This was a crime scene and I was analyzing it; I would be all right. I said, "Have you ever watched a cleaning person at work? The first thing they do is strip the beds and shove the sheets and towels in the washing machine, so they'll be done by the time they leave. That bed in the master bedroom is still made—sloppily, with the used linens. There are still dirty glasses and ashtrays in the living room. She never got started this morning. You're sure there's no evidence of a break-in?"

"None. And Sharanov says he leaves the place locked

tight as a drum when he leaves on Sunday. Anyway, he told me nothing's missing.''

"He might say that anyway."

"Why?" Scully was looking less and less like Sherlock Holmes and more like a wide-eyed schoolboy.

"You don't know he's almost certainly a crook?"

Chuck shook his head in wonder. "He is? How would I know that?"

"He's not big-time," I said, "but not that small either. Extortion, smuggling, who knows."

Chuck's eyes widened even more. "What! He gives to every charity in the area."

"Don't they always? But if something was stolen from here that he'd have a hard time explaining—how about a bundle of cash?—he might bite the bullet and not report it missing."

"A crook…" Chuck was still absorbing this. "Then again, if the *girl* discovered something here she shouldn't have, Sharanov might have been boxed into killing her himself. Or having her killed."

"In his own house? I wonder. But you're right, you can't rule that out either. Especially since there was no forced entry."

"My guess is, she let someone in," Chuck said firmly.

"If she did, it was someone she knew—knew well enough so that she went down to the bedroom level with him before he killed her." Her limp body swam before my eyes.

"Unless she was forced down here to be raped."

"You'll have to wait for the medical examiner on that," I said, "but she's fully clothed, and—I don't know, this doesn't look like a rape to me."

We turned at the sound of footsteps—the heavy, plodding steps of someone who might be carrying a sack of potatoes on his back. The figure that appeared at the bottom of the ramp—oversize cartoon shoes and floppy socks first—carried no load, but his bent back did suggest he had been burdened all his life, probably by life itself. Dough-faced and dull-eyed, with arms that dangled uselessly from the too-short sleeves of a baggy dark suit, he looked less as if he had lost his last friend than as if he had never had one. I smelled a cop who had been at it too long. And I wanted to sketch him, then and there.

His dull eyes moved from Scully to me. "John Docherty," he growled, as though he expected to be challenged on the claim. He flashed a county sergeant's shield at me. "You Scully? You want to show me the body?"

"I'm Scully," Chuck piped up. "This is Lieutenant Sid Shale, NYPD." Grudgingly, he added, "Retired."

Docherty's heavy lower lip dropped; it may have taken a conscious effort to keep it raised. He turned to face me again, and he took a moment to inventory my features. "Shale, huh?" he said. "Formerly NYP fucking D?"

"That's right."

Docherty pursed the big lips and allowed them to widen into a half-smile before he spoke. "Mr. Shale, we had an inquiry about you just this morning at County," he said.

"About me?"

"From a lawyer. In New York." He didn't like the taste on those bulbous lips of the last two words.

Chuck said, "I forgot, so did I," He turned to me, a slight strain in his voice. "In fact, that's what I called you about at nine-thirty or so, but you were out."

"A lawyer? Inquired about me?" I had to be sounding stupid.

"Asking if you've done anything nasty," Docherty said. "Gotten in any kind of trouble since you've come to live out this way."

I was beginning to get an idea of what he was talking about, but I didn't invite him to expand on his statement.

He did anyway. "I suppose he's looking for ammunition. In the suit he's bringing against the NY fucking PD." Pause. "On behalf of his client you beat the shit out of. Got a little bit of a temper in there you can't control, Lieutenant?"

I had waited so long for that shoe to drop that I had stopped listening for it.

FOUR

THE PROBLEM ITSELF was relatively simple, but it trailed a long history.

Shortly after my grandfather, Sam Shalkowitz, came to America, he somehow got it in his head that, poor as he was, ignorant as he was, he could hold his head up in any company, be the equal of any American, if he wore a pinky ring. Who knew what went on in the heads of immigrants at the dawn of the twentieth century? His boss on Seventh Avenue wore a pinky ring. He also wore a heavy gold watch chain, but my grandfather knew that would always be beyond his means.

So out of his meager salary as a garment center presser my grandfather paid fifty cents a week for I don't know how long to buy a gold ring with a tiny ruby embedded in it and SAM S. etched on the inside. That ring came to mean a lot to him. When he lay dying at an early age he gave it not to his older son Carl ("the bum would only lose it in a crap game") but to his seventeen-year-old son Bernie, decades later to be my father, and made him promise to wear it always.

Bernie didn't need to be bound by a deathbed plea; the ring had already come to stand for his father. And except for one time, Pop never took that ring off his finger. So for me it always seemed as much a part of him as his broken nose or his arthritic limp. Maybe more.

The one time he took the ring off was the day of my bar mitzvah. He wanted me to wear it in the synagogue that morning so that when I read the Torah portion that would fold me into the company of the men in the congregation I would be bonding as well with the grandfather I never knew.

In considerable awe, I tried it on. "Pop," I told him, "it's too loose for my fingers, it's going to fall off."

"No, it won't," he said. "You'll keep your hand bent a little. And you'll be careful, because you're wearing your grandfather's ring."

How careful could I be? It was my bar mitzvah, I was excited, and I had to pay attention to a lot that was going on.

After the service, as we were leaving the temple for the reception my mother had arranged in our backyard, I noticed that the ring was no longer on my finger. I remember staring at my hand in disbelief, as though I could will it back. I had never been so scared in my life. What could I do? Where could I hide?

Thirty minutes earlier I had been recognized as a man. Manfully, I drew my father aside and told him the ring was gone.

If I live long enough so that my early years dissolve in a hazy dream, I will never forget the look, first of incomprehension, and then of rage, that flooded Pop's features. He yanked me back into the now empty sanctuary, my feet barely touching the floor, and the two of us searched inch by inch on our hands and knees for forty minutes while our friends and relatives waited for us at home, the toasts unmade, the food uneaten, the concern growing.

We found the ring on the bimah, where it had embedded itself under the cantor's chair, but it took the rest of the day for the color to come back to my father's face.

Twenty-one years later, when Pop's body was found in the driver's seat of his cab, his brains splashed on the windshield and his blood coating the steering wheel, the ring was gone, along with the cigar box containing the day's receipts that he kept hidden under the passenger front seat. There was no sign that the cab had been searched, so he must have given up the cash willingly, as he always said he would. ("It's only money, am I crazy?") But my guess is that he had been reluctant to turn over the ring, and the perp had things to do and places to go and not much patience. The .38 slug in the ear had possibly served no purpose but to speed the transfer.

By then I had been a detective first for several years, and it didn't take long for the word of my father's murder to spread from my squad in Washington Heights to all of Manhattan. I was alerted to every arrest stemming from a violent crime involving a taxicab, sometimes even before the perpetrator was booked.

There was a rash of such crimes back then, and I followed wild geese all over the five boroughs. I must have grilled a couple of dozen suspects over the next few years. You never close the books on a homicide, but the faint trail my father's killer left went gradually cold. I began to believe it had become close to impossible to link this crime to a particular perpetrator.

By the fifth year after Pop's murder I interrogated only two or three of the likeliest prospects. I had recently become a lieutenant, with my own detective squad in lower Manhattan and a desk piled with paperwork. After nineteen years as a cop I was looking forward to retirement and full-time painting. I could get out nicely at twenty years, but I had decided to stick it out to twenty-two or -three. With college looming for two kids, the pension would be better, but I had another reason: There was a shortage of lieutenants around that time and I figured I owed the department the benefit of my experience a while longer.

FOR ALMOST ALL of my twentieth year on the job there wasn't a taxi crime I thought worth my time to check out. But late that winter word reached me of a suspect in a cabby murder in the South Bronx. Ballistics didn't match the bullet that did in Pop, but that in itself meant little; some shooters trade off their guns after they fire them, so as not to lay down an MO profile.

What drew me to this case—and it wasn't much—was the single shot that killed the victim. The gun had been hooked into the upper curve of his right ear, and faced slightly forward—exactly the placement of the weapon that had killed my father. A hunch, more than reason—a gut feeling—sent me up to where the suspect was being held for arraignment in the Bronx County Courthouse on 161st Street. His name was Ray Drummit.

His back was turned when I entered the interview room where they had left him for me to question alone. The first thing I saw was the ring. He had been rear-cuffed, and the tiny ruby glowed dully.

He turned to face me with a sullen smirk, but I spun him around and he let out a gasped "Hey!" when I pulled the ring off him. I knew it was Pop's without checking, but I checked anyway. The engraving was now so faint I had to turn the ring this way and that to find it. It was there.

I spun him to face me again. "Where'd you get this ring?" I demanded. I usually kept my voice friendly at the beginning of an interrogation; I couldn't manage it this time.

He was thirty, pipe cleaner skinny, with a ferret's face and tiny eyes. "What do you mean? What the hell you doing?" he spit out. "You can't do that, man. Take my property."

"Where'd you get this ring?" I repeated.

"It was my grandmama's," he said, meeting my eyes. "Her ring. She left it to me."

"You had a grandmother named Sam?"

He had never read the inscription, but he barely took a beat. "Yeah, that's what they called her. For a nickname." His tiny eyes were taking my measure, and his tone became conspiratorial. "Listen, man, you want the ring? Hey, it's yours. It ain't worth shit to me."

Without thinking, I drew back my fist and drove it into his face. It was just the one punch, but I felt something give. He staggered back against the wall. A moment later he spit out a tooth, maybe two, and blood bubbled from his mouth. And he let out a howl of anguish.

I had never done anything so dumb in my life—striking a handcuffed prisoner. At my worst, I had never been a physical cop; in the course of a long career I had used force only in the heat of an arrest where there was resistance. I was known on patrol and then in detective squads as "one of those talkers." I had found that talking usually got me what I needed to know.

That moment of dumb cost me. The suspect beat the charge he had been arrested on (the missing teeth helped; he looked like a lost waif to the grand jury), and there was not nearly enough evidence to tie him to my father's murder. He claimed he didn't know where his grandmother got the ring. I ended up with it, and with a twenty-year retirement hastily forced on me by a department eager to distance itself from a possible charge of police brutality.

Apparently, after nearly two years, here it came.

THE CRIME SCENE Unit arrived three minutes behind Detective Docherty, and I invited myself out of the house. The county cop seemed to have a festering sore he blamed on the NYPD, and this was not the time to pick at it. Even before I left the corridor he was saying to Scully, "What the hell business did he have here anyway?"

On the way up the ramp I could hear Sharanov on the phone in the guest bedroom, his high-performance engine of a voice idling smoothly, but ready to be gunned if that was called for. I stopped to listen.

"Yes, yes, terrible, terrible…" He betrayed no emotion. "Kitty, I am not dismissing it, I am giving you the facts…. What does this have to do with me? Nothing. Not one damn thing… You are not listening to me…. Kitty, if you don't shut your mouth I will have it shut for you so that it never opens again." He had dropped his voice for the last sentence but it was spoken with no more revs per minute than the others.

One of the CSU people above began waving for me to keep moving. Reluctantly, I continued on up the ramp.

OUT ON THE driveway a photographer was taking general shots of the house and grounds. There were now three vehicles I hadn't seen before, but among them no van from the coroner's department. I asked Walter, the cop on duty, if a medical examiner had gone in the house.

"Nope. They told me the doctor on duty is out on a case, and they're still looking for his backup."

Unlike the county people, Walter had no interest in shoo-

ing me off the property, and I wandered around to the side
of the house and then out to the back—not after anything in
particular, just not ready to leave. I was finding that I couldn't
walk away from this crime scene as I had from so many
others. I hadn't realized how strong my connection was to
the girl in that bedroom lying in a pool of her blood; beyond
help, she still hadn't given me permission to leave.

I walked down to the ocean's edge and looked out at the
pulsing waves of the advancing tide. There was reassurance
in their unfailing rhythm. The universe rolled on; Cassie
Brennan, barely a woman, had been folded into it. Our loss,
not hers.

After a few brooding moments I felt the water lapping at
my sneakers. The tide had sneaked up on me. The mood
broken, I backed off and turned to face that blindingly white,
excessively whimsical house. Only this morning I had included this facade in a beachscape sketch—by my calcula-
tion, some two hours before Cassie's throat was cut. I would
never again look at this house without thinking of her. It was
all wrong, insultingly so, for the scene of her murder.

Something was nagging at me. I stared at the house. Something was different. Had I been less than true to it in that
drawing? And then I decided after all that I hadn't; it seemed
different now only because I had drawn it from far down the
beach, and in the totally different light of early morning.
Nothing more than that.

My peripheral vision picked up someone approaching from
the west along the water's edge. Paulie Malatesta again. Walter had chased him away from the house, but the beach was
open to everyone; he must have parked in a driveway somewhere up the road. He came closer but kept a wary distance
between us.

"You're the guy lives in that shack down the beach," he
decided. "The one painted different colors." His tone was
friendly; he seemed to have forgiven our wrestling match.

"How did you know?"

"I've passed it. Weird-looking. Anyway, you're a painter,
right? She told me."

"Cassie?"

He swallowed hard and nodded; if he said the name he was going to break down. "She was working for you a couple of hours a week as a model when I met her."

That was where I'd heard the name. Malatesta; it sticks with you. He came up during, I remembered now, my next to last session with Cassie. She was her usual chatty self. She'd met this guy in Mel's, where she bused early breakfast several days a week. He was kind of new in town, good-looking, older. (This was older?) In answer to my question she had said sadly, no, she wouldn't go out with him, was I kidding? She liked that he was from somewhere else, but her mother would kill her, didn't she say he was *older*? Anyway, she didn't have time for that stuff.

Paulie was kicking sand and probing. "She said you were a cop from New York. Right?"

"Used to be."

"But you're a pro. Not like these clowns. How long you think before they arrest that creep? That pervert Sharanov?"

"Easy, Paulie. The investigation's just getting under way. They have to build a case that'll satisfy a grand jury. They'll likely want to talk to you, to a lot of people. Meanwhile, why don't you go back to the garage? Work'll calm you down."

He had only heard one phrase. "What do you mean, build a case? While Misha hires himself some high-price lawyer? The man's a gangster."

"How do you know?"

"I *know*. I can smell it. Dirty money. He's a crook, crazy mean, and he's been after"—his mouth jammed up—"after her since last year."

"She was a pretty girl, Paulie. He wasn't the only man who thought so."

"He was *after* her."

"Did she say that?"

"She wouldn't, or I'd have made her quit. But she didn't have to say it. His wife got so jealous she hit him with a chair. I'm surprised he didn't blow her head off. That's got

to be his style." He paused. "Is that what he did to...to...
He shot her?"

"I don't know how Cassie died." Telling him was not my
call. "You'll have to ask the police."

"That kid Scully? What the hell does he know? He was
probably after her himself." And then, "I'm sorry, I don't
know what the hell I'm saying."

"That's why you should go back to work."

"Yeah, I guess..." He considered the option, but not for
long. "Do they have what did it? The gun, knife, whatever?"

"Speak to Scully."

"If they haven't found it yet, they can forget it. Misha's
got thirty miles of dunes to bury it in. They should have run
him in by now. Is he still in the house?"

As if in answer to the question, Sharanov's voice, smooth
and assured, carried to us from the driveway around front.
"Officer, this car will have to be moved before I can get
mine out."

Paulie was stricken. "They're letting the son of a bitch go.
I can't believe it."

Before I could stop him he had raced around the side of
the house and disappeared in front. I followed, but at a more
measured pace. I had done my bit; let Walter handle this one.

By the time I got around to the front of the house, Nikki,
the massive yam head, had a thick arm wrapped around the
struggling Paulie's throat; his other hand had Paulie's head
pulled back by his hair. Poor Paulie, a glutton for punishment, had been licked twice in twenty minutes. If he couldn't
handle me, he was a fool to tangle with Nikki, who had a
good five inches and fifty pounds on him.

When I didn't see Walter at first, I thought he had departed
to a less stressful location, but then I spotted him in one of
the police vehicles. He had been trying to move it out of the
way of Sharanov's red Cadillac. Now he was wriggling his
bulk out of the seat so he could handle the "altercation," as
he would call it in his report.

Meanwhile, Sharanov had walked up to within a foot of
the pretty much helpless Paulie. He moved as though he was

on a track; if you wanted to change his course you would
have to derail him. Quietly he said, "Did you have something
to say to me?"

"No," Paulie managed, "nothing." Then, "I just wanted
to kick you in your fucking, murdering balls."

After which he tried that. But Nikki yanked him back and
Sharanov dodged with a quickness I wouldn't have expected
from him. The flailing foot met only air. Now Nikki in-
creased the pressure on Paulie's throat and Sharanov stepped
forward and slapped him smartly across the face. Once, with
his weight behind it. The sound carried.

Few things humiliate a grown man more efficiently than a
slap in the face. A punch is a man-to-man act, a slap a punishment from one's betters. Paulie's eyes glistened with held-
back tears. Sharanov, energized by what he saw, hauled off
for a second slap.

"Hey!" I called. "Cut that. Right now."

Sharanov turned to me; his face registered surprise. He was
not used to being dissuaded from anything he did.

"Or what?" he asked mildly. It was not a challenge; not
yet. He was merely curious. But his eyes were glacier chips.

"I'll tell you when your hired hand releases Mr. Malatesta.
By the count of three." I wasn't going to give him time to
think. "One, two—"

Calmly, not in the least intimidated, Sharanov muttered
something in Russian. Nikki unwrapped his hand from Paulie's neck and let go of his hair. Paulie adjusted his coveralls
and assumed a defiant stance—sheer, face-saving bravado on
his part. His dark cheek had an overlay of red.

Nikki turned toward me; he was waiting to be unleashed
by his boss. Walter was somewhere in my peripheral vision;
he was letting me handle the situation because I had done so
well with the last one.

"Or what?" Sharanov repeated, soft but insistent.

Jesus, this guy didn't let go. I walked up close to him, but
the cop's trick of looking him steadily in the eye didn't work;
he looked back just as steadily.

I said, "That's information I release on a 'need to know'

basis. You no longer need to know.'' I turned to Malatesta. ''Paulie, shouldn't you be getting back to work?''

Paulie knew when he was outgunned, and he was grateful to be able to leave in response to a suggestion from me; there would be no loss of face in that. With a final glare at each of his adversaries, he marched out the driveway.

And now Walter lent his weight to the scene. ''I'll clear the Caddy for you folks,'' he called and waddled back to the police car that was blocking it.

''That young man may have come on too strong,'' I said to Sharanov, by way of a half-assed apology for Paulie; I didn't want some Russian goon sandbagging him late one night. ''But you have to understand why he's upset. Cassie Brennan was his girlfriend.''

''We are all upset,'' Sharanov said evenly. ''And I don't think Cassie was anybody's girlfriend.''

That ended our close eye contact. He turned and walked toward his car, Nikki at his heels.

He said, ''Nikki, we will stop in the village for something to eat.''

It was lunchtime and he was going to eat lunch. Period.

FIVE

I SURFED the radio dial on the drive home. The story hadn't broken. It would soon enough, and reporters would climb over each other to get to Beach Drive. "Teenage Beauty Murdered in Beachfront Mansion." Couldn't miss.

It was now close to two and I had forgotten to confirm with Lonnie that I would come to the city to meet her Texas "collector" at the gallery. It was the last thing I wanted to do that day, but I couldn't afford not to.

The phone was ringing as I opened the front door. It was Gayle, nearly breathless. "I've been calling you for half an hour. I heard. Sid, I feel awful. Sick."

"You knew Cassie?"

"She's been working for me. Two afternoons a week holding down the shop while I was upstairs doing my line for the new season."

"Could she do that? Wait on trade?"

"The number of walk-ins I get this time of year, believe me, she could handle. And she had the figure for the beach things I make. I knew that the minute I saw your sketches of her. I pinned patterns on her, draped fabrics, used her body to try out ideas. I never told you?"

Maybe she had; everything about Cassie had taken on new importance in the last half hour. Why hadn't I realized before that Cassie and Gayle had pretty much the same body in different sizes? Clearly, it was the kind of body I wanted to draw.

"Damn, I'm sorry about that girl," Gayle went on. "Why does this kind of thing have to happen?"

I thought I heard a note of guilt in her voice. I said, "Gayle, did you see something like it coming?"

"Nothing like this," she said quickly; she may have

started down a road she hadn't meant to take. She took a moment, maybe to plan how she would say it. "But looking back I can't say I'm totally bowled over with surprise."

"What does that mean?"

"It means it takes one to know one." She was surer now. "Sid, she was *me* at that age—spreading her wings, ready to take chances. I don't know how or why, but she may have stuck her nose in where she shouldn't have."

"A straight-ahead kid like Cassie? Feet on the ground, all-around good?"

"Basically, sure. Hey, *I* was basically a good kid. But if you hadn't come along I'd have ended up modeling a body bag on Adam Clayton Powell Boulevard."

"Don't compare your world with Cassie's. She had a real home, a religious mother who fussed over her—"

"Yeah," Gayle murmured. "That'd keep her in line."

"From what I could tell she stayed in line."

"If she did it was because she was afraid her old man would show up to give her a good whipping. That's about the only thing he ever did show up for."

"She talked to you about that?"

"Not much. But maybe more than with you. Girl to girl. He was bad news."

"Did he make moves on her?"

That startled her. "What? She never said anything about that. Where'd you get it?"

I started to backpedal. "Was it something she said once? I'm not sure."

But I remembered it clearly: She said some man had seen her naked and she didn't like it. What had made me make the leap to her father?

Gayle said, "The worst I heard about her old man is that he's a boozer. Like half the people in this town. That other, ugh. Maybe I was lucky."

"That your father never came after you?"

"That I never knew him."

Because she and Cassie had been girl to girl, I wondered what she knew about Paulie Malatesta. I never got to ask; a customer had walked into the shop and Gayle had to hang up.

With the phone still in my hand I remembered to call Lonnie. I got the machine:

"You have reached the Leona Morgenstern Gallery. Please leave your name and number and we'll return your call at the very first opportunity."

This wasn't the shrew who phoned me just after the crack of dawn, but the woman who had taken a lease on my heart when we first met two decades ago. Lonnie now mostly reserved that liquid, come-hither voice for the paying customers.

After the beep I said, "Lonnie?...Lonnie, where the hell are you? It's nearly two o'clock. Rule one for selling art—open the door." No wonder my work wasn't selling.

I waited a few seconds for someone to pick up. Nothing but tape static. I said, "Okay, I'm coming in. I'll be there at six to meet your Texas fat cat. If he shows before me, warn him to stand back from my paintings with his pointy alligator boots."

I thought that this might stir her to pick up her phone. When it didn't, I added, "And, Lonnie, would you tell Alan I'm coming in? When I'm through at your place, I'll take him out for spaghetti or another budget dinner of his choice. Just the two of us, we haven't talked in a while. And no, in answer to your reminder, I haven't forgotten I have a daughter at college."

I glanced at Sarah's laughing photo at the back of the desk and I was reminded again how close in age she was to Cassie Brennan. I said, "And yes, I will come up with my half of the tuition—if I have to earn it painting the white line down the middle of the Montauk Highway."

And suddenly the phone was being answered. Perkily. "Hel-lo?...Hello?" It wasn't Lonnie. "Leona Morgenstern Gallery. May I ask who's calling?"

"Jackie, is that you?" It was; I had recognized her voice. Lonnie's assistant.

The voice dropped an octave. "Oh, Officer Shale." Meaning, I wasn't a customer, just her boss's dreary ex-husband, and a hard sell, to boot. Jackie could get all of that into three words. Even Lonnie had told her not to call me "Officer Shale."

I bit my tongue and made nice; this woman was sometimes the bridge between me and a possible buyer. I said, "Hi, Jackie, how you doing? Leona around?"

"Ms. Morgenstern?" God, this woman was exasperating. Did she think I meant Leona Helmsley? "I'm expecting her in about an hour. I'm just opening up."

"At two o'clock? You open the gallery at two o'clock in the afternoon?"

"This isn't a doughnut shop, Officer Shale. Our clients don't buy paintings in the morning." Subtext: They're unlikely to buy yours at any time of day and maybe your work would do better hanging in a doughnut shop.

She went on in that fake cultivated voice that probably fooled nobody, "Did you wish to leave a message?"

"Thanks, Jackie, it's on your tape." And I got off before I said something that would be reflected in my future sales.

ON A FRIDAY AFTERNOON at three I would be driving against the main traffic flow between here and the city, and well before local people left their jobs in the area for home. If there was no major repair work on the LIE, I could make it to the gallery in well under three hours. Lonnie claimed that my usual beachcomber attire failed to inspire confidence in the "collectors," as she always called them, so I would have to trick myself out in city clothes before I left. That gave me about an hour to work on *Large*.

Before I climbed up the scaffold I took a moment to pull out the sketches of Cassie that I hadn't looked at in months. They hurt. My drawing hand had been more cunning than I remembered. The girl came alive on the paper, her body lithe and playful, her pixie face alternately sly and open. I was no doubt reading more into these drawings than was there, but Cassie Brennan invited that.

These maudlin thoughts were doing me no good. I put the

drawings down on my worktable. Next to them were the two I had done this morning—the beachscapes.

Was it only this morning? The second drawing, pen and wash, with the Sharanov house filling the foreground, held my eye—as that same elevation of the actual house had held it half an hour ago, when my troubled contemplation of it was interrupted by the arrival of Paulie Malatesta.

I picked up the drawing. It was true to the occasion; it caught the feeling of that harsh early sun flooding the beach-side facade of the many-windowed house—the windows, in my wash, throwing the blinding light back out to sea. The ocean was fretful, the dunes unruly, the rubble-strewn beach forlorn. It said, Will summer never come? A good sketch.

And yet, something about it bothered me. Was it too facile, or what? Was it the sketch that bothered me or the house itself? Because I had this same feeling when I looked at the house, life size, half an hour ago.

Maybe *bothered* was the wrong word. Miss Clavell popped into my head—Madeleine's custodian in the Bemelmans classic I must have read to my children a hundred times. Miss Clavell, who woke in the middle of the night and said, "Something is not right."

Something was not right here, and I didn't know what it was. It couldn't be much, and if I took the time to try to figure it out I wasn't going to get any work done. And I had acres to fill on *Large*.

I climbed the scaffold and wet my roller.

SIX

EVEN UNDER FAVORABLE conditions the trip to the city on the Long Island Expressway sometimes made me feel like a medieval knight on a quest. There would be the dragon of the overturned trailer truck, the black knight in the careening Porsche, the malevolent road gangs with their ever-narrowing construction lanes, and at the end of the journey the dreaded city that held the fair princess. Well, not quite. The city held Lonnie Morgenstern.

I hadn't seen Lonnie in months, and I filled the endless drive by reviewing, as I did every second or third trip to Soho, our troubled history. An exercise in masochism.

When Leona Morgenstern and I met in 1977 I had been going to the Art Students League for years. On my first evening in a life drawing class that semester I spotted her opposite me through the model's arched leg, intent on her work. Her eyes, Jewish and blue, were set in an oval face of flawless alabaster ringed with unruly dark curls. My heart—there is no better word for it—sang.

After class a few students gathered on the ASL's shallow front steps facing the trundling buses on West Fifty-seventh Street and talked art. Art theory talk was the kind of gasbagging that set my teeth on edge, but I wanted to get to know this beauty, so I hung around the periphery of the group, contributing just enough platitudes so that I didn't seem a mere voyeur. On the third such evening I was able to position myself next to her on the second step.

We made small talk. She had a voice somewhere between sultry and smoky. But liquid. Not so liquid as to pour too easily; slightly viscous. She was taking just the one class, she told me, but as soon as she had some savings she'd be adding another, under a well-known painter whose work she admired. Luckily, so did I.

Her name was Leona, but she had been called Lonnie since she was six months old. I figured her for twenty; I was twenty-one. She worked for a department store chain as a buyer-trainee in sleepwear, but she didn't think of herself as on a career track; all she was looking for right now was to earn enough money to further her ambition to paint seriously. The alabaster face turned full on me, like a newly risen moon. And what was my day job?

"I'm a cop."

She laughed. "No, seriously."

"Seriously. I'm a New York City police officer."

She stared. "Sid Shale..." She was tasting the name.

"Yes, I'm Jewish. It was Shalkowitz. My father shortened it to speed passengers' complaints against him with the Hack Bureau, but then there never were any. And yes, there are lots of Jewish cops. But not nearly as many as Irish or Italian cops. Too many Jews get suckered into physics and microbiology."

"Still...," she said doubtfully.

"Think of the Tel Aviv police force. A hundred percent Jewish."

"The firemen too, I suppose," she said earnestly. At barely twenty she had not yet fashioned her razorlike sense of humor. There was something endearing in her helping me make my points.

It took another six weeks to persuade her to go out for a cup of coffee after class. She was heavily booked. She had boyfriends by the job lot, and a waiting list. Doctors, lawyers, microbiologists. Nobody, so far as I could tell, on the civil service rolls. What finally got my toe in the door was my drawings. She locked on, and she said the right things—almost the same things I would have said about them. Then I showed her a small painting, and that was the clincher. Her instincts were nearly infallible. She knew where I was good, and true, and where I was faking.

She started fitting me in on Tuesdays, after class. Not all

Tuesdays, but most. Eventually, as my paintings improved, I got an occasional Friday. It wasn't easy for me to manage the more important Fridays. I was working out of a busy precinct in the east Bronx, and Lonnie lived with her parents on the Upper West Side of Manhattan. We weren't sleeping together. Someone significant had been in the picture for a while, and she was one man at a time. I would have described us as moving tentatively in the direction of becoming an item.

Not to put too fine a point on it, I was wild about her. So far as I could tell, only one thing stood in the way of my being hopelessly in love: I hated the way she drew. There was strength in her line, and conviction; she drew what she thought she saw. The trouble was, she looked, but she didn't see. Her superb critical eye failed her totally when it came to her own work. Not uncommon.

How could I tell this object of all my desires that she drew lousy? I couldn't. Neither could I lie. I found myself saying about the drawings she showed me, "I see what you're trying to do here," and "I like that one better than this one" and, when I ran out of ideas, "Uh-huh, uh-huh." Weaseling was not easy, but it was the only difficult part of our times together.

As my work improved—my paintings were becoming looser, more fluid—so did our relationship. And art finally won out over commerce, or was it science? The commodities trader or heart specialist, or whoever—I never did find out—faded from the picture, and Lonnie and I became lovers.

I was intensely happy. We were perfect for each other. This was the woman I wanted to be my life's companion, my critic and inspiration, and also the mother of my children.

She wasn't as sure. She never said so, but I had the sense that she was still shopping. I didn't feel we had a permanent deal until, a couple of months into our sleeping together, she said two things. The first, after a particularly steamy session of lovemaking, was, "Nobody's ever made me feel like that before." It was a naked admission more intimate than the lovemaking.

The second, the next day, was more like thinking out loud

than speaking. She was lying on her back after sex and it
was addressed, dreamily, to the ceiling. "If you become a
famous painter—and I believe you will—attention would
have to be paid to whoever was painting at your side.
Wouldn't it?"

We were married three months later.

THE FIRST FIVE years couldn't have gone better. We were
crazy in love, and everything in our lives looked good—our
jobs, the dirt-cheap loft space for painting we found above a
Colombian restaurant next to the el on ethnic Roosevelt Avenue in Queens, even our so-so apartment on Queens Boulevard. When the kids came along—Sarah and then Alan—
we were still able to manage long painting sessions together
because we set up a corner of the loft for the kids' play and
nap space.

The bad times began, as I suspected they might, when
Lonnie realized she was not going to make it as an artist. To
her credit, she figured it out by herself. It was a long time
coming, but when it did, everything turned to ashes. Her job
became unbearable, she hated the apartment, everything. It
was about then, during our increasingly nasty arguments, that
the sultry, smoky, semiliquid quality went out of her voice.
You could have used her voice to slice salami.

The marriage was on the skids and would have soon
crashed but for a small miracle. Lonnie's grandfather died
and left her a small inheritance, just enough to do what her
superb critical sense suited her for: She opened an art gallery.
She already had her eye on three or four promising artists
(including her husband), and she found a space in SoHo far
enough off West Broadway so that the rent didn't hurt.

The Leona Morgenstern Gallery lost money its first year
but never again. Two years later she moved it to better quarters. She had more than a superb eye: She knew how to sell.
If she had stayed in sleepwear she would have had the whole
country in her pajamas. She found her way to the moneyed
"collectors" the way a dowser finds his way to water, and
they bought. I myself was a hard sell despite respectful, or

better, notices from the critics, but they even bought me; not often enough, but Lonnie fetched me some handsome prices.

She began to wear designer clothes, and why not? She was earning big bucks. Her dark hair no longer ringed her alabaster face in wild curls but was pulled back into a sleek French knot. We had an apartment in Manhattan now and a sleep-in Jamaican woman Lonnie referred to as "the nanny." Okay.

The collectors invited her to charity events and cocktail parties, and if I wasn't working or painting I tagged along. Sometimes she had to remind me to change out of my cop shoes. A couple of times someone at these events asked what I did, and before I could answer Lonnie said, "Sid is with the city." She said it as if I had the mayor's ear.

When I called her on that she said, "Sid, it isn't easy to sell paintings by a cop at serious prices." But I told her to cut it out. So the next time a collector asked what I did, Lonnie piped up, "Sid is in counseling."

When we were alone I said, "Counseling? What the hell did that mean?"

"'Put down the gun.' Isn't that counseling? 'You have the right to remain silent.' *That's* counseling."

The relationship wasn't working on any level and all that kept us from a divorce at that point was my father's death. And then, less than a year later, Lonnie called off her lawyer again when my mother died. So it took us three years to unwind from our marriage. By then we were more worn out than angry and we declared a civilized peace.

I had moved back to Queens. That was that.

THE LEONA MORGENSTERN Gallery was a spare, high-ceilinged space, cool in tone but not as cool as Jackie, who always reminded me of a vanilla frozen custard. She greeted me near the door with, "Officer Shale. Ms. Morgenstern is expecting you in the office." Subtext: I can't imagine why.

I tried not to look at the walls as I made my way back through the gallery. They were hung with recent works by two of Lonnie's favorite artists, neither of them half bad, and

I didn't need that. The office door was open and I went straight in. I said, "Officer Shale reporting for duty."

Lonnie took off her glasses—since when had she started wearing glasses?—and rose from behind the paperwork on her desk to come and greet me. She looked good; she usually looked good, even with that slicked-back hair.

She said, "Is Jackie still calling you that? What can I do with her? Sid, you're on time. How nice."

She had allowed some of the old smokiness to creep into her voice, and when she touched her cheek against mine it was smooth and warm, and her hair smelled bedroom-y. I felt the lick of desire that still brushed me once in a while when I was with her. This time I chalked it up to a record dry period; I had been up on that scaffold too long wrestling *Large*.

Lonnie had stepped back to lamp my wardrobe; I could see an instructional lecture coming. I wasn't going to let her go down that street, so I shortcut her with, "I don't hear the jangle of spurs. Where's your Texan?"

"They should be here any minute. They're coming separately."

"They?"

"A father and daughter. They're darling. You'll like them."

"I will, if they buy. And Alan and I will go for steak instead of pasta."

"About Alan." She made a face. "Turns out he has a date. With a girl, if you please. You want him to cancel?"

I said, "And make me the heavy? Bad enough I'm the absentee father." But I was disappointed.

"You'll see him soon enough. He expects to go out to the beach when school ends."

"For as long as he likes." The kid painted better than I did at his age. "I'll put him to work on *Large*." Of course I was looking to needle her; I didn't know why, except that she was so goddam serene. "There's an acre of canvas on the west border that'll take less skill than painting a back fence."

"Oh, God," she exploded, "then you *are* still on that kick." *Touché*. "Sid, will you please grow up? You're not functioning in the real world."

"Because I'm painting big? There are tapestries in European castles that make my piece look like a commemorative postage stamp."

"Because the *rooms* in European castles make this gallery look like a broom closet," she snapped. "It's bad enough that your work fails to communicate to most of my clientele—"

"Not my problem," I cut in. "Did I forget to tell you? I'm not in the communications business." I was losing it.

"Sid, Sid," she said wearily. "You really are a spoiled, contrary child."

The arrival of Jackie at the door saved us from taking each other apart like boosted Caddies in a chop shop. "Your Ms. Turkinton is here," she announced in a hushed voice.

Before leaving the office we took twenty seconds to breathe deeply and come off the boil.

Ms. Turkinton—"Tess," as she insisted I call her—didn't look like Texas cattle money, and if she was oil money she lived closer to Neiman Marcus than to "Daddy's" wells. Turkinton Senior hadn't shown yet, but Tess had called him "Daddy" at least four times in her first three minutes with us, clicking her tongue smartly against the roof of her mouth with each *d*, giving the word a certain spring. Daddy seemed to be a kind of god—the patron saint, I hoped, of filthy lucre.

Tess was in her late twenties, pretty, auburn-haired, and very slim; she only had it where it counted. Her generous smile, I decided, had been designed to excuse frequent excesses in her behavior; she was used to seeing people jump when she made known her whims. After the briefest of introductions she had announced that Daddy would want to see a representative sampling of my paintings, so she had ordered that a spread of them be set up in a viewing room next to the office before his arrival. Daddy was not to be kept waiting.

Lonnie chose to assist Jackie and their handyman in bringing up half a dozen of my best paintings; I was assigned to entertain the guest. "I think she's a little sweet on you," Lonnie managed to whisper as she passed me on her way toward the basement door.

"So," I said, turning to Ms. Turkinton with a show of interest, "you're big *D*?"

"Fort Worth, to be precise," she replied. "Does it matter?"

"Sid had his eye peeled for a rhinestone belt," Lonnie called from the basement stairs. She had her ear tilted to miss nothing.

"That's Daddy's belt," Tess purred. "I'm afraid Bryn Mawr and the Sorbonne knocked the last rhinestones out of mine."

That surprised me; neither school had knocked the Texas twang out of her. But she was too self-confident to wonder if she had been patronized—and probably too secure to want to lose the accent. She didn't even look to me for my reaction to her show-off bio. She had already left my side to get close to a painting Jackie was propping on a chair. She leaned over it and squinted: She may have been fighting off eyeglasses. She was wrong; they would have softened her angular good looks.

Still bent toward the painting, she cocked one arm behind her and snapped her fingers; it may have been the way she called her horse, but this time she meant for me to trot over. I went at a slow walk.

She didn't notice. "So far I like this one best," she said. That meant shit; I must have said something like it half a dozen times to Lonnie while gritting my teeth over her lousy drawings back at the Art Students League.

Tess glanced around at the other paintings being set up. "Uh-huh, uh-huh," she said. To be fair, there was no way she could know she was enraging me further. She said, finally, "Am I wrong, or do I find in your work an unusually healthy dose of German Expressionism?"

More bullshit. Not quite throwing caution to the wind, I

said, "Tess, I just paint them. Whatever you find, you get to keep."

Now she turned to look at me. She gave me a flash of the generous smile, and then, "Did I say something to offend you? Because I'm on your side. If you don't explain your work to me, how am I going to explain it to Daddy?"

"I have no idea. If I could explain my work I'd do that instead of paint it. If your daddy takes one of my pictures, he and it will have to get to know each other all by themselves. You and I would just be in the way."

Tess's smile had long since gone. She said, "My, we are just a little bit touchy, aren't we?"

Lonnie had come up from the basement lugging a painting, and she had caught the last exchange. Her alabaster face took on a purple tinge. She shot me a look and turned sweetly to Tess. "Is there something I can help with, Tess?"

But Tess had forgotten what we were debating. She had locked on to the painting Lonnie was carrying. "That's the one Daddy must have meant," she gushed. "The one he told me he especially liked."

A moment of sadness had passed over me like a scudding cloud. I hadn't seen the canvas since I'd brought it in to Lonnie months ago. It was my portrait of the nude, fragmented Cassie Brennan.

"Yes," I heard myself saying from somewhere in the middle distance. "It's one of my favorites, too."

It was the first thing I had said in agreement with Tess, and I could see that Lonnie approved.

ment, Tess. I pay plan them. Whatever you like, you got to ...

Now she turned to look at me. She gave me a flash of the gorgeous smile, and she wanted me to somehow to dread you. By her standards it amounted to a plea. But how you work to me, how am I going to explain it to Daddy?

"I'll have no idea. If I could, darling my week, I'd do that

SEVEN

DADDY SHOWED THREE minutes later, direct from "some high-collar directors' meeting I'd have come out a winner if I'd passed." He was pretty much the free-spirited Texan a casting director would have sent—leather faced and squint eyed, surrounded, figuratively, by tumbleweed. He wasn't wearing boots or a multigalloned hat, but that may have been a grudging concession to New York. His expensive suit bowed discreetly to western tailoring, and it was cleverly cut to conceal a massive gut. He was fifty-something, as good-looking as his daughter but with a strong Roman nose instead of her turned up one, and a voice that often boomed, whether he wanted it to or not.

Tess ran to peck him on the cheek, skillfully sidestepping the big belly to do so. He accepted the homage and slapped her on the rump. Wild horses at play.

What would attract this cartoon of a man to an idiosyncratic nude, heavy on the impasto? My shattered, scattered, multilimbed, twin-faced take on the ill-fated Cassie Brennan?

But *Seated Girl* was the painting he wanted, no question. After a final routine squeeze of his daughter's neck he pushed her gently aside and went for it with the purposefulness of his mount heading for the stable.

"Yeah, that one—that's the one hit me when I came in the other day. I could make out like it was otherwise, Leona, try to jerk you around on price, but we're two grown-ups here. What's your best deal? What would you charge your momma for it?"

Lonnie grinned tightly and went pale, but said nothing. She never spoke prices; she once told me that doing so made her feel like a rug merchant. She extended an arm, and Jackie rushed to hand her a clipboard with my pieces and their prices listed on a computer printout.

"It's number nine," Lonnie said, handing the clipboard to Turkinton. *"Seated Girl."*

"Seated Girl, my ass," Daddy said. "Girl with World Class Hooters."

"Daddy," Tess admonished and rolled her eyes heavenward by way of apology. The moment Turkinton showed up the tough independent woman had become Daddy's little girl.

Turkinton was looking at the price list. "Mmm," he said thoughtfully; he managed to make even "Mmm" boom. Then, "Leona, when did the cost of a brush and a few squibs of paint go through the ozone layer?" And then, "I suppose a frame is an extra, huh?"

"I can recommend a good framer," Lonnie said smoothly. "Franz will know exactly what to do with this canvas."

"Mmm," Turkinton said. And waited. For a price concession, I assumed.

Impasse filled the room.

Lonnie was not going to be diddled. She sized up the situation and drifted over to another, smaller, painting—totally abstract and loose as a rag doll. A good canvas, but in a different voice.

"Mr. Turkinton, might I suggest this as a sensible place to begin collecting Shales?" she murmured smoothly. "It's a work central to Sid's themes, but somewhat less of a strain on the pocketbook." And then, briskly, "Number six on the list in your hand, *Untitled Number Three."* It was of course a negotiating ploy: She was testing his balls.

Neither of them knew Cassie was dead, so it was unfair of me to harbor the thought, but they were like a couple of cadaver merchants dickering over the price of the corpse.

Turkinton didn't even look at the price list. *"Untitled Number Three* is not talking to me," he said. "I'm not getting so much as a belch."

He waited another moment, then shoved the clipboard back in Jackie's hand. He may have decided he had a better chance waiting out the millennium than Leona Morgenstern.

"Number nine is the one I've got to have," he said. "That naked little girl." He turned to me. "But I tell you, Sid, I'd have preferred her with fewer legs and more titties."

"Dad-*dy*, for God's sake."

Turkinton paid her no heed. He was giving me the full piercing squint he used against a relentless Texas sun. I was afraid that having failed with Lonnie he was going to start bargaining with me, and I have zero bargaining know-how. But he was on a new tack. He boomed, "How'd you come to paint this little girl?"

"The usual way. She sat. It was a job. Why do you ask?"

"You caught her. Real good. In separate little bits, but I can glue them together right side up in my head. That's her, all right."

"You"—I almost said *knew*—"know her?"

"Hell, yes, I know her. Carrie? Cassie. She didn't say she posed for you." He was studying me narrowly. "I wouldn't mind getting some of that."

"Modeling work?" I had decided to play it dumb. "Real boring. Takes patience. Where'd you meet her?"

"She's a hired girl for a friend of mine. Out on Long Island. Where you do your painting."

Now I understood where we were at. "Your friend is Mikhael Sharanov?"

"That's him. You knew she works for Misha?"

"A drawing of mine hangs in his living room. You may have seen it."

"Very good, Sid. Misha must be a big fan. It's the only picture in his house."

Where was he coming from? I said, "And that drawing made a fan of you?"

"Enough to have you looked up. Truth? I've been Misha's guest at the beach three or four times this spring. I took Tess with me just last week. Misha's a fine host, a *mi casa es su casa*, so take it, please, kind of fella. I was looking for a thank you that would be appropriate and also surprising. *Seated Girl* fills the bill."

"I'm flattered, Mr. Turkinton, but a gift of"—out of re-

spect for Lonnie, I checked myself from saying the formi-
dable dollar figure—"a painting?" Lonnie was shooting dag-
gers at me; I wasn't doing our side any good, but something
made me push on. "You could have gotten away with a
couple of pounds of Godiva chocolates."

Turkinton chuckled his appreciation. "Sid, you must know
the story of the Texan whose son wants golf clubs for his
birthday, so he buys him St. Andrews and Pebble Beach?"

"Daddy, you are a *card*," Tess giggled.

"Fact is," Turkinton went on, and he was trying to moderate the boom, "Misha and I are doing a little bit of business
together. Trying to. You'd be surprised how something *personal*—not chocolates—can grease the wheels when you're
paying a man back for his hospitality."

He laughed. "Which hospitality might be his way of greas-
ing *my* wheels." He cocked his head slyly. "I never said
that, you understand?"

Sharanov and Turkinton. They could be the spider and the
fly. But which was which? "How well do you know Sharanov?" I asked.

"Well enough. He near knocked my socks off with that
Russky nightclub he runs out there in Brooklyn. An honest-
to-God money-making machine." He turned to Leona, who
was standing by fidgeting; the conversation had veered dangerously off the only subject she was interested in.

"Leona, remind me to write you a check before we
leave," he said casually. "Send the little *Seated Gal* out to
Franz and make sure she gets delivered to the address at the
beach Tess will give you."

Deal. Leona broke out an ear-to-ear grin and a burble of
appreciation. Turkinton waved it aside and returned to me.
He had just given me a healthy head start on my share of
Sarah's school bill, and I was elated but also determined not
to show it; why should he think I had gotten the better of
the deal?

Turkinton wasn't interested in my reaction. He was saying:
"What I'm going to do, Sid, is duplicate Misha's restaurant
thing in Dallas. The whole package—maybe bigger, if you

can picture that. We're ready for it. The last few years we've taken on all the French and Italian chowdowns we can handle. I'm betting I can sell the Russian scene from bleenies right up through beef strongenuff.''

"Stroganoff, Daddy. And I told you, it's a stew that's full of *sour cream.*'' Tess shuddered for her innocent father.

I shuddered for him too. For his well-being. He was buying my painting, so I had a rooting interest in his staying healthy, at least for the next few days. If he was a con artist, I needed him to wait until his check to Lonnie cleared before he tried a swindle on Misha Sharanov; that foolish error could lead to his turning up in some distant airport, portioned out in a set of matched luggage.

"So you and Sharanov aren't set yet on your deal?" I probed.

"We're down to the short strokes," he said dismissively; he had tired of the subject. "Listen, Sid, Tess and I are heading out for a couple of steaks. We'd be pleased to have you join us."

He was not likely to reveal any more about his relations with Sharanov and I could think of no other reason to spend an evening with this pair. "I'd like that," I lied, "but I promised some buddies I'd join them for dinner."

"What buddies?" Lonnie asked; she was making it clear with eloquent facial tics that it would be a sound business move for me to cultivate this pliant customer across a yard of charred beef and a parade of bourbons.

"My old gang," I said. "They still go to Muccio's Friday nights."

That much was true; a few of the guys I went through the police academy with continued to meet for sentimental reasons, or maybe out of inertia—certainly not for the food—at a primitive Sicilian restaurant off Mulberry Street that had been the best we could afford in our early days on the force.

Lonnie's expressive eyebrows were saying, Your stomach could take that joint in your twenties; is it up to it in your forties? But she kept her mouth shut: Tess had the floor.

"Mr. Shale, I am a little bit dismayed," she said, mock-coquettish, a coiled spring at the back of her voice. "Daddy and I don't get turned down that often."

Her father was watching her with amused interest. "I know *you* don't, Tessy. I sure as hell do. Maybe I'm the fly in this strongenuff."

I said quickly, "Nothing like that. Let's do it another night. I'll call."

"Or we'll call you," Tess pouted, not much nourished by my vague offer. "I'm sure Leona knows how to find you."

This party was going rapidly downhill. Before it hit bottom I repeated my feeble excuse and beat it out of there.

Another thought had sneaked into my head, and it expanded to fill it as I made for the door: Wouldn't Turkinton stop his check when he heard that the subject of the painting he was buying to charm Sharanov had been brutally murdered?

I shoved that nugget to the back of a high shelf, where it nestled beside the accusation against me of police brutality. I reminded myself to start thinking positively: I had sold a painting.

Cassie Brennan, poor Cassie, had come through for me.

EIGHT

SHARANOV HAD APPARENTLY abandoned his Brighton Beach roots. When I couldn't find his phone number in the Brooklyn book it took a call to my old buddy Tony Kump, still working a precinct in Manhattan I had left years ago, to locate him through the DMV on Central Park West. The phone was unlisted, and NYNEX doesn't routinely give unlisted numbers even to the police, but Tony got me that too. I didn't ask how.

"So you're in town," he said when we had finished our business. "You going to Muccio's later?"

"Some of the guys'll be there?"

"It's Friday, isn't it?"

I thought maybe I would go. I had an understandable itch to find out what was so compelling about my "oeuvre," as Lonnie called it, that Mikhael Sharanov had to have a drawing by me hanging in his living room—his only wall adornment—while a business associate of his fell all over himself to gift him with one of my paintings. If Sharanov himself wouldn't enlighten me, one of my old bunch might have some recent news on him that would help clear the air.

Meanwhile I called the Manhattan number Kump gave me.

A woman answered with a sour, "Yeah?"

"Mr. Sharanov, please."

"You have got to be kidding." She was beyond sour; she was bitter.

I said pleasantly, "Does that mean he's not home?"

"You pick up pretty quick." She wasn't only bitter, she was drunk. "Who wants him?"

"My name's Shale. We met at the beach today." Did she know what had happened there? "At his house."

"You sound like a cop. Are you investigating Cassie Brennan's murder?"

Okay, she knew; that would save some explaining. "I'm not a cop. I'm a neighbor. But I knew Cassie." This woman wasn't Russian. "Are you Mrs. Sharanov?"

"Kitty. 'Mrs. Sharanov' makes my teeth ache."

Now I knew how she knew. She had to be the Kitty I heard Sharanov talking to on the phone. I said, "Do you know where I can reach Misha?"

"I have no idea, thank God."

She sounded as if she might be more forthcoming than her husband. "I'm in the neighborhood," I lied. "Could I drop up for a few minutes to talk?"

"What about?"

"Cassie's death."

Pause. "Why don't you just do that?"

IT WAS A SOLID prewar Central Park West building, but almost certainly a rental; no co-op board with half a brain would approve a purchase by an applicant whose proudest reference was that he had never been indicted. The doorman phoned up to Mrs. Sharanov for an okay and then sent me to the tenth floor.

Kitty answered the door herself. She certainly hadn't spent the ten minutes since my call gussying up for a visitor. She was wearing a pale silk robe that she may have been living in. A yellowish nightgown drooped forlornly below its hem. Her lank pale blonde hair matched her pale blue eyes. Her face was drawn with an unhappiness that had all but robbed her of her Nordic good looks. She was probably under forty because even in her present state she didn't look more than forty-five.

I stepped into a large foyer with lime green walls that were completely blank; except for my work, Sharanov didn't seem interested in art. During my quick glance around, Kitty looked me frankly up and down. Apparently she approved because she said, almost pleasantly, "Can I fix you a drink?"

I didn't want a drink; if I went on to Muccio's, I'd be

drinking as much as I could handle before the ninety-mile drive home. But this woman would take a refusal as an insult.

"Sure," I said. "Whatever you've got."

"I've got everything," she growled, as though I had challenged her bar. She was leading me into a good-size living room with dark, clunky furniture and the same lime walls. The minimalist style of Sharanov's beach house was definitely a mood change for him.

"Why don't you surprise me?" I said, and then, "You know something? You've got a great view of the park, but you'd like it even better if your walls were bone white."

She stopped her beeline march to the bar to give me another scrutiny, this one more intense. "What are you, a decorator?" she said in dismay. I was beginning to think she had plans for me, and if she didn't like my answer I might be given the door instead of the drink.

"No, I'm a painter." Now she wrinkled her straight arrow nose in disdain. I added, "Of paintings. Cassie used to model for me."

Visibly relieved that she was not entertaining a handyman, she resumed her path to the booze. "I can see why. She was a pretty young thing."

She had suddenly remembered the tragedy and her face sagged; behind the booze and the brittle facade may have lurked a woman of substance. Abruptly she said, "I should never have hired her..." She had reached the sanctuary of the bar and her voice trailed off under the sound of rattling bottles.

"Why not?"

"Do you bring candy to a diabetic? Misha has a serious sweet tooth when it comes to women. Cassie was only fifteen when I hired her last summer, but she turned sixteen in the fall. Sweet, sweet sixteen. And Misha started going out to the beach more. Good weather and bad."

"They were having an affair?"

"I hope not. But who'd ever know for absolutely sure? He was smitten, and he doesn't give up easily. If she had any sense she turned him down. And please don't dignify

Misha's every score with 'affair.'" She was drunk but she wasn't stupid.

"I gather you two aren't getting along."

"Never better. I haven't seen the bastard in weeks. I got what I deserved."

"How's that?" I prompted, although this woman didn't need prompting.

"Thinking I could civilize him after two wives failed. But they were Russians, raised to expect nothing from their man but a kid or two and a belt across the chops on Saturday night." She handed me a generous Scotch on the rocks. Her own was even bigger. "I forget. What was it brought you here?"

"I care what happened to Cassie. I think you do too."

The brittle shell was easily punctured. She said softly, "I wish I knew who did that. And why. Misha is cunning and he's got the conscience of a house plant. But *that*..." She couldn't say it, and her sculptured jaw quivered. "What happened. That's not his style. Not anymore. Cassie may have brought it on herself."

"How?"

"Exploring the world of grown-ups. Testing her powers and going too far. What do you think?"

I didn't want to speculate about that. I said, "I don't know what she was like at the end. We'd been out of touch for months."

She let me off the hook. "Yes, at that age months can be years. God, can they." Her face softened further at some memory. I took a closer look. Tarnished gentility now, she must have been something at that age.

I changed the subject. "All those wives, including you—did any of you teach Misha to make a bed?"

"Misha? He resented having to tie his own shoes. Russian men!" And then, shrewdly, "Didn't you say you weren't a cop?"

"I'm not. But a question keeps nagging me. I don't figure your husband for a nester. And yet his bed at the house was made this morning—not made well, maybe too quickly, but made. Sheets, blankets, pillows, cushions, bedspread, the works. And not by Cassie—she hadn't even begun her housework when she was killed. That bed must have been made up when Misha left for the city last weekend. Any idea who might have done it?"

"None. Except, you're right, it wasn't Misha. In all our years together I never saw him make a bed. Even badly."

I took a shot. "Is there someone else here who can help us with this?"

She dug a hand in her yellow hair. "What do you mean, someone else?"

"Am I sticking my nose in where I shouldn't?"

Kitty stared at me, but she said nothing. She hadn't stopped drinking since I arrived but she had been growing progressively less drunk.

I said, "Okay. I'm looking at two sections of the *Times* on two chairs, one folded neatly, the other badly. By different hands?"

She took a moment before she said, "You *are* a cop."

"Again, no. But I used to be. I got it right, huh?"

She called, "Roy!" And then, "Roy, would you come in here, please?" And then, to me, "It's no big deal. My brother moved in when I threw Misha out. They've never gotten along. You'd never say anything about his being here...?"

I shook my head. "You threw Misha out because of Cassie?"

"No. How could I compete with that? My blood boiled over only when he went after women past thirty." She looked at me and she was no longer vaguely flirty; she was suddenly too insecure to go on using me for target practice.

I took a swipe at reassuring her. "The better-looking the woman, the more she hates rejection. I'd hate to be near when your blood boils. I hear you pitch chairs."

She may have seen through my flattery, but she rallied. "I've heard that too. It's not true. Sunbathing breeds gossip. All that lying around with nothing to do."

The brother had walked into the room; he had pulled on a sweatshirt over rumpled cords, but he hadn't taken the time to comb his hair. I had figured, brother my eye; she's taken a live-in lover. But he did look like her—a softer version, pudgy, with drooping eyelids and a self-conscious languor. I'd have given odds that he had been out of work for two years while he looked for "a really suitable business opportunity."

Kitty introduced him as "Roy Chalmers, my baby brother," and me as a "Mr. Shale." She hadn't been so drunk as not to remember my name. Roy allowed in a faintly preppy voice that he was pleased to meet me, as though I had shown up for an audience. I decided that this pair might be the remnants of a once proud WASP family that had gone through the last of the money.

"Roy," Kitty said, "if I told you someone was currently playing house at the beach with my dear husband—even made his bed for him—would you take a guess?"

"Only if there's a prize for getting it right the first time." He didn't wait. "Let's see, I'd look for someone witchy, greedy, and calculating—a woman who may be better at unmaking beds than at making them, but who'd better nail him before her looks fade and her chances vanish."

Kitty's lips tightened; the tail end of that description cut too close to the bone. But she said, "You do have someone in mind."

"Of course. So must you. Olivia Cooper. Or you wouldn't have thrown that beach chair last summer. Kit, have you given any thought to dinner? What would you say to the little Turkish place we discovered last week?"

He had dismissed me. I stayed only long enough to learn that Olivia Cooper lived in Manhattan, and I left brother and sister arguing dinner plans over fresh drinks.

NINE

CHINATOWN WAS CREEPING up on this part of Little Italy; in five years it would vanish in a sea of wonton soup and black bean sauce.

Muccio's didn't seem to notice. I hadn't been to the joint in nearly two years, but it might as well have been ten. The front room never changed; I suspect it had looked this way since Rocco Muccio opened the doors in 1922 to share with the world his wife's punishing version of Sicilian cooking. Rocco's son Jack was not so much maintaining a tradition as failing to see that the moldering place had one. The regulars didn't care; if they didn't object to the food—Jack's cousin Angelina was keeping up the standard in the kitchen—why would they complain that the decor was fifty years out-of-date?

That front room still had all the warmth of a storefront gypsy mitt joint. A long bar, scarred and bruised, was the main attraction here. Above the back bar hung an overripe nude in overripe colors I had painted for Jack Muccio twenty years ago in exchange for meals. Looking at it now gave me the same heartburn as Angelina's cooking.

A few drinkers could usually be found at the bar, but diners ate in the large backroom. I had never seen any of the four tables in here occupied. Forty years ago two mob hit men had lurched through the front door and sprayed this room with submachine guns, killing two patrons and wounding four, although none was the rat fink they were after. He was in the john at the time, upchucking Mrs. Muccio's linguini *con vongole*. Ever since the massacre, the tables in the front room had been considered undesirable.

I had forgotten that on Friday and Saturday nights a pudding-faced woman named Mona held forth in the front room on an electric dreadnaught; when I came in the door she was winding up a bone-rattling "Volare." "Lieutenant Shale!" she yelled happily, over it.

It was good to be remembered. "How goes it, Mona?" I asked and stuffed a couple of bucks in the cloudy tooth glass she kept next to the keyboard.

"Not bad," she yelled, "except for a touch of arthritis in the fingers."

"Mona, you mean you haven't always had that?"

She laughed appreciatively and launched into "Sorrento." It was as though I had never been away.

I bellied up to the bar and a full-throated greeting from Jack's nephew Enzo, the bartender. "Sid-ney!" he said; he always gave me the measured two syllable treatment. "Long time. You been dead or something? Your gang is in the back-room."

"In a while, Enzo. Good to see you. I'm expecting a lady."

"*Here?*"

I wasn't surprised at his surprise. "Not to eat. Would I lay a lawsuit on the joint? What's new?"

"Here?" he said again, and looked confused; I had forgotten that nothing was ever new at Muccio's. "I miss you, Sid-ney. The guys miss you. I think even the button men miss you."

He was pouring me a red wine, my usual drink here. I said, "No, Enzo, I'm on Scotch."

He gave me a look that said, Aren't we fancy tonight: expecting a lady, drinking Scotch. He poured the wine back in the jug and reached for the well scotch. I wasn't so fancy that he would offer me a premium brand.

I looked at my watch: five to eight. Olivia Cooper had agreed to meet me here at eight.

After Roy Chalmers's unflattering capsule description of her I had expected to be given a hard time when I phoned, but she had been receptive, even cordial. Cassie Brennan's murder had made the six o'clock newscasts, she told me, and although she knew the girl mostly from having seen her at work at the Sharanov house, she was, of course, shocked by the news.

When I started to explain who I was, she interrupted to say, "Of course. I know who you are. I've passed your house." She paused, and I sensed she was stifling a giggle. "It's right out of a kindergarten crayon drawing. You do know how to express yourself."

"Thank you."

She lived on Gramercy Park, not that far uptown, and yes, she was agreeable to meeting me for a drink—just for a drink, she made clear—to talk about the murder. I suspected she was at least as interested in taking a look at the painter who lived in the weird house east of Sharanov's. I had to repeat Muccio's address twice; I think if I had given it to her before she agreed to come, she might have turned me down.

She showed at eight straight up. Mona's mighty organ had just finished returning us to Sorrento when Enzo said, "That's got to be your lady."

I gave her a gold star for punctuality, turned on my bar stool, and gave her another for looks. I had been half prepared for the femme fatale Roy Chalmers had described; what I got in the doorway was a trim, vital woman in her thirties with an easy smile and dirty blonde hair worn what the hell. I went to meet her, and while I introduced myself she sized me up and seemed reasonably satisfied.

As an icebreaker, I suppose, she began describing the difficulty her Pakistani cabdriver had finding this place; meanwhile she was drifting toward the table area. I took her arm and steered her, with apologies, to the bar, where the four or five other patrons were seated.

She looked around as she climbed onto a stool. "Doesn't anyone sit at the tables?" she asked.

"Not since they peeled the bodies off them in 1957."

Her lips formed a respectful "Oh." She didn't have a follow-up question, and I asked her what she would like to drink. Enzo was standing by attentively.

"A gin martini?" she said doubtfully. "Straight up?"

I said, "Enzo, this is Ms. Cooper." As they shook hands,

I continued, "Enzo can tell the red wine from the white and he can read the labels on whisky bottles. Mixed drinks..."

Enzo chuckled and produced a dusty pitcher. "For a friend of Sid-ney, why not?" He set to work and we averted our eyes.

I said, "I'm sorry to drag you down to this joint. I'm joining some friends for dinner."

She raised an eyebrow. "Here?" she said.

"It's a manhood test. You've seen Indians walk on hot coals?"

"Okay." She was satisfied.

I had been studying her. She was even better-looking than I first thought. She had a glow. And high cheekbones, a straight-ahead nose, well-shaped lips. Sharanov had taste. "So, are you still seeing Misha?" I asked.

"If I was seeing Misha, would I be free on a Friday night on thirty minutes' notice to have a drink with a stranger?"

"You might be, if he was under arrest."

That brought her erect on her bar stool. "Is he?"

"I have no idea. I wanted to see if you were paying attention."

She leaned toward me and bit down on the words. "Does this satisfy you? I am not 'seeing' Misha, I never 'saw' Misha. Misha is a married man."

"Technically."

"I'm a stickler for technicalities. Where did you get that story?"

"His brother-in-law."

"Roy Chalmers." She nodded her full understanding and relaxed. "The original lounge lizard. No visible means of support, except what he earns as his sister's cheering section. And Kitty was never my fan."

Enzo deposited the martini in front of Cooper. "Enjoy," he said with a flourish. The drink was in a heavy-duty wine-glass, and it was flush with the rim.

"That's a healthy martini," I said.

"You know my customers," Enzo said. "Fill the glass halfway and they bitch."

"That's with *wine*."

He shrugged and Cooper said, "Enzo, could I trouble you for a twist?"

"I'll try the kitchen," he said. "They'll have lemon for the veal piccata."

I shook my head. "Not unless you plan to peel the RealLemon bottle."

"Never mind," Cooper said. "Not important." She lifted her glass in a graceful arc and didn't spill a drop. "Cheers," she said.

Enzo beamed as she brought the glass to her lips. He waited for a verdict. And waited.

"Mmm," Cooper said.

Enzo nodded his appreciation of what he decided was a compliment, and moved down the bar to serve another customer.

"How long has this place been here?" Cooper whispered.

"Seventy-five years," I said.

"That explains the vermouth," she mused. "It was the best they could get during prohibition." She raised her glass again. "Here's looking at you." She took another sip.

"How come Kitty Sharanov doesn't like you?" I asked. "What's not to like?"

She put the glass down and turned it with long tapered fingers while she composed her answer. Finally she said, "Do you know Misha?"

"We met for three minutes."

"Think of a sleeping tiger. Power at rest. Scarier than the out-front kind because you never know how much is there waiting to be unleashed."

"That's close to my impression."

"Then you know a lot about Misha. People say he may be a gangster. Whether it's true or not, the rumor alone makes him appear dangerous. That's catnip to many women. Very sexy. There are usually women around the Sharanov place, around Misha. Much better-looking women than me."

"That's hard to believe."

"I wasn't angling for a compliment, I'm simply telling you

the way it is. Some real stunners. So why does Kitty single me out as a threat? I'm the one who's not interested in Misha. He takes that as a challenge, and he hits on me. Kitty thinks I'm playing a game to snare her husband, and that makes her mad. If it was true I wouldn't blame her.''

"So how come Misha's charm escapes you?"

"Because I've been down that road. I had a man like that in my life. Not a gangster, but macho, controlling."

"What happened to him?"

"I divorced him. One is enough."

"You're not interested in Sharanov, but you do hang around the Sharanov house."

"I sure do. It's *entertainment*. I've got this little place in Southampton, and I go out most Fridays after a bitch of a work week. During the day I play tennis, and in the evening I wind up at Sharanov's a lot. I find what goes on there more interesting than the scene at this week's cutting-edge East Hampton restaurant."

"Like what?"

"Like the furtive comings and goings of broken-nosed hunks Misha growls at in Russian; I always imagine he's sending them out to break the noses of other people. Whatever he tells them, they jump—in front of a train, I bet, if he told them to do that. There are memorable house guests. The last few weeks the best guest bedrooms have gone to a loudmouthed Texas software tycoon and his pushy daughter. Daddy, poor sap, thinks he's going to hornswoggle, if that's the word, Misha in some scam or other. He thinks he's dealing with a Slav off the steppes and still not totally defrosted. Misha will not only pick him clean; he's already, I wouldn't be surprised, had his way with the daughter."

Could anyone ever really have "his way" with Tess Turkinton? Any "way" was likely to be hers. But I could see where observing Sharanov at work and play might hold the same fascination as watching a pit of rattlesnakes.

I said, "What about Cassie Brennan? Was she much of a presence in that house?"

"Not really. Misha would have her in when there was a

big crowd on a Saturday night. She'd fetch, clean up, whatever. She seemed eager to please. A really pretty kid, full of life. But I'm not telling you anything you don't already know."

She knew I was waiting for more. After a moment she said, "Maybe he had an itch for her, but I never got a hint it went the other way. Is that what you're looking for?" She gave me a hard, clear-eyed look. "What exactly is your interest in Cassie's death?"

"She was a friend. I'd like to see her killer nailed. Maybe I can help with that. I used to work homicide for a living."

"You were a cop!" she exclaimed. "That's what this place is—a cop's hangout. I should have guessed." She seemed pleased at having solved the puzzle of why we were at Muccio's.

"About Cassie," she continued quietly. She was looking at me with new interest: What kind of friend was I to Cassie? "I don't see what more I can contribute. We never got personal. She did clean my place once last fall. She was good, too, but she didn't have that much to say." Her eyes slid off me for a moment, then back. I didn't like that.

I said, "That doesn't sound like the Cassie I knew. She was a nonstop talker."

Again she didn't meet my gaze. "If I had to guess I'd say she was more open with men."

I said, "You may still be able to help." Here it came again: I was beginning to obsess about that damn bed.

"Yes?" Now I had her full attention. Good-looking woman; I almost forgot my point.

But I hung in and made my pitch. "Somebody made the king-size bed in Sharanov's bedroom when he left the beach last weekend. It wasn't Kitty—she hasn't been there in weeks—and I'll bet my house it wasn't Tess Turkinton—"

"You've met her?"

"Long enough to know she wouldn't make anybody's bed except under a court order. Do you have any ideas?"

"The Turkintons were Misha's only house guests last weekend. If you were wondering if it could have been Cassie,

I don't see why. And I certainly don't see how. Misha heads back to the city on Sunday morning. I know this much about Cassie—she goes to church with her mother Sunday morning. Anyway, why does it matter?''

"I'm not sure it does. But that made bed—complete down to the spread, the throw pillows, the works—is the only thing about the murder scene that doesn't belong. It's a What's Wrong with This Picture, and it bothers me."

She was studying me frankly. "Because you *are* afraid Cassie might have been in that bed."

"I don't know."

I wasn't about to protest that I had no sexual interest in Cassie. It would sound self-serving, and anyway, it was a no-win position; the denial itself would be a sign of interest. So I changed the subject.

"You agreed to meet me for a drink only. Can I expand the invitation? Will you stay for dinner?"

She was not in the least surprised. "Now that you've checked me out?"

"Not really," I lied. "I'd have asked you on the phone, but I was afraid of scaring you off."

She looked amused as she weighed the offer. "Dinner with a bunch of cops? Sounds safe."

"The company will be safer than the veal. So that's a yes?"

She looked even more amused. "Only because I can't trust myself to navigate alone after this ocean of martini."

Mona had just plunged into a spirited "Funiculi Funicula." What timing.

TEN

IF THIS BUNCH of mostly bruisers had shown up on your street you might have called the cops, but *they're* the cops. Red Buchanan sported an ear that had been redesigned in the Golden Gloves. Tom Ohlmayer wore a scar from his jaw to his collarbone, souvenir of a bomb squad screwup. Tony Kump had two joints of a finger missing; somebody had tried to keep him out of an apartment, never mind the search warrant. There were a few size-eighteen collars, although there wasn't much collar-wearing in this crowd. Some of these guys wore a suit only as a disguise, and to weddings. And not all weddings.

The cast at the Friday night cops' gathering in the noisy backroom at Muccio's had evolved over the years and it changed from week to week, depending on the demands of duty rosters and wives. I recognized only seven or eight of the dozen or so guys at the long table, which could be ex- panded as needed by joining more tables at either end.

Rocky Peretti and a couple of others were from the original group I knew as far back as the Police Academy; Steve Sta- vrianos had been my partner for three years, and so on. They were mostly detective firsts who had earned their gold shields the quick but dangerous route—undercover in narcotics. They had not been totally at ease with me when I first made lieutenant, but we soon went back to the old gang feeling, at least here at Muccio's. I was reminded of that now.

"Yo, Picasso, over here!"

"Beach bum, where's your tan?"

"Look who showed—it's the poster boy for the shuffle- board league."

And more of the same. When they simmered down I in- troduced Cooper. A woman did occasionally show at these gatherings—even an occasional policewoman—but women were not encouraged. I could see right off that there would be no problem tonight. The guys had registered their unspoken approval.

Stavrianos said, "Miss, if you've got your eye on this one, forget it. He's got a very small p-p-p"—he pretended to struggle with the word while the others held their breath—"*pension,* and he paints with his feet."

"His feet?" Buchanan objected, through the laughter. "His teeth—when they're in."

This got the required hoots of derision. That was the way the guys did it; I had been out of touch, and I had to be folded back in. Slowly. After more ragging and some general catching up they were satisfied, and Cooper and I were waved to the next two places at the table.

She was feeling the martini and she ran her eye hungrily down the menu, not that easy to read through the stains. Finally she murmured, "I have an itch for linguini with clam sauce, but I can't find it."

"It's called linguini *il salvatore* here, because it once saved someone's life, but if you ask me how, you may not order it." I turned to Rocky, sitting next to me. "How's the ziti?"

"The same. Try the osso bucco."

A guy down the table called, "I've got the osso bucco. Have the ziti." And so it went.

I had been giving Tom Ohlmayer eye signals, and after I grabbed one of the overworked Muccio cousins waiting table and Cooper and I ordered, I excused myself to pull up a chair next to him at the head of the table. Tom and I hadn't worked together in years and rarely saw each other anymore, but when we did it was as though the last time was yesterday.

I asked about his kids, he asked about mine, and I said, "You heard about the homicide out at Mikhael Sharanov's beach house?"

"Yeah. Doesn't that scumbag live near you?"

"My good neighbor. Do you know what he's up to these days?"

"Aside from milking his cash cow in Brooklyn?" Tom had once given me a pop-eyed description of a drunken evening at the Tundra with his wife and some friends. "I have no idea."

"Wasn't a rackets team put on his ass a couple of years ago?"

"That's over. Couple of damn good detectives. They've been reassigned."

"How come?"

"In the first place, after two years they couldn't even find a way to ticket him for spitting on the sidewalk. Do you need a second place? The order to knock off came from the commissioner's office, no explanation."

I said, "The Department's wrong to give up on Sharanov. He's smart, but he'll make a mistake. Don't his kind always?"

"Has he already made his, Sid? Did he do that young girl out there?" He raised his thumbs prayerfully. "Wouldn't it be sweet to tag him for murder?"

I had gone over this ground before. "A killing in his own home? Would he take that chance?"

"He would if he had to. Remember that homicide at the Tundra three years ago?"

"The body in the coatroom. They never touched Sharanov with that one."

"Or anyone else. There were five hundred Russians in the place. Half of them owed the victim money, every one of them was juiced to the scalp. The suspect list read like the Brooklyn telephone book."

I said, "You mean, whereas at his beach house Sharanov is the only suspect?"

"Who better? Suppose the girl was dusting the furniture or vacuuming the drapes, and she found the gizmo that could put him away forever? Could he avoid cutting her throat? Or having it cut for him?"

"What is this gizmo you're talking about?"

"Who the hell knows? Not our problem. Suffolk County will have to sort it out."

Cooper was signaling. They were delivering our dinner. Time to face the ziti.

COOPER PASSED ALL tests as a dinner companion. She gave the guys as good as she got, and she managed to choke down most of her linguini *il salvatore*. We were on coffee and cannoli when I spotted a wide-eyed Enzo beckoning me from the entrance to the bar. I mimed that if he wanted me he would have to come to me, and he did, dragging his feet. His body language was, This is entirely on your head.

He bent to my ear and breathed, "In the bar." And waited.

"What, in the bar?"

"A lady."

"For me?" I said stupidly.

"She would have come in here but I told her I would bring you out." He spoke in a respectful whisper. To invite a lady to Muccio's was something; to follow with a second was awesome.

Enzo was glancing at Cooper, who pretended not to listen. He went on, "I figured you wouldn't, you know, want this one to see…"

Too late; the second lady was in the doorway. Tess Turkinton. Her eyes swept the room like a prison yard searchlight, and she made right for me.

I murmured to Cooper, "Excuse me a minute?" and went to head her off.

We met midroom. "Hello, Tess, what a surprise."

She was still taking in the place. "What a dump," she said in a try at a Bette Davis reading that was spoiled by her Texas drawl. "And you turned down a steak at Gallagher's for this?"

"Didn't I tell you I was meeting friends?"

She was focused on the cops' table. "I noticed. Isn't that Olivia Whatever?"

"Cooper."

"Whatever. She does get around. I suppose you know her from the beach…"

I had her by the elbow and was steering her to an empty

table near the door. It wasn't easy; I had met less resistance from suspects reluctant to enter a police car.

I said, "What's on your mind, Tess?" Lonnie must have told her where to find me. I was hip deep in women tonight, not necessarily a plus.

We sat down and Tess snapped her fingers at a passing waiter, Angelina's son Benno. She may have planned on linking up with me for some after-dinner pub crawling—she had, after all, shown up without her father—but since I appeared to be here with a date, she was regrouping.

"I have to talk to you," she said. And to Benno, "Do you serve any wines by the glass?"

Benno looked confused. I said to Tess, "Not many people here order the entire two-gallon jug. Benno, a glass of red. On my tab."

He nodded and took off. This woman's father had bought my painting, so I tried to sound politely regretful. I said, "Tess, I'm afraid you'll have to drink that either fast or alone. I can only give you five minutes."

"You're not going to introduce me to your friends?"

"It's a sort of club, and they've got an ironclad rule. You're allowed to introduce a woman once a year. Two women, never."

"They're policemen, aren't they?"

I nodded.

She nodded back. "That's what Leona said. And you're a policeman too? A detective?"

"Used to be."

"That's what Leona said." She was testing to see if my story matched Lonnie's; she must have laid on the power of a tornado to get Lonnie to admit that she was peddling the oeuvre of an ex-flatfoot. She said, "How long are you off the force?"

"Going on two years." Why the question? Was she looking to renegotiate my price downward on the theory that I had painted *Seated Girl* on the taxpayer's dime? "Painting is my day job," I said firmly.

She got my drift. "Oh, I'm not here about your painting,"

she said. "That's a done deal." That was a relief. "I came to ask about a possible police matter."

The upward slant at the end of that sentence invited me to inquire further. I didn't.

Okay, she would have to do it herself. She said, "The thing is, the business my father's engaged in with Mikhael Sharanov? Where Daddy's going to have to invest a great deal—I mean, a *great* deal—of money?" She was searching my face for a clue to I wasn't sure what.

She said, "I mean, you're a policeman..."

"Was."

"But you'd know."

"What?"

"Whether this Sharanov is some kind of crook. Whether the police are investigating him. Because Daddy is starting to hear rumors that are...well, they're just a little bit *unnerving*."

It was hard to tell whether she was worried or merely trying to appear worried. She and her old man, a pair of big winds out of big *D*, were almost too good to be true.

I quickly reviewed the bidding, not for the first time. These two could be naive straight shooters. But if they were pulling a confidence stunt, they hadn't done enough research and they were zeroing in on the wrong mark; Mikhael Sharanov would eat them for lunch and feed their bones to his dog. Then again, they were buying my painting to give to Sharanov, and I couldn't afford to alarm them into stopping their check to the Leona Morgenstern Gallery, the check that represented an investment in my daughter's future. I had a fine ethical line to walk.

I said slowly, "Since I'm no longer on the police..."

"Not at all? No connection?"

"The NYPD doesn't have part-time employees."

"Are you telling me you don't know anything about Misha?"

"I've been out to his club in Brooklyn..."

"The Tundra." Impatiently, "So have we, of course." Benno had set down her wine and she pulled it close to her.

"It looked to me like a good business," I said. "But your father would be a better judge of that than me."

Even more impatiently, "Daddy says it's a gold mine. So you think, as a cop—okay, an ex-cop—that he's legit? We can do business with him?"

"Your father must have checked his credit standing and so forth. He'll have to go with his best assessment." And then I felt honor bound to say it. "But watch your back."

Her eyes widened in alarm. Or, again, was she faking it? "Damnation," she said and took a long pull on her wine.

I said, "I'm sorry, Tess, I don't see how I can help. And now I'm afraid I am going to have to get back to my table." I stood up.

I could see her eyes boring in on Cooper. Her mouth was set in a grim line. "Let me give you tit for tat," she said. "Watch your back."

She put down her half-finished drink, pushed back from the table, and strode out of the room. Trailing smoke.

I counted to ten, in case she decided to come back. Then I draped the napkin loosely over her glass and picked it up carefully by the stem. As I started back toward my table with it, Benno appeared at my shoulder and shuffled along beside me.

"Here, let me have that," he said, reaching for the glass. "No way can you get lipstick off with a napkin. I'll put the wine in a fresh glass for you."

I had to switch hands to keep the glass from his eager grasp. "I don't want the wine, Benno, I want the glass."

"Why?" He looked astonished.

I couldn't think of a reasonable explanation. I shrugged. "Sentimental reasons."

I left the bewildered Benno behind and delivered the glass to Ohlmayer. I was pretty sure the prints were unsmudged.

ELEVEN

BY 11:25 P.M. eastbound traffic on the Long Island Expressway moves at a good clip, even on a Friday. I would be home in near record time, if I could keep my eyes open. There is no sleeping pill half as effective after a few drinks as two hours behind the wheel on a limited-access highway.

Olivia Cooper hadn't invited me up for a nightcap when I dropped her off at her Gramercy Park address. Thank God; one more Scotch would have nodded me off by Syosset. Of course, if Cooper had invited me up not for a nightcap but for the night, the possibility of a road accident would have been avoided. But there was no hint from her that she was interested in playing house, and after Tess Turkinton's dark "watch your back," my guard had gone up again.

What was there about Cooper that stirred bitchiness in other women? I had gotten barbs about her from two in one evening. Cooper, for her part, had almost nothing to say about Tess Turkinton's pushy visit to Muccio's. She had looked mildly amused but asked no questions when I returned to our table with the boosted wineglass. She murmured, "Ms. Turkinton does get around, doesn't she?" and never mentioned her again.

My trick for staying awake on that drive home was to dwell on thoughts angry enough to keep blood pumping to my brain. I thought of Lonnie nudging me into a one-on-one with Tess Turkinton: Lonnie the sales pimp. I thought of Misha Sharanov—unscrupulous and so far unindictable—and how Cassie's death had left him totally unmoved. And when I felt my eyelids pressing like paperweights, I began to think back a couple of years to Ray Drummit, that piece of dirt who more than likely put a bullet in my father's brain and might now collect a king's ransom from New York's taxpayers because my single outraged punch to his mouth had knocked out a couple of teeth.

And as I neared home I thought of Cassie Brennan, cut down in full flower, her blood crying out for justice in a long arc on Sharanov's bedroom wall.

I DIDN'T EXPECT lights on Beach Drive at one-thirty in the morning at this time of year, but I did spy one in a distant window. A moment later I realized that the window was mine. I had gone to the city in daylight; I wasn't likely to have left a light on. I floored the gas pedal and gravel flew.

A police car, its lights out, was pulled up at my front door beside my found-object sculpture. The light spilling from the house made *Flotsam* look like a weird sci-fi take on an Easter Island statue.

I peered through the windshield of the police car. Walter, the chubby village cop, was slumped over in the driver's seat, his hat on the dash, his cheek mashed against the side window. For a moment I thought he might be dead, but he was only asleep. I couldn't blame the poor blimp for cooping, he was running up hefty overtime. In aid of what?

My front door was unlocked. That didn't trouble me; I leave it unlocked about half the time. But as soon as I walked in I saw that person or persons had laid heavy hands on the place. Furniture and painting supplies had been moved, boxes unstacked, drawers opened, canvases spread.

Houses in summer resorts are routinely burglarized out of season, but the houses of year-round residents usually are not: The family might show up to surprise the burglar. And it was widely known around here that I owned nothing worth stealing but my paintings. Local thieves would find those more of a headache to sell than their time was worth. Ask my dealer.

And on closer inspection I concluded that what had gone on here was not the work of thieves. The place had been searched, not ransacked. For what? The answering machine was blinking and I punched it on. There was one message, and it held no answers. Leona Morgenstern had called:

"Sid...? Sid, are you there...? It's after midnight, and you're still out on the town? Does that mean the Turkinton woman found you? I trust you two are getting along. Do you know how long it takes for a check to clear on a Texas bank? Many love affairs blossom and wither in less time. Sid, you must have seen the bill from Bennington sitting on my desk. The figure on the bottom line is not my Social Security number. Act responsibly. Talk to you tomorrow." The woman was urging me to screw my way to solvency.

I went back out to the police car; Walter must have been assigned to keep an eye on the house after it was violated. Some watchdog. I opened the driver's side door, and my knees buckled as he slid into my waiting arms. His eyes snapped open.

"Right. Yes. Move along here," he barked into the night before he understood where he was. He glanced at me sheepishly, said, "Uh, good evening, Lieutenant." And then, with some help from me, he wriggled to an upright sitting position and tried to look professional.

"What's going on, Walter?" I asked in a reasonable voice.

"I've been watching for you," he said. "Waiting for you," he corrected, in the interest of accuracy.

"Do you know who broke into my house?"

"They wouldn't do anything like that. Not nearly. They went in perfectly legal."

"Who?" But I had already guessed.

"Chuck Scully—the chief. And that detective from County. Mean son of a bitch, isn't he?"

I was beginning to get a creepy feeling deep in my bowels. "What do you mean, perfectly legal?"

"They had a search warrant. Good day or night. Got hold of a judge in Riverhead and came back with the paper. Perfectly legal, all the way down the line."

I wished he would stop repeating "perfectly legal." The creepy feeling was working its way along my extremities. I said, "Walter, what would make a judge sign a search warrant when there was no good cause?" I was asking for it.

"Scully and that other one—Docherty—had their reasons.

Don't ask me what, I wasn't in on that part, but they were perfectly legal. The judge went down their list and it didn't take him five minutes to issue the warrant.''

"They had a list?''

"They did. I'm supposed to bring you over to the village, Lieutenant. The chief is waiting to see you at police headquarters.''

I was in some mild form of denial. "No, Walter. Not at this hour, he isn't.''

"Yes, he is. He said to tell you he'd be there all night, if necessary. He meant it, too.''

POLICE HEADQUARTERS occupied the entire ground floor of the village hall. At that hour too many fluorescent lights were burning in too much empty space. No one was on hand but an officer at the switchboard and Chuck Scully, who was nervously shuffling paperwork at his desk. As I approached the open door of his office he jumped up like a startled cat and broke into a relieved grin. It was as though he had been half-expecting word that I had been spotted crossing the Mexican border.

He said, "Come on in, Sid.'' He wasn't calling me Lieutenant tonight.

Walter, a step behind me, said, "Is it okay if I sign out now, Chief?''

Scully barely hesitated. "Tell you what. Why don't you wait a while?'' I supposed that was in case it was going to take the two of them to subdue me. Walter was going to be a lot of help in that situation.

I could see that Scully was bracing for a roundabout approach to a delicate problem. I cut through the underbrush.

"I understand you searched my house, Chief,'' I said, looking him steadily in the eye. "You must have had a pretty good reason.''

"You want to see the application for the warrant?'' he said eagerly, and thrust a Xerox copy at me. He looked miserable.

I laid it on the desk without looking at it; I wasn't going

to make it easy for him. I said, "Why don't you just tell me the high points?"

He sat down and gestured for me to do the same. We were going to be informal about this awkward business. Walter had ambled out of the office to chat with the man at the switchboard.

"You want a laugh?" Scully said, his way of showing he was on my side. "Docherty thinks you could be unstable, possibly dangerous."

"Because of that possible lawsuit from the felon I belted a couple of years ago?"

"That ticked him off. I don't know why, but he's not a fan of the NYPD."

"I noticed." Where were we going with this? "I doubt he used that argument with the judge who signed the warrant."

"No, he didn't." It was too late at night for irony; Chuck hadn't picked up on mine. He said, "Cassie Brennan's killer may have wiped the crime scene clean. The only liftable prints were two fingers on the headboard." He mumbled, "They were yours."

I couldn't believe this. "Chuck, I was with you when I touched that headboard. When I stood up after bending over the body."

He brightened. "You think that's when it was?"

"I *know* that's when it was. Are you telling me Docherty's crime scene people found the prints and scrambled to check them against my file at the NYPD?"

"I don't remember if it happened exactly that way." He shifted gears. "That drawing of yours hanging at Sharanov's? Sharanov says it was Cassie persuaded him to buy it. He says she pressed him about it until he had to get her off his back."

"What does that mean? I had something going with her?"

Reasonably, "I, for one, don't think so, Sid. But you can't rule it out."

"And then what? In a fit of jealousy, or a lover's quarrel, I killed her?" I was doing a slow burn. "Aren't we getting a little silly here?"

"Not necessarily." I was hitting him where he lived. That

was stupid; I could see his back stiffening. We were becoming adversarial.

He said, "Would you like me to read you your rights?"

"I know my rights," I snapped. "And Chuck, keep your pants on, you haven't scored a killer. I was *home* when Cassie Brennan was murdered. Waiting for my model to show. Gayle Hennessy."

He shot back, "Sid, you're the one who showed me how Cassie had to have been killed soon after she came to work. That fit pretty good. And you say you were home then? I called you around nine-thirty. I got your answering machine."

"I was home." Did I have to explain that I was draped across a beam, and why? After a very long day I wasn't going to pick my way through all that at two something in the morning.

I said, "I couldn't get to the phone." In a house not much bigger than a hot tub? It sounded lame even to my ears.

The most painful part of this business was that at heart Scully really was on my side. But that county cop, Docherty, had steamrollered him good. And now I could see poor Chuck getting ready to hit me with something worse.

"The thing is," he began slowly, "it turns out Cassie's throat was cut with a knife that had a jagged edge. We checked Sharanov's kitchen and there was an empty slot in the knife holder. Sharanov is sure it's the bread knife that's missing."

"Sharanov knows what's in his kitchen?"

"I asked him that. He said Russians eat a lot of bread and the house couldn't function without that knife." He was pleased with how his inquiry had gone. "A knife with a serrated edge."

"That's on Sharanov's say-so? That it was a bread knife that was missing?"

"At that point, yes."

"Good detective work, Chuck." I wondered how much of it had been Docherty's. "Anything else?" I knew that there had to be more; his eyes kept sliding off me to his wall calendar.

He said, "When we left the crime scene Docherty thought we ought to stop by your place. To see if you had anything to add that might be helpful. Because you're the nearest neighbor."

"And?"

Now he was looking totally miserable. He said, "You know that weirdo statue outside your door?"

"Beach side or road side?"

"I didn't know there were two. Road side."

"*Flotsam.*"

"Doesn't matter. There's two sixteen-ounce Schlitz beer cans stuck to, I don't know, I guess what might be the chest. Those are breasts?"

"If that's what you see, Chuck."

"That bread knife was sitting nice and neat in the left boob. We only noticed because the blade stuck out and glinted in the sun. Naturally we were surprised. And then it turned out you weren't home. You can see why Docherty thought we should go for the search warrant."

It took me a moment to find my voice. "Chuck, this is probably your first murder investigation."

"You know it is."

"Tip. Not many killers hide the murder weapon outside their front door. Especially if they've got thirty miles of beach at their back door."

"That's what I'd have thought. But what do I know? Like you said, this is my first murder investigation. So we got the warrant."

He was still feisty, but now he began to soften. He said, "And then when we did go into your house..." He trailed off.

"Yes...?"

"We found those drawings of Cassie," he blurted out. "Those naked pictures."

Oh, boy. "Nude studies, Chuck. It's what artists do."

"Her mother was horrified."

I groaned audibly. "You told her mother?"

"Docherty did. That news came on top of... You know, everything else. She's a religious woman, Sid. She said Cassie swore there'd be none of that when you asked her to model. Nora Brennan would never have allowed it."

"There was no reason for you to tell her mother. That was cruel."

"I know. But Docherty said we had to do what we had to do. He thinks you have an obsession. And that it led to a compulsion. He says you're bad news."

I SPENT the first twenty minutes back home putting the place in order. It was almost three-thirty in the morning, roughly twenty-one hours since I had climbed up on the scaffold to repair that clumsy hand on *Large*. I was burned out but too keyed up to sleep; some time in the next couple of days, unless an ADA with some common sense was put on the case, that jerk Docherty was going to find a way to arrest me.

If I had any smarts, I would find myself a lawyer as soon as the sun came up, although every lawyer I had run across since moving out here was a real estate specialist. To a man, they would advise me to shop for the best deal I could get on a thirty-year mortgage on my life.

I could retain a lawyer, or I could pay the damn college fees; until I absolutely had to holler for help I would try to fence with the law on my own. With luck, Cassie's killer would tip his hand before then. With luck.

The last thing I put away were the drawings spread out on my worktable. The cops had taken almost all the Cassie drawings; they were solid evidence, I supposed, of my sick compulsion. The two they left behind—none of the nudes—competed for attention in my mind with the memory of that limp body beside the bed. I taped one of the drawings to the wall; by keeping that vibrant image before me, maybe I could overcome the one of the dead Cassie lying in her blood. Not a chance. That was the way I would remember her, probably forever.

I had forgotten that I had taped another drawing to the wall—this morning's sketch on the beach with the Sharanov house in the foreground. I took another hard look at it; what was in that sketch that had bothered me?

Damned if I knew.

By now my eyes were losing their focus. I stripped off my clothes, turned out the light, and crawled into bed.

In a probably vain hope that I would find sleep.

2

...A SHORT WEEK

TWELVE

ARE YOU GOING to the wake? If you are, okay if I tag along?"

This was Monday morning, and it was Gayle Hennessy on my answering machine. I was up on the scaffold, working near the top left corner of *Large*. I was on a roll and not inclined to scramble down to pick up.

Except for a few hours of sleep and an occasional bowl of canned chili, I had been painting almost nonstop since Saturday afternoon. Once Chuck Scully turned down my admittedly foolish offer to help in his murder investigation ("Are you kidding? Docherty would kill me."), I turned to the best therapy I knew—work—to help me lose, or at least temporarily put aside, my laundry list of angsts about recent events.

Since I usually paint for long stretches seven days a week anyway, it was not easy to tell when my regular work habits began to spill over into therapy time. But something was working. Gayle's call startled me into realizing that I hadn't thought of Cassie Brennan in hours. I still had the sketch of her posted on the wall, but there was damn little left for me to chew over about her death. Scully had cut me off when I tried to feel him out about the results of the autopsy. I was so out of touch that Gayle's call was the first news I had that the body had been released to the family.

Next time I climbed down, to clean brushes and replenish my paints, I called Gayle and said, yes, of course I would go to the wake. She said she had the Brennans' address, and I said I would pick her up at eight.

I knew I had to go, but I don't do well at wakes. Almost all of those I had been to were of cops killed on the job. (Or by the job; suicides.) Days after the death the painfully young widow and orphaned children would still be in a state of shock, and the photographs of the deceased that took up so much of the crowded living room always seemed to be saying to me, "Why didn't it happen to you instead of to me?" I'm more comfortable with the Jewish death ritual: Plant them fast, grieve afterward.

Only once had I gone to a nonpolice wake. The deceased was a murder victim. I had a hunch that his killer might be on hand and in some way signal his guilt, the way an arsonist sometimes gives himself away at the scene of his fire. All I picked up on this occasion was a buzz from the alcohol I had to consume to blend in with the mourners.

I stayed aloft on the scaffold until six, then showered and dressed in clothes suitable for showing respect for the departed. They were roughly the same clothes I had worn the previous Friday to show respect for that pair of Texans who were interested in buying my painting of her.

That, I decided, was letting Cassie down. But I had nothing better to offer.

GAYLE LIVED in a small apartment behind the workroom over Gayle's Provocativo on Covenant Street. She was waiting for me in front of the shop when I drove up, casually but calculatedly draped in a dark purple whatever the hell, somber but striking, that she may have whipped up just for this occasion. Gayle worked that way.

The news burst from her as she climbed into my pickup. "The prodigal has returned."

"Who's that?"

"Cassie's old man. Mel, at the diner, saw him drive into town this afternoon. For the wake, I suppose. Cassie told me she hadn't seen the bastard in months. I guess he couldn't resist the chance to belly up to the free booze."

I said, "Come on, Gayle, you're not being fair. If he hadn't shown, you'd have said he had a heart of stone. You'd damn well want your father at your wake."

"Just long enough for me to stand up in the box to see who the son of a bitch was and kick him in the teeth."

She fished the driving directions out of a fold of her garment and said, "Sid, be careful what you say to the mother. The way I heard it, she was not all that crazy about Cassie posing for you." She perched her reading glasses on her perfect Lena Horne nose. "I mean, even before you got the girl to do the nude stuff. I guess you must regret that."

No kidding. Thank you, Gayle.

"Another thing. Let me warn you: Cassie's body's at the house. It's the way they did it at Nora Brennan's grandmother's wake, and she insisted."

This was not going to be my favorite wake.

THE BRENNAN HOUSE, a cracker box, stood in a cluster of near relatives in a wooded area about equal distance from the ocean and the bay, with easy access to neither. Resale values here would never climb much above rock bottom. But the Brennan house was tidily landscaped, painted, and curtained, and had a well-maintained path to the front door.

I parked behind half a dozen vehicles. Four or five people were on the path, some leaving the house, one couple arriving with a tray of food. At Gayle's suggestion we had stopped at the Cake Box, and she carried our contribution to the evening, two pounds of assorted cookies. We edged the front door open against a sea of bodies and squeezed inside.

The front room was so crowded I couldn't even make my usual eyeball check for pictures on the walls. A plain pine casket took up a good chunk of floor space, and a long table set up with the bar and free lunch consumed much of what was left.

The shoulder-to-shoulder mourners spilled into the kitchen and a bedroom. These people were all locals; they appeared to be neighbors and co-workers of the mother. Cassie had told me that Nora Brennan worked for the tax assessor in the village office. Oddly, I saw no young people—no one Cassie's age. A priest was the youngest person in the room. Where was the boyfriend, Paulie Malatesta?

I let Gayle lead the way and we pushed through to the casket. A low stool had been placed at the open end, and she dropped to it in a practiced kneel and bowed her head for a moment of silent prayer. When she stood up and moved quickly off her eyes were glistening and her lip trembled. Gayle had grown up surrounded by death, but she had long ago shed her inner city veneer of detachment from it.

I moved forward to the casket but remained standing; I don't come from a tradition that includes kneeling. The mortician had done an okay job. That wasn't the Cassie I knew in the box, but at least the slashed neck was mostly buried under makeup and a weird-looking high collar that had nothing to do with the real world. The waxy face had been made up by a cosmetician who didn't know the girl. His work reminded me of a boardwalk caricaturist's—it delivered everything but the essential Cassie. But he had achieved a repose that may have given comfort to the bereaved.

I was not moved; I felt nothing. I was not reminded of Cassie; Cassie was somewhere else. But I stood for a long moment with my head bowed, so as not to be thought callous—the man who had looked on this girl naked but refused to kneel and look at her dead.

Gayle had told me she had met the mother with Cassie once or twice in the village, so again I let her take the lead. She threaded her way across the room to a high-backed chair against a window and waited for an opening in the cluster of women surrounding its occupant. At the first break she elbowed through and bent over. She grasped the seated woman's hand in both of hers, said a few words, and turned to make sure I was behind her—as though she was afraid I might have chickened out.

She said, "Mrs. Brennan, this is Mr. Shale, who drew so many lovely pictures of Cassie, caught her so beautifully with his pencil and brushes."

Gayle was doing her damnedest to smooth the moment. She stepped aside and I said my piece.

"Mrs. Brennan, I knew Cassie only a short time, but I grew to respect her a great deal. I feel her loss deeply, so maybe I can begin to imagine your pain. I am terribly sorry."

I had expected a woman of middle years; Nora Brennan

was almost certainly younger than me. She was, in fact, an older version of Cassie—Cassie with the juices partially drained. Putting aside the current grief that had her eyes red-rimmed and her face drawn and sickly pale, she was a Cassie stamped with bitterness; her mouth had been set in unhappiness years before her daughter's murder. Only a Velázquez could have captured her mixture of pain and pride.

She looked at me steadily, without change of expression, and I looked back just as steadily. If she was going to dump on me, let's get on with it. Meanwhile the three women who had been chatting her up turned and moved on; they had sensed that something private might be in the works here.

Finally Mrs. Brennan's tight lips parted. Her voice had an edge, and it cut. "Was Cassie's body suitable for your purpose, Mr. Shale?"

Jesus, this was going to be even harder than I thought. "Cassie was a good model," I said. "Maybe the best who ever sat for me. She was disciplined. I admired her spirit. It was a privilege for me to get to know her during our sessions together. I came to think of her as a friend."

"Did you? Then why did you dismiss her?"

"I never did. I'd have used her as long as she was willing to sit. At the time there was a question of money. There still is. As soon as I had some I'd have called her."

"To pose naked again? Was that your plan?"

"No. That happened once. There was...a miscommunication. But you must understand that Cassie was proud of her body." I took a gentle shot, on the theory that the best defense is an offense. "Why wouldn't she have been? God gave her that beautiful body. She had no reason to be ashamed of it."

The red-rimmed eyes were fixed on me, the mouth again set. Eventually she said, "Your behavior toward my daughter was entirely inappropriate."

Inappropriate didn't sound too bad. I said, "I assure you, Mrs. Brennan, nothing happened during those work sessions that would have troubled you."

"I know that," she snapped. "Cassie would have told me

if you had acted in a way you shouldn't have. She shared everything with me. Always. And she had so little to confess to in her brief life. So very little."

She had kept a tight rein on her daughter, and for a fleeting moment I wondered if she regretted that Cassie had not had the opportunity to taste certain earthly pleasures. But then she said, "She was a religious girl, thank God, and I take comfort in that. She's with her little sister now. And the angels."

THE ORDEAL WAS OVER. Gayle and I were each holding a Scotch, and we were circulating. I had ended my audience with Mrs. Brennan by offering to bring her one of my sketches of her daughter—by implication, one in which she was clothed. She had turned me down, and I quickly assured her that in any case none of the sketches were for sale; they would all remain in my files. That got no response and I backed off with another expression of sympathy. It hadn't been good, but neither had it been as bad as I feared.

Gayle had hooked up with a couple of village merchants and I looked around for a familiar face. I found only one— Jack Beltrano, the fire chief. He was a small-time contractor, a young and fit fifty, weathered like barn siding by too many hours framing up summer homes in bad weather. He was deep in conversation with a man whose back was to me. Jack and I caught each other's eye at the same time and he said a few words to the other man and made his way to me.

After we exchanged greetings I said, "Did you know Cassie well?"

"My mother lives next door. She needs a lot of attention, so I'm around. Sid, did I ever thank you for the drawing you donated to the auction? We had some hot bidding on that one. A picture of the village where you can make out every shop? Who wouldn't want that?"

People who wanted it because it was a good drawing, that's who. But I said, "You sent me a note. You said it went to someone who asked not to be named. I was impressed."

"I didn't mean to be mysterious. I have no idea who bought that picture. But can you guess who showed up to bid for the buyer?"

I wanted him to say it. "Who?"

"Cassie. It was poor Cassie Brennan. She came in that night with a bundle of cash. And I guess instructions to buy your drawing, whatever it took. She hung in until she'd worn out the couple of other bidders. She laid out a healthy chunk of dough on behalf of some fan of yours out there somewhere."

He allowed himself a small chuckle. "Unless she was buying for herself. Beautiful kid, it's a damn shame. What about it, Sid?"

"What about what?"

"Was she a little bit hung up on you?" He was uncomfortably flip for this setting, and now I could tell he had already had a couple of drinks.

I said, "Cassie worked hard for her money, and she was too smart to be that reckless with it—even if she'd had a schoolgirl crush on me." He looked as though he was about to say something wiseass, so I quickly added, "But she was too smart for that too."

The man Beltrano had been talking to had idled up to the makeshift bar and fixed himself another drink. Now he was walking toward us—to retrieve Beltrano, I thought. But it was me he turned to.

"Jack tells me you're Sid Shale."

"I am."

He was in his forties, another construction worker, I figured, two hundred pounds, much of it flab. He had once been handsome, but his softening features, mottled skin, and eyes nearly lost behind cushions of flesh gave away a drinking problem. I knew who he was half a beat before he announced it.

"I'm Jim Brennan. Cassie's dad." There was confrontation in his voice.

I said, "She was a beautiful young woman. I'm truly sorry for your loss, Mr. Brennan."

"Are you? There's a laugh." He tried to force a laugh and failed. "Mr. Painter."

Beltrano cut in soothingly, "Okay now, Jim. Easy does it."

Brennan shook off the steadying hand. His attention was fully on me. He said, "Showing up here."

He was having trouble forming his thoughts and he repeated, "Showing up here." He had a good head of steam by now. "I want to talk to you."

"Fine. What about?"

"What about? What the hell do you think about? My daughter." He was beginning to shift his weight like a boxer waiting for the starting bell.

"I don't know what I can tell you that you don't already know," I said. I didn't like his air of menace and I added, "But Cassie did tell me you had been out of touch lately, so maybe there are things you missed. Your Cassie had grown up lately."

"She had? Not to her father." What there was of his eyes had narrowed to the vanishing point. "And I'm here when I'm here. When I'm needed. Understand? I go where the jobs are, that's the way it is in my line of work. I'm not some frigging artist who never has to move more than five steps from his own crapper."

Jack Beltrano took his arm again. "Jim, keep your voice down. And I think you should save this for another time."

Brennan said, "No. This is the time I'm here. Right now. When I'm needed."

He took a step toward me; we were nose to nose, all but touching. He was claiming the territory. Angry husbands used to do that when I was a patrolman on "domestic dispute" calls. Their home was their castle and I seemed to be a threat.

Now Brennan said, "But yeah, Jack's right, this is not a good place to be talking." The tiny eyes were riveted to me. "We won't bother anybody out back."

Beltrano said, "Look, Jim—"

Brennan ignored him. "There won't be anybody in the yard."

He waited for a reaction from me. When I gave him none he said, "Through the kitchen." He nodded in that direction. "You get what I'm saying?" He turned to Beltrano. "We won't be needing you, Jack."

Beltrano said, "Don't be a damn fool." But he made no effort to stop Brennan, who was already on the move.

Jesus. Better out back, I supposed, than here with the coffin and the grieving mother. I followed the beefy guy as he lurched toward the kitchen and through it. People got out of his way. Two women making sandwiches at the kitchen counter didn't even look up as he swept past them.

Without looking back to see if I was there, he held open the kitchen door, and I went through it to the small backyard. Is this where he took Cassie when he believed she had earned a good thrashing?

A frayed hammock that had barely survived the winter hung over a balding lawn. Nora Brennan kept a tidy house, but it was clear that she never came back here to put this area in shape. I wondered if Cassie had lain in that hammock last summer when her father was nowhere around, and dreamed of the bright future for herself that didn't include this town.

Brennan turned around and faced me. "Okay. What the hell were you doing with Cassie?" he demanded. "With my girl?"

"I was drawing her picture. It's the way I make my living. Cassie sat for me." Was I going to have to pick my way through another labored explanation? "Your wife knows about our arrangement. Talk to her."

"I'm talking to you. I don't have to talk to her."

"Okay, talk to me." With luck I could talk him down off his high.

He wasn't prepared to talk, only to confront me. "She was a kid," he offered weakly. "Still in school, for Christ's sake."

"Cassie graduated last January. Didn't you know?"

He possibly didn't; the red blotches stood out in his face. He didn't want me asking questions, only answering them. He shouted, "You son of a bitch, were you humping my daughter?"

"No." I was tempted to say, Were you? "The work we did together was intense but it was strictly business. And it brought good results. For us both."

"Bullshit. You did her bareass naked."

He knew that if we stuck to words I might get the better of him. With no further warning he lurched toward me and threw a roundhouse punch. It came slowly, and I was able to move out of its path. And then, almost by reflex, I stepped forward and drove a fist deep into his soft belly. I was sorry the instant it connected.

He said, "Oof," and doubled over.

Now people were spilling out of the kitchen door, and a low rumble of disapproval floated my way. I had done a dumb thing; they saw the mourning father sunk to one knee and looking like a whipped dog.

He straightened up and I read the humiliation in his mottled face. He was getting ready to deliver another punch. I braced myself and moved to take this one. He was drunk; how much harm could he do?

More than I guessed. He wasn't all flab, and there were nearly two hundred pounds behind his meaty fist. It caught me on the left shoulder, and I spun around and went down on my butt. A shock wave traveled up my spine to the back of my neck.

When I looked up, Jack Beltrano had grabbed the outraged but now satisfied father of the deceased by the waist. "Easy, Jim, easy," he said and led him away. Someone behind me was helping me to my feet.

It was Chuck Scully. He said softly, "Don't these people have trouble enough? What are you doing here?"

"Paying a condolence call."

So much for my noble sacrifice; I hadn't damaged my hand, but my shoulder and neck were killing me. If that kept me from painting I would brain that drunk Brennan.

"Some condolence," Scully was saying. "Jeez. Can't you control your temper?"

He was spanking yard dirt off the back of my good clothes. He said, "No wonder Docherty locked on to you. And in case you thought he'd forgotten, he wants you in tomorrow morning. To answer some questions. Nine a.m. at police headquarters. Meanwhile, why don't you go home and paint a picture or something?"

I said, "I think I'll do that."

THIRTEEN

I DIDN'T NEED Gayle to point out that I had behaved like a damn fool; my shoulder explained that to me all the way back to her place.

"I found out why Jim Brennan has that chip on his shoulder," she said. "Did you know the Brennans had another daughter?"

"Cassie told me she died."

"She was run over. Five years old. Her father was supposed to be watching her, but he'd slipped off to a bar for a quick one. How's that for a load to carry around?"

As she got out of the car she invited me up for comfort food—cold chicken and a beer.

I thanked her but explained that I was eager to go home; I could still get in a few hours of work before sleep. What I was thinking was, Chicken, Gayle? I've already eaten crow tonight.

THE MINUTE I got home I changed into sneakers and sweats. My neck was almost back to normal; I figured a half hour's jog on the beach, working my arms vigorously, would keep that shoulder from stiffening when I started painting. It was not much after nine o'clock, and the May air was still mild. Good weather for a run.

Out on the sand I took a precautionary first step in aid of the shoulder; arms extended to the sides, I cut small circles in the air while I listened to the whispering ocean. I happened to be facing west, and up the beach a quarter of a mile I could see a light in the Sharanov house. Not a room light, more like a small lamp. If there were any more ambient illumination it wouldn't have shown, but the moon was no bigger than a fingernail paring.

And then the light winked, bobbed, threw a beam, and slid from one upstairs window to another: I was looking at a flashlight. Sharanov was in the city, and someone was in his house, almost certainly without an invitation. A persuasive argument for my jogging west rather than east.

I weighed one other decision: Should I go back in the house for my off-duty pistol? The compact Smith & Wesson five-shot had been a comforting weight in the small of my back for years, my faithful companion on long subway rides and latenight trips to the convenience store. Like all retired cops I was licensed, but the S&W lay in my desk drawer unloaded. I hadn't fired so much as a single practice round in half a dozen years, and I might do more harm than good with the piece.

The clincher was that I couldn't remember where I had stashed the .38 ammo. By the time I found it, Mr. Flashlight might vanish. So I jogged off unencumbered. Toward the Sharanov house.

When I was a cop, if I had gone to investigate a possible crime in progress without both a weapon and backup I would have drawn a reprimand. So why was I so hell-bent now? It was beyond hope to expect Cassie's assailant to be sniffing around the scene of his crime at this late date. But something was up; it certainly wouldn't hurt to take a look.

I advanced at less than warp speed. In the pitch dark along the beach I had to be wary of where I placed my feet; the scattered rivulets and gullies changed shape and position from day to day. And every time I lifted my head from my sneakers the distant flashlight had moved to a new spot. By the time I got close to the house, still working my arms therapeutically, the light had long since floated down the ramp to the bedrooms. That was one busy prowler.

Without taking the time to stop and decide exactly what I intended to do, if anything, I moved around the house to the front entrance and glided up the corkscrew ramp to the door. I would shape a plan at the top.

One choice was to wait beside the door for the intruder to

leave, and jump him as he came out. Another was to knock firmly and see what that stirred up.

The choice was made for me when I touched the knob. The door was unlocked.

I slipped in and eased it closed. Here in the dark of the living room I expected to have a moment or two to make a further decision. Should I look for the switch and turn on the lights? Should I slip down the ramp in the dark and assess the situation? Or should I find the phone and make a whispered call to the police? And why hadn't I thought of this last before I jogged the quarter of a mile up the beach?

The choice, it turned out, was not to be mine. Almost immediately, I spied the flashlight beam bouncing back and forth on the interior ramp. The visitor was making his way back up to this level.

I flattened myself against the living room wall at right angles to the top of the ramp. And realized I had now more than half-committed myself to mixing it up with whoever was on his way up. Conscious of the dull ache in my shoulder, I was probably about to go one-on-one with someone for the third time in four days—more often than I had in my last ten years on the job. My out-of-shape and aging body was protesting, and so was my cautious mind.

At least I had surprise on my side. I had better use it decisively.

That light beam was pointed dead ahead while the feet that moved it up the ramp dragged. This clod was taking forever to make it to my level. When he did, I was ready. I came out low and charging.

I connected with a hip. The attached body toppled over backward and I landed on it. The two of us rolled a few yards down the ramp, first me up, and then him, before we came to a stop. With me, as luck would have it, on top. Meanwhile my opponent, who was softer than a jelly doughnut and had about that much fight in him, had been yelling "Hey! What the hell! Damn it, stop!"

The yell was urgent and frightened, but its undertone was

almost languid, as though urgent and frightened were alien
to this voice. I had heard the voice before.

Still straddling my adversary, I yanked the flailing flashlight out of his hand and shone it in the face of Kitty Sharanov's lounge lizard brother. What was his name? Roy Chalmers. He still couldn't make out who was sitting on him, and
now he was shouting, "It's no use, all I have is six dollars.
Take it, it's yours."

I said, "You'll need it for gas and tolls, Roy. Unless the
village police hold you for breaking and entering."

I turned the light to my face. Chalmers took a moment to
place me and then I felt his body untense. He said, "What
do you mean, breaking and entering? I have a key to the
front door. What are you doing in this house?"

It was a reasonable question.

WE WERE SEATED in matching chairs on the west side of the
living room. By agreement the only light came from a small
lamp we had placed on the floor between us. There would
be no one in residence in the summer homes to the west,
practically no likelihood of the light being seen to the east,
where the nearest house was mine. But why take chances?

Chalmers was relaxed now, comfortable in the designer
chair; he knew how to lounge, all right. He was dressed in
his snooping clothes—a pair of good lightweight wool slacks,
a maroon cashmere sweater over an open shirt, and Italian
shoes with adjustable buckles, in case, I supposed, he lost
weight in his feet during the caper. I had already explained
that as a conscientious neighbor I had come over to investigate what I thought was a prowler. And what was his excuse
for being here in the dark?

He said he didn't need an excuse; he reminded me that his
sister was mistress of this house, and she had given him the
key to pick up a few things for her.

"With a flashlight?"

"With a flashlight or a flaming torch," he said languidly.
"What the hell business is it of yours?"

"None," I said. Then, "But don't you think your brother-

in-law might be interested in your reason for this visit? If he
is, you'd have to give him a full explanation because I happen to know he gets impatient with people who are less than
totally candid with him. Have you ever seen Misha impatient? He's really bad news.''

Chalmers's posture shifted noticeably. No longer lounging,
he now veered toward cringing. ''The man's impossible to
live with,'' he whined. ''Temper, temper, temper. Plus, he's
a flagrant adulterer.''

He wrestled with himself briefly before delivering the rest
of the news. ''You'll hear about it anyway. Kitty filed for
divorce today.''

''No kidding,'' I said; she had plenty of cause but I hadn't
thought she had the guts.

''Misha's furious,'' Roy went on. ''She's afraid he won't
allow her access to some things here that are indisputably
hers.''

''Why not?''

''Sheer spite. Clothes, accessories, personal items. There's
no reason for you to fan the fire by bringing my presence
here to his attention. You met Kitty. She's a decent woman
but dreadfully pliant. Misha will roll right over her. She may
end up with nothing. After nearly fifteen years with the creature from the black lagoon.''

If she ended up with nothing, so would brother Roy. I said,
''You've been poking around here in the house for—what?—
a good twenty minutes. If you're collecting Kitty's personal
effects, where are they?''

He wasn't prepared for the question. After a painful silence
he murmured, ''I was basically doing an inventory this time
out. I plan to return with a minivan in a day or two.''

I wasn't going to let him off with that lame excuse. I said,
''Kitty's things would likely be in one or two places—the
bedroom and her bathroom. You were running all over the
house with that light. Looking for what?''

His mouth pursed. He didn't want to go into that.

I pressed. ''How about you were looking for something
you didn't need a van for? Like cash.''

"Don't be ridiculous. Whatever wretched little money Kitty has is in the bank."

"I mean Misha's cash. A bundle or two he might not be able to put in a bank. Skim from his restaurant in Brooklyn."

Dismissively, "The Tundra? I wouldn't know anything about that."

My hunch was that possibly he did. He would if Kitty did. But if that was it I wasn't going to get it out of Roy Chalmers. Cash money was serious business. Hot irons to the soles of his feet wouldn't coax that truth out of him.

Two minutes later we left the house together, and Chalmers locked the front door. I watched him get into his Mercedes—his sister's, I supposed—and drive off.

I called after him, "Be sure to give my regards to Kitty."

I REALIZED WHEN I got home that at least one good thing had come out of the encounter. Jogging hadn't done the job, but rolling down the ramp in an embrace with Roy Chalmers had readjusted my shoulder; the pain was almost gone. I would have to remember the remedy.

The answering machine was blinking. It was Lonnie, uncharacteristically subdued, a note of sympathy in her voice.

"Sid...? Sid, bad news, I'm afraid. Ben Turkinton called. He's heard, of course, about the death of that young girl. Who hasn't? My God, it's been all over the news. He tried me over the weekend, but I was away. He thinks, no surprise, it would be counterproductive at this point for him to gift that man Sharanov with the portrait. Even I would be hard put to deny the element of the ghoulish in such a gift.

"Sid, I'm sorry, he's stopped his check. The picture had already gone out to the framer, so he's agreed to pay for the framing, but that's it. For now, anyway. I got him to agree to reassess the situation in a few weeks, when the picture might again seem appropriate—'a way for Sharanov to remember a young friend who was cut down as she began to flower.' But I don't think Bennington will take that vague promise in lieu of tuition. So that's it.

"Oh, Alan said to tell you he's sorry he missed you on

Friday and he looks forward to seeing you when school ends. He's still painting like mad evenings. Very good stuff. He reminds me of the young Sid Shale.''

End of message.

I formed an image: Mikhael Sharanov in his living room proudly showing a visitor the tastefully framed portrait of a dismembered naked girl who happened to have been butchered in his bedroom.

Yeah.

I climbed up on the scaffold and lost myself in painting.

FOURTEEN

WITHOUT ANY OUTSIDE stimulus that I was aware of, my eyes sprang wide open at about three in the morning. I had been dead asleep for less than an hour, but I was as fully awake now as if I had been roused with a cattle prod. An idea had sprung full-blown into my consciousness, totally unbidden. It had to have been germinating somewhere in the back of my mind because the sketch I did early in the morning of Cassie's murder—the beach scene with the Sharanov house in the foreground—had been troubling me ever since.

I hopped, literally, out of bed, turned on the desk lamp, tilted it back, and took a close look at the sketch, still taped to the wall. Yes, the answer to "What's wrong with this picture" that I had seen in my head was right there on the paper. If you were looking for it, it hit you in the eye; if you weren't, you slid right past it. Nice work, Sid.

I secured the sketch between cardboards. Before I went back to bed I put it in a shopping bag at the front door.

As if I might forget it.

I WAS ALMOST never in the village at ten to nine in the morning. That was another thank-you I owed County Detective Docherty. Except for the Super-ette, Mel's Deep Sea Diner, and the Coffee Cup, none of the downtown shops were open this early. The only activity on one-way Covenant Street was in front of Gayle's Provocativo. Gayle Hennessy was outside the shop fussing with something on the window. She flagged me down when she spotted my pickup. I stuck my head out the window and she stepped aside so I could see the sign she was posting:

PRE-SEASON SPECIAL—ALL MERCHANDISE 20% OFF

Sale Ends Saturday

"Is this okay?" she said.

"Good color, nice composition," I called. "But I don't like the message. With the season coming you should be charging twenty percent *more*."

"Thank you, I wasn't looking for a critique," she said. "I just want to know if the damn sign is straight."

"It's straight."

A tow truck had pulled up alongside my pickup. Paulie Malatesta was at the wheel, looking ghastly; he obviously wasn't getting much sleep.

He leaned toward me and yelled, "Yo, Lieutenant, have they arrested him yet? Sharanov? Have they nailed the creep?"

That kid had only one tune in his head. Understandably. I was tempted to shake it out of him with, No, but they may be about to nail me for the crime. Instead I cranked down my other window and said, "I don't know any more than you do, Paulie. You could have asked Chuck Scully if you'd been at Cassie's wake last night." I wanted to see what that would stir up.

He blinked, drew back as though he'd been slapped, and roared off down the street.

Gayle said, "That was cruel, Sid. I don't think Cassie's mother even knows Paulie exists. And what are you doing in town at this ungodly hour?"

If I told her I was on my way to be grilled, the whole village would know in fifteen minutes. I said, "I like to get my shopping done before the stores crowd up."

DETECTIVE DOCHERTY WAS almost genial this morning. He greeted me in Chuck Scully's office with what I took to be a smile, although his heavy lips had trouble cranking it up. He was not a frequent smiler.

He sent Chuck for a couple of chairs and he arranged them so that we sat at the desk as a circle of equals, three professionals gathered to discuss a murder investigation. A cozy start, and I didn't care whether it was an interrogation ploy or Docherty responding to someone in the DA's office who had instructed him to cool it until he built a reasonable case against me. I had my own agenda for the meeting.

But first I gave the county cop what he asked for. I started with an account of how I came to do a couple of nude sketches of Cassie, despite Mrs. Brennan's prohibition. That wasn't easy. Then I had to lurch through an explanation of why I happened to be hung up on a ceiling beam the morning of the murder and therefore unable to get to the phone when Chuck Scully called me at nine-thirty. I wound up by congratulating Docherty's crime scene people for lifting my prints from Sharanov's headboard. I explained, as I had to Chuck the other night, how they got there, and I admitted that I had possibly been careless in allowing that to happen. I couldn't help adding that in my previous life when we found an officer's prints at a crime scene we considered the source.

"I did," Docherty said, but mildly. He was exercising restraint.

Chuck looked embarrassed through this part of the meeting. Until Docherty had goaded him into the role of attack dog he had been my totally uncritical fan. Now that Docherty was easing up on me Chuck was out there all by himself, an attack dog without a mission. I sensed his tail curling between his legs. He would start biting it the next time Docherty reversed himself.

So before the questions grew sharper—I expected a grilling on my relationship with Cassie and a close examination of my movements the morning of the murder—I shifted the focus by going into my own pitch. Out of courtesy, I directed it at Scully: This was his police station.

"Chuck, I brought something in I thought you'd want to see," I said and took the sketch from the shopping bag at my feet. I slipped it out of its protective cardboards and laid it on the desk facing the chief.

The move got Docherty's attention. He leaned across

Scully and turned the sketch to face him. "That looks like the Sharanov house," he announced. He hadn't made detective for nothing.

"It is," I said. "I drew this sketch the morning of the murder."

Docherty jumped all over that. "That morning? You were out there on the beach, near the Sharanov house, the morning of the murder?"

"Yes, somewhere around seven. I was back home well before eight."

Chuck spoke up for the first time. Eagerly he said, "Yeah, you can see the sun hitting the house flat, bouncing off the windows head on." He was edging back to my side. "It would do that real early."

"So?" Docherty said.

"You see how I did that?" I said. "The glare whiting out the windows? Turning them blank?" I had done it with a wash.

"What are you looking for, compliments?" Docherty growled. "Or what?"

But Chuck got it. He was leaning across Docherty. "Here, the bottom of this window, see? A band of black. No glass. No reflection from the sun." He let the rest roll triumphantly. "Like this window was partly open."

I had to hand it to him. The double-hung bedroom windows were tiny in the picture, and more suggested than drawn in detail. It had taken me three days to spot what I had done with a couple of strokes of my black pen.

I said, "People may leave their weekend house without making the beds, but they make absolutely sure the house is locked up tight."

"Sharanov's was," Chuck said excitedly. "Almost the first thing I looked for was forced entry. Every door, every window, was locked."

"So what that means...," Docherty said slowly. He was waiting for someone to tell him what it meant.

I let Chuck do it. He was coming into bloom. He said, still excited, "That open window is in the master bedroom. It

If offer card is missing write to: Mystery Library Reader Service, 3010 Walden Ave., P.O. Box 1867, Buffalo NY 14240-1867

NO POSTAGE
NECESSARY
IF MAILED
IN THE
UNITED STATES

BUSINESS REPLY MAIL
FIRST-CLASS MAIL   PERMIT NO. 717   BUFFALO, NY

POSTAGE WILL BE PAID BY ADDRESSEE

MYSTERY LIBRARY READER SERVICE
3010 WALDEN AVE
PO BOX 1867
BUFFALO NY 14240-9952

Play The Lucky Hearts Game

and get...

FREE BOOKS, a FREE GIFT... and MUCH more!

Yes! I have scratched off the silver card. Please send me my **2 FREE BOOKS** and **FREE MYSTERY GIFT**. I understand that I am under no obligation to purchase any books as explained on the back of this card.

415 WDL CNGT

Scratch Here!
then look below to see what
your cards get you...

© 1998 Worldwide Library

Name _____

(PLEASE PRINT)

Address _____ Apt.# _____

City _____ State/Prov. _____ Postal Zip/Code _____

Twenty-one gets you
2 FREE BOOKS and a
FREE MYSTERY GIFT!

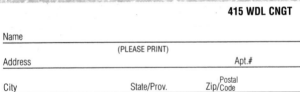

Twenty gets you
2 FREE BOOKS!

Nineteen gets you
1 FREE BOOK!

TRY AGAIN!

Offer limited to one per household and not valid to current subscribers. All orders subject to approval.

PRINTED IN U.S.A.

could have been open at seven in the morning because Sharanov had slept there the night before and opened it for ventilation. If he did, he was still there when you drew the picture. And then he closed and locked the window sometime later—maybe because he didn't want anyone questioning him about having been in the house.''

Now Docherty came aboard. "And if he closed it after nine, was it because he was there when the girl came to work and they had some kind of dispute?" To make sure we got his point he ran a finger across his throat.

I let the cops bounce the ball back and forth between them: They were on salary.

Chuck said, "Sharanov claims he arrived at the house around eleven, hours after the murder."

"And according to him, he never went inside," Docherty said.

Chuck agreed. "He says he left the chauffeur with the bags and drove into the village to pick up a few things. That's an easy check."

"*Toward* the village was the way he put it to me," Docherty corrected. "The chauffeur called him on the car phone and told him about the murder. Sharanov never got to the village. He turned around and went back to the house. That can be checked with the chauffeur. What's his name?"

"Nikki," I said; I couldn't resist finally joining in. "Nikki wouldn't be much help. If Sharanov told you he was delayed en route by space aliens Nikki would swear he saw the mother ship. The cellular phone record would be more reliable confirmation."

"I'd better get hold of this Sharanov," Docherty said; he was keyed up. "For a sit-down."

He had lost interest in me, at least for the moment. He smelled blood somewhere else. It couldn't have gone better.

TEN MINUTES LATER he was gone. He had located Sharanov after a blizzard of phone calls, and he left to meet him in Brooklyn at the Tundra, "to secure your additional assistance in our ongoing investigation." I gathered that the Russian

had not exactly leaped at this chance to help in the figh
against crime.

Chuck offered to accompany Docherty, but Docherty
smelled a possible collar somewhere down the road and he
declined the offer. Not unless he absolutely had to was he
going to split credit for the arrest with a village policeman
who was still on his first can of Gillette Foamy.

Once Docherty left the building I pulled Chuck back into
his office and closed his door. He gave me a what's-going
on-here? look.

I said, "If Sharanov slept at his house that night there may
be a quicker way to find out than driving all the way to
Brooklyn. If you can help me with this."

I looked around for something to draw on. A large cal
endar from an insurance company hung on a wall. I pulled
the April sheet from off the back and laid it on the desk
blank side up. I selected a ballpoint pen from half a dozen
in a coffee mug.

I said, "While I was settling down on the beach to sketch
that morning, a man came toward me over the dunes from
Beach Drive. He was heading west to east with fishing gear
looking for a likely spot to surf cast. In walking to the beach
he had almost certainly passed the front of the Sharanov
house. If he did, no way could he have missed a red Cadillac
out front."

Scully nodded his agreement. "Not at seven o'clock on a
Friday morning."

"Out of season."

Scully's eyes sparkled with anticipation. "You know who
that was, Lieutenant?" Suddenly I was no longer Sid.

"No, but he would almost certainly have to be a local
And you've lived here all your life."

"Except for college."

I had already begun sketching in quick, bold strokes. The
image was clear in my head, but I left the bony face blank
to do the easy stuff first—the long skinny body, the boots
and hat, and the gangling arms that stuck out of the T-shirt

one holding the shoulder strap of the creel, the other the fishing rod.

Then I carefully filled in the features as I remembered them—the squinty eyes in the narrow Don Quixote face, the jutting cheekbones, bent nose, long jaw, and thin mouth. It was an easy face to caricature.

Chuck stared at the sketch. "What would you say he was—under thirty?"

"Probably. About your age."

"Darkish complexion?"

"I'd say. Anyway, in the sun a lot."

He continued to stare, then took his shot. "I think it's Harry Gregg."

"He lives out near the beach?"

"Near enough to walk. And I know he likes to fish. We were in high school together. He played pretty fair basketball."

"What does he do now?"

"Last I heard he worked at the Gulliver—the boatel over on the bay side?—as house engineer. I've run into him at Mel's Deep Sea."

"You going to talk to him?"

"Yeah." Sheepishly, "You want to come along?"

FIFTEEN

WE DROVE OVER to the Gulliver in Chuck's chief's car. We seemed to be easing back to our old relationship. En route I said, "Will this make a problem for you?"

"What?"

"My coming along. Docherty's favorite suspect?"

"Docherty's on his way to Brooklyn," he said, as though that explained a lot. "And you're the only one who can make a positive ID of this possible witness." Then, as an afterthought. "Anyway, until there's an arrest, everyone east of Patchogue is a suspect. People are edgy. The hardware store is selling door and window locks like there's a fire sale. It's a sad time for this village."

"How well did you know Cassie?"

"Mostly to say hello. She was a genuine Ten, wasn't she? A real winner. If I wasn't married I'd have asked her out. She seemed to light up around older guys."

By Cassie's standards Chuck was an older guy. I said, "She had an older boyfriend, didn't she?"

"That mechanic at the Huggins station. Malatesta. Yeah, he's twenty-five. If he was her boyfriend."

"What do you mean?"

"We talked to him. Were they going together? We mostly have his word for it. After she died."

"I can't think why he'd make that up."

"And I don't know anybody who ever saw them together."

"They'd have kept a low profile," I said. "They didn't have Mrs. Brennan's blessing. Paulie wasn't even at the wake."

I had a question that was likely to draw a None of your business, so I turned it into a statement that didn't have to be answered. I said, "I'm sure the ME checked for a possible rape."

Chuck took a moment to decide whether to share the information with me. He came down on my side.

"She'd had intercourse recently. There was no indication of rape." His voice was tight with embarrassment. "They found traces of a lubricant used on condoms."

The news shouldn't have surprised me, so why did my pulse quicken? Sometime after Cassie proclaimed her virginity to me the previous fall she had obviously had a change of heart. And body. She had left her constricting home, and this world, somewhat more woman than girl. I devoutly hoped her exploration of the senses, no matter how brief a time she had for it, had been fulfilling, and that it had been accompanied by love in all its glory. I was rooting for that.

THEY TOLD US at the Gulliver that Harry Gregg wasn't due at work until 2 p.m., so we doubled back south toward where he lived. Chuck remembered the house from a single visit he had made to it as a teenager. "I think Harry was born in that house. North of the highway, but not that far north," he said.

North of the highway meant a less valuable property; not that far north meant that Gregg lived a brisk walk from the beach. Chuck said the house was old even when he saw it years ago, and declining. And, he warned me, so was the present-day Harry Gregg.

According to Chuck's thumbnail sketch, Gregg was from an old local family and possibly the product of too many generations of distant cousins falling in love with each other. His father died when he was a child and his mother had a hard time of it. She died when Harry graduated from high school. He married soon thereafter and moved his bride into the family house. The marriage didn't last. The bride took him for whatever little he had, and Gregg, always something of a loner, started drinking and became even more awkwardly antisocial.

All this was a prelude to Chuck's warning me that we would have to be slow and careful with Harry Gregg.

"Take it as slow as you want," I said. "I'm basically along for the ride."

THERE WAS a ten-year-old Ford truck in the driveway, so we figured Gregg was at home. The two-story-plus attic frame house was old, all right, and needed paint and patching and a new porch rail, but age gave it a certain dignity. Toward the back of the weedy property a huge storage shed had gone to its knees with rot. The place looked like the cornerstone of a standard Suffolk County potato farm that had long ago been divided and subdivided to extinction. The surrounding houses were not nearly as old, but they stood helter-skelter, as though they had been dropped at random from above.

We climbed onto the sagging porch, and Chuck knocked on the front door. And again. And again, louder. Finally we heard shuffling and bumping deep in the bowels of the old place. Eventually the door opened.

I saw at once that I had caught him in my sketch; this was my Don Quixote, minus hat and fishing gear. His sandy hair was uncombed and he looked sleepy, but his narrow eyes widened some when he recognized Chuck.

"Chuck Scully," he said. "What the hell, I do something wrong?"

"Hello, Harry. Nothing like that. How've you been? My wife—you remember Jean—said to be sure to say hello. Did I catch you at a bad time?"

"I'm all right. I was napping, is all." He paid out the words the way a miser does dimes. "I don't have to be at work until two o'clock."

"So they told me at the Gulliver. Okay if we come in for a minute? Oh, this here's Sid Shale."

Gregg glanced my way and nodded, but I didn't register with him. He said, "Yeah, hi." Then, to Chuck, "Jean, right." He nodded again, but I don't think he had a fix on Jean either. "I was out fishing real early is why I was napping. So the house is kind of a mess. Can we talk out here?"

I suspected the house was always a mess and maybe nobody ever got inside. As Gregg grew older and more eccentric people would call it "the crazy Gregg house" and kids would scale stones at it.

There was no place to sit out here but the porch rail, and that looked chancy, but Chuck said, "Sure, here's fine." He perched on the rail and it swayed. I continued to stand and so did Gregg. He was signaling that he was not expecting a long visit.

"You don't recognize Mr. Shale?" Chuck asked.

Gregg shook his head slowly. "What's this about, Chuck?"

"Did you go down to the beach to fish last Friday morning?"

"I fish three, four mornings a week."

Suddenly he understood. He said, "The morning the girl was killed. Yeah, I fished that morning." Then, his face darkening, "Now, wait a minute—"

"Relax, Harry, I just want to know what you may have observed on your way to the ocean. Did you walk along Beach Drive?"

"Mostly, same as always. Then I cut across the dunes to the beach. I didn't see anything special along the road. Or anybody, if that's what you mean. Nobody's in any of those houses this early in the season on a Friday morning."

"How early was it?"

"Somewheres about seven. Wait, there was a guy on the beach drawing pictures. I remember it was that day because when I heard about the murder I thought maybe... But then I figured he must be the artist lives in that crazy-looking shack down the beach and I forgot about it."

Chuck nodded toward me. "Is this the man you saw drawing?"

Gregg took a better look. Under his deep tan he flushed. "Could be him."

"It was me," I said. "Did you have any luck fishing?"

"That day? I think maybe I did get me one. I've got a freezer full, so what I catch don't matter. My neighbors get the overflow."

Chuck said, "Harry, try to remember. You came east on

the beach road at seven or so in the morning. You must have
passed the house where the girl was killed.''

He nodded. ''The big white house with the winding ramp
out front. Yeah, I know it.''

''Think back. Did you see a car parked out front?''

He didn't hesitate. ''No.''

''You're sure? Maybe a red Cadillac?''

''I told you, that stretch of road was dead. Any car would
have stuck out like a sore thumb. A red Caddy? Forget it.''

So there went my theory of why Sharanov's window was
open early that morning. The only comfort I could take from
its having proved a lemon was that my nemesis, Docherty,
was making the long, dreary, and hopefully traffic-y drive to
Brooklyn for nothing. Beyond that, I surmised that when he
got back out here he'd start leaning on me all over again.
Unlikely a suspect as I was, I was the likeliest he had.

CHUCK SCULLY DROPPED me where I had left my pickup,
not far from the village hall. I spotted Jack Beltrano across
the street checking a length of hose stretched out in front of
the firehouse. He sauntered over to me as I was opening my
door. After a perfunctory greeting he said what he had come
to say.

''About that business at the wake last night. Jim Brennan
acted like a damn fool. But you have to understand, Sid. The
man was loaded.''

I climbed in. ''Is there a time when he isn't?'' I was bored
with listening to excuses out here for what people did because of drink.

''Okay, he's like a lot of people in this town who drink
too much. I don't have to tell you, the winters are a dead
time. Especially in construction. But you have to understand
the added factor with Jim. He's never got over what he did
to Cassie.''

That got my attention. ''What he did to her?''

''The guilt he laid on her. When his little one was run
over—Angela, she was five—Jim was supposed to be watching her. But he'd slipped away for a while, leaving Cassie in

charge. And that's when it happened, Cassie reading in the schoolyard and Angie running into the road after a ball. Cassie was ten or eleven, and it took her years to get over it. If she ever did. You can guess how Jim felt. One daughter dead, the other blaming herself. He really did love Cassie something fierce.''

"If he was so crazy about her, how come I hear he was never around for her?''

"That was Nora's doing. She and Jim haven't gotten along in years. No surprise there. So he keeps his distance. You and I would have gotten a divorce by now—in fact, didn't you tell me you did?—but that's not the way it works with couples like the Brennans.''

"Jack, if you're apologizing for Brennan, apology accepted.'' It was a wrenching story, and it rang true. "Tell him I'm sorry for his troubles.''

And I took off for home. I had gone the whole morning without painting, and a morning without painting is a morning without meaning.

THE ANSWERING MACHINE announced two messages. I punched it on and climbed the scaffold with a fresh supply of brushes.

From Leona Morgenstern: "Sid, *Seated Girl* is back from the framer, and it is much enhanced. The piece is nuanced, fluent, powerful. A man who paints like that I would marry in a minute if I hadn't already been disastrously married to him. Tess Turkinton dropped by this morning with a check for the framing, but mostly to ask a lot of questions about you, including what's your phone number. You have no doubt made a conquest. Maybe that's why I am looking at you with new eyes. Anyway, I'm determined to sell those moneyed Texans something of yours. For both our sakes.'' Lonnie did have her good moments.

But the other call was not from Tess Turkinton: "Sid, I never did thank you properly for a lovely time the other evening. Oh, this is Olivia Cooper—in case, as is likely, you have trouble sorting out the ladies who are grateful to you for recent lovely evenings. Anyway, will you give me a chance to reciprocate? I'll be out at my beach place this weekend; without being boastful, I believe I can cook you a dinner to equal Muccio's. And if you don't like what I do in the kitchen"—a ripple of laughter here—"maybe there's a room somewhere in the house where I *can* please you."

She left her number and hung up. She had come on like the Macy's parade; this was a side of Cooper I hadn't seen.

I was suddenly a hit with the women currently in my life. If the soon-to-be ex-Mrs. Sharanov checked in, I would be batting a thousand.

SIXTEEN

By Tuesday evening a semblance of normality had returned to greater Quincacogue. Chuck Scully had gone back to tracking down the phantom bicycle thief (five missing, in all); the media had moved on to more active stories; the weather continued seasonal; and a house painting crew and a decorator were hard at work in the Sharanov master bedroom. (Out, damned spots, and everything associated with them. I could understand Sharanov's impatience to get that job done.)

Detective Docherty had now taken complete control of the murder investigation. I figured I was still high on his suspect list. I had heard nothing further from him directly, but Chuck Scully dropped by to warn me that Docherty had learned of my "weird temper tantrum" at Cassie's wake; he wondered whether I might be "going off the deep end—cracking under the intense police scrutiny."

And then Tom Ohlmayer phoned from Manhattan South to report that the county detective was nosing around the NYPD, trying to build a "psychological profile" of what he believed was a dangerously angry man with a fatal obsession. I hoped that kept Docherty busy into the foreseeable future.

Tom had struck out locally on the prints from Tess Turkinton's wineglass; he was going to try the national file in Washington. The hell with them all; I was painting up a storm.

Cassie Brennan's funeral had been held that afternoon. I didn't go. I had already attended a funeral for Cassie in my heart; an appearance in church might have set Jim Brennan off again. Not to disappoint Detective Docherty, but I had reached my quota of hand-to-hand combat for the week.

Gayle Hennessy called after the funeral to report that both Sharanovs had shown up at the church. Mrs. Sharanov she recognized because she had bought a beach outfit from Gayle the previous summer and paid by check. Mr. Sharanov she figured out because he looked just about the way she guessed he would, right down to the jacket not worn but draped over his shoulders, "Hollywood gangster style," and by the way he and Mrs. Sharanov kept ten yards between them at all times.

By nine at night I was painted out; my brush hand was going numb. What I needed was a forty-minute jog, followed by a drive into the village to finish unwinding over a few beers. My pub of choice was Pulver's; the locals hung out there to escape the frantic second-homers with their trendy gossip and cutting-edge wardrobes. Nothing at Pulver's was cutting edge except the knife that sliced the salami for the free lunch. I intended to end the evening with some serious sack time.

I stripped off my painting shirt and found another that wasn't yet ready for the Laundromat. I remembered it as the one I wore when I went over to the Sharanov house the day of the murder. White, but remarkably clean. Waste not, want not.

The salt air was relatively still, the rolling surf calming. I jogged east for a mile or so. There were locals in the houses in this direction, lights were on, and shadows moved behind the windows. Except for the gentle sound of the ocean it was too much like a city suburb. I preferred the feeling of Colorado ghost town I got when I headed west toward the belt of summer homes there. I turned in that direction and jogged to the Sharanov house and beyond, past half a dozen in deep slumber.

When I doubled back I slowed to a walk as I passed the Sharanov house. I had thought the master himself might be in residence tonight, since he had come out to the beach for the funeral, but the lights were out. With nothing special in mind I made my way around to the front. A couple of painter's ladders were stacked beside the entrance ramp, ready to be picked up in the morning. The repainting was finished.

I realized Sharanov probably wouldn't use his bedroom again until the paint was dry, the smell was gone, the new furniture was in place, and the memory of the tragedy had faded. For most people that last might take months or years; for Misha, I figured, violent death would be less of a nuisance than having to keep two sets of books for his restaurant. He would be over Cassie's in a day or two.

I had worked my way to the Sharanov driveway, so I set out for home along Beach Drive; under a thin moon this was a less treacherous route than the beach, with its ever-shifting gullies. When I made the dogleg turn a couple of hundred yards on I could see my property dimly silhouetted against the sky—house, dune grass, *Flotsam,* pickup.

And another shape, a bulky sedan, possibly a Volvo. It was not a police car, thank God, but I had an unknown visitor sitting out there in the dark waiting for my return.

There was no point in trying to steal up to this vehicle for a sly preview of my caller. If he hadn't already heard my sneakers crunching on the gravel he certainly had kept an eye peeled for my return. So I slowed to a saunter: Let him wait.

Closer, I was able to make out two heads in the car, one in the driver's seat, one in the back. Both were turned my way. The backseat visitor opened his door and got out— unfolded out, would be a better description. He was big. A couple of steps closer I saw that he was Nikki, Sharanov's chauffeur, maître d', whatever. Man of a thousand disguises, he was in an ill-fitting houndstooth jacket and a sweater with a baggy turtleneck. A country gentleman from a Third World country. But perched on this backwoods squire's outfit the yamlike head looked more aristocratic. Clothes do make the man.

"Nikki, nice to see you," I said pleasantly. "To what do I owe the honor of this visit?"

He had been prepared for an argument, and he took a moment to regroup. "Is no honor, is no visit," he muttered. "Mikhael Sharanov wants you."

"Fine. Is that him in the driver's seat?"

It didn't look like him, and anyway, it was unlikely he

would be driving; but as Winston Churchill once said, "Jaw, jaw, jaw, is better than war, war, war," and I wanted to find out what Nikki meant by "wants you."

Nikki said, "No, dat's not him."

I said, "I just passed his house. He's not there."

"His house smells bad. From paint."

"So where is he?"

"I will take you."

Damned if I was going to drive to Brooklyn with this goon. Patiently I said, "Nikki, Sharanov wants me, I don't want him. The way we do here in America, the person who wants does the traveling."

"Not Mr. Sharanov."

"You know what? Neither do I. You've delivered your message. Thank you. I'm on my way into the village." I was testing the waters.

I started around him toward my pickup. Now the other man slid out of the driver's side of the Volvo. Squat, big-bellied, bouncy. Another Russian. He rocked from side to side to show he was ready for whatever, and he looked to Nikki for instructions.

Nikki took a couple of steps toward me, and now the two of them had me in a loose sandwich, about two feet of air to my front and to my back. I stopped walking.

"Is Dimitri," Nikki said by way of introduction. "We have a big car. Plenty of room." Did he think I was worried that I might feel crowded during the drive?

We were at an impasse. While I considered my options the Russians each sidled a half step closer. Their argument was growing persuasive.

Finally I said, "Hey, if Mr. Sharanov is this anxious to see me, why not? Just give me a minute to duck in and use the john. The bathroom?"

In a minute I could grab the Smith & Wesson and possibly find the ammo. I would feel more comfortable with the gun tucked in my belt under my loose sweatshirt.

But Nikki said, "Mr. Sharanov has bathroom, very nice. Is not far."

So we all climbed into the Volvo. Plenty of room.

NEITHER OF THE RUSSIANS was a talker, and we made the trip in virtual silence. It turned out that Sharanov was staying at the Gulliver, no surprise when I thought about it. The village was not eager to encourage casual visitors; it preferred the stability of summer people who were homeowners. So the Gulliver, a totally ordinary two-story motel on the bay that could have been built from mail-order plans, was the only decent public shelter in the area. Its one distinction was an attached marina. In season it attracted boaters who wanted a night in a real bed after taking a real bath; the rest of the year business was, at best, slow.

The parking area was sheltered by the two wings of the motel. Dimitri drove to the center section and turned the car so that the door on my side was exactly facing a room door I surmised was Sharanov's. Dimitri was either being careful not to overexert me with a long walk or he was making sure nobody saw me go into that room.

The caution seemed unnecessary; of the several dozen oversize motel windows we were facing, only two or three leaked ribbons of light around the edges of the closed drapes, and there were no more than half a dozen cars in the vast lot. That reflected the predictable occupancy rate for a Wednesday in May.

Dimitri switched off the motor. Nikki reached past me and opened my door. I felt less than totally at ease; I supposed I was being paranoid, but if Sharanov chose, he could play Roach Motel in this setup. His visitors might check in, and if they didn't check out there would be nobody around to notice.

I stepped out of the car. Nikki was resting a big mitt on my shoulder, in case I wondered if he was still behind me. Four short paces and I would be at Sharanov's door.

And then I came into a small piece of luck: It turned out we were not alone. A room door sprang open a few yards along the walkway and a man in overalls emerged. He was steadying an air conditioner on his shoulder and carrying a tool kit in his other hand. He pulled the door closed behind him.

Nikki's mitt was urging me to move. Dimitri was already knocking on Sharanov's door. But now the man in overalls turned just enough so that his face emerged from behind the air conditioner. It was Harry Gregg.

"Harry!" I yelled in exactly the voice I would have used to greet a brother I thought had perished years ago in a jungle air crash. "Harry Gregg, well I'll be damned."

Sharanov's door had opened a crack, but now it quickly closed, and the parade of which I was the centerpiece came to a halt. So far, so good.

The trouble was, Gregg looked, but he didn't recognize me. I couldn't blame him: He had barely glanced my way the few minutes I had spent on his porch yesterday, and this walkway was poorly lighted. He seemed rattled by my larger-than-life greeting. All he said was, "Huh?"

"Harry, are the bluefish still biting?" I called. Dimitri was rocking, as though his spring had been overwound.

I said, "Chuck Scully and I were wondering if we could get in line for some of your overflow catch." I was laying it on with a snow shovel.

Gregg took a harder look and put together who I possibly was. "Oh, yeah, right," he said vaguely. "Well, I haven't been out since, so there isn't any."

He had started off across the area and I called, "I'm visiting a friend here. You want to meet me for a beer at Pulver's when you get off?"

A lot he cared. He had already disappeared into the dark.

But I had made my point with my escort. Behind me, Nikki muttered a few words in Russian that were not complimentary.

SHARANOV WAS WEARING a black silk dressing gown with contrasting trim. Had I seen Edward G. Robinson in a vintage movie on the tube relaxing in a similar robe after a hard day with his submachine gun? I had to admit that Misha looked good in his, almost good enough to make my palms sweat.

When he nodded recognition of my arrival it was with an air I remember Miss Lombardo in second-year high school French describing as *de haut en bas* when we were studying idioms.

The boss was occupying what I supposed the Gulliver called a suite—two identical motel rooms with an open connecting door. The first room he had personalized with a vodka bottle and a clutch of glasses. He waved me with a show of politeness to the second room, but I held back while he took a brief apologetic report in Russian that he didn't like from his two goons; I supposed they were telling him about our encounter on the walkway.

He shook his head as though to say, What can you do with the kind of help you get these days? Then he left the boys to shift for themselves—or were they standing guard?—and he led me into his personal quarters. Except for an open suitcase this room was no more personal than the other.

Without an ounce of irony he murmured, "I'm glad you could come, Mr. Shale."

He nodded me to the king-size bed while he took the single chair. He said, "Please excuse this place. I'm supervising some redecorating at my house. Would you care for a drink? I can offer you a vodka—Swedish, not Russian."

"I'll pass."

He watched me sit and said, "You're comfortable there?"

I wasn't, nor was I with his purring tone, which again reminded me of a high-performance engine in idle. Enough politeness. I said, "What the fuck do you want?"

If my response put him off he didn't show it. He waited till he had lit a thin cigar and then he said, "I want to talk to you. You know, you've caused me trouble."

"No, I don't know. How?"

"The detective. Doggerty? Docherty? He came out to Brooklyn to see me. At my restaurant? I don't like to see policemen come to the Tundra. It upsets the staff."

I bet. I said, "What does this have to do with me?"

"Docherty asked me questions. He wanted to know where I had slept the night before the little girl was murdered. Cas-

sie.'' The idling engine lost its purr for a single piston stroke
on the name.

He was becoming more interesting. I said, "You had trouble with that question?"

"I did. My wife and I—it is no longer a secret—have been
in a serious marital dispute for some time. We are now going
to be divorced. Where I slept that night is a matter of no
damn business of the police. But it might be of some interest
to Kitty's lawyers. Mrs. Sharanov."

"You're not legally separated?"

"Only physically. I have been staying for the past couple
of weeks in a hotel in Manhattan. Docherty believes I slept
that night in my house here at the beach. As it happens, I
could prove to him otherwise in a minute, but I don't want
it anywhere recorded that I was in the company of a woman
that night."

"I can understand that. But I repeat, what does any of this
have to do with me?"

He leaned forward and blew smoke not exactly in my face
but close enough. "You are the person who—how does it
go?—put the bug on his ear."

"In his ear."

"That my bedroom at the beach had been slept in that
night. You gave him a picture you drew that shows a window
open in my room. You said you drew it early on the morning
of the murder."

"That's right, I did." Docherty had been needlessly generous in giving me credit for the deduction. He may have
hoped that the Russian would reciprocate by having one or
both of my legs broken.

"But what you claim is impossible," Sharanov purred. "I
did not sleep in the house that night. And I never leave that
house until it is locked up. *Tight.* I see to that myself." He
leaned back into his chair, totally confident. "So there remain
two possible explanations for the picture you drew with the
open window."

He waited for me to ask what they were. When I didn't,
he volunteered. "One. You drew the picture on a different

day than you originally thought—possibly a day during the previous weekend, when I *was* staying in the house."

"Nope." I knew he wouldn't like that answer. I said, "Okay if I take a stab at number two?"

"Do that."

"I exercised artistic license and drew the window open because I liked the look of it that way. But it was actually closed."

"Excellent. You said it much better than I could have."

"Thank you," I said, and shut up.

I had guessed where he was headed, but contrary to his expectation I was damned if I would follow. More and more the man was bugging me. And more and more I didn't like this bed heaving under me at my slightest move while Misha sat back in his comfortable chair and we played his game to its predictable end.

He was searching my face for a clue. Finally he had to spell it out. "So that is what happened? You drew what you liked, what pleased you, not what you saw that morning?"

"No."

His face didn't show it, but he really hated that answer. He said, "Mr. Shale, you are not making a careful search of your memory." His voice was still in idle, but now he touched the accelerator. "Think again. It is important that you do so."

"Not to me." Slowly and carefully I added, "And, Mr. Sharanov, that last sounded like a threat."

"Did it?" He was unmoved.

"You must know that would be foolish."

"Because you are a New York City policeman? But retired." He had his ducks in a row. "And under investigation for having beaten a prisoner."

My eyebrows may have lifted because he took the trouble to explain. "How do I know? Your victim's lawyer found me. To ask if I believed it was you who murdered my cleaning person. Since you have a history of sudden explosions of violence."

"And what did you tell him?"

Again he tapped the gas pedal. "I said I would have to get back to him on that."

"He knew where to come," I said, "for an expert opinion on explosive violence."

Sharanov acknowledged the validity of my point with a tight smile and a jab of the cigar: touché. "Ancient history," he said.

"That's comforting to hear."

His eyes shifted purposefully to the other room. "I'm speaking for myself," he said. "I can't answer for the actions of anyone else."

"So you *are* threatening me, you son of a bitch."

He erupted in a short staccato laugh and his slate eyes returned to me; there was no laughter in them. He said, "My apologies. That came out of an old habit. I haven't threatened anyone in years. All I ask of you is that you set the record straight when Docherty gets back to you. Which he most certainly will. And very soon, I predict."

"Are you going to tell me why?"

"He has to be interested in your involvement with Cassie Brennan. Don't you agree?"

"What involvement?" I hated the taste of the word. "There was none."

"No? Then why did she push me—push me hard—to buy that drawing of yours from the firemen's auction?"

Cassie had promoted me to Sharanov in all innocence, and now he was turning it into something dirty. But at the same time he was giving away something about himself.

I said, "Do you usually take artistic advice from teenage girls who clean your house?"

A mask dropped over his face. "Sometimes. Why not?"

But I had pressed the right button. The Turkintons believed the way to please Sharanov, the way to his pocketbook, was with a painting of Cassie Brennan; they were prepared to bet a bundle that he was hung up on Cassie. Kitty believed as much, Paulie Malatesta smelled it, and Olivia Cooper would not have been surprised. All that was new to me now was how much the aging thug had been like an eager puppy with the teenager. He must have been far gone to buy my drawing for no better reason than that Cassie wanted him to buy it. He wouldn't have told Docherty that he had a drawing of mine; he certainly wouldn't have said why he had it.

So Misha and I broke even on the question of "involvement" with Cassie. He couldn't hold that club over me without calling attention to himself. And I could see that he understood that.

So he reached back again into his enforcer past and tried to play from that strength. "You will think about what I asked you?" He was purring again. "To remember correctly how that drawing with the open window came to be? To set the record straight? I would hate there to be a misunderstanding between us."

The man had tunnel vision. "I'll think about it," I said. "Absolutely." Screw him; but not while I was still his "guest."

"Good. Done. My people will drive you home."

And the hell with that. "Thanks anyway, I'm not going home."

I WALKED TO Pulver's, about half a mile. The night air was still mild and people were out; they were leaving restaurants or strolling on Covenant Street, but I still glanced back a couple of times to see if I had company.

And at Pulver's instead of the beers I had planned on I knocked back a few scotches and unwound by listening to the soothing sounds of the locals arguing zoning code changes.

I phoned for the village taxi. It was not as roomy as Nikki's Volvo, but it was worth every penny of the ten bucks it cost me to get home.

I thought I would put in a couple of hours on *Large*. But first I spent ten minutes rooting around for the ammo for the Smith & Wesson. I never found it. By then I was too disgusted to paint and I went to bed.

SEVENTEEN

ON WEDNESDAY MORNING I was forced to lay down a brush heavy with paint and climb down off the scaffold. Someone had been pounding on my front door and wouldn't take no response as an answer.

For my trouble a bowlegged marshall with bad breath favored me with a subpoena to appear the following Monday at 11 a.m. before the grand jury at the county courthouse forty minutes to the west. Docherty was casting his net.

I had put off hiring a lawyer, and I was going to have to do something about that; but not until I absolutely had to.

Inspired by my cash flow drought, what I was going to do was clean my brushes, close my paints, and take a stab at what I had done for a living all those years: investigate a murder. My money problem aside, didn't I at the very least owe Cassie Brennan, friend and loyal booster, a serious try at bringing her killer to justice? Especially since neither John Docherty nor Chuck Scully had moved a millimeter closer to doing that.

I eased into my sleuth mode slowly. I began with a variation on a ritual that had worked for me in the past when I wasn't making headway on a case. I used to park my car on a side street, tilt back the seat, and free-associate everything I knew about the case while I stared at the ceiling light. What I did now was kick off my shoes, lay back on my bed, and let myself be hypnotized by that giant hand I had repaired on *Large*.

People, facts, and events formed three-dimensional pictures in my head. They knocked against each other and spun away like fun park bumper cars. In the past when I did this two cars would sometimes lock.

After I'm not sure how long, a couple did now. Anyway they clung for a moment. Long enough to get me started.

THE HUGGINS SERVICE Station was at the west edge of the village, along the highway, a last chance for residents heading for the city to keep their gas money local. I steered clear of the pumps and parked at the side of the garage. A mechanic was at work in each of the three bays.

Paulie Malatesta was just emerging from the open jaws of a Jeep in the middle bay, his jet black hair tumbling onto his generous brow. I could see why Cassie might have gone for him; he had the dark, brooding looks of a Heathcliff, if not the style.

I called his name, and his face lit up when he saw me. He wiped his greasy hands on a paper towel with only moderate success and hurried to meet me.

"Hey, Lieutenant, what's up?"

"Can we talk?"

This was not what he wanted to hear; he was expecting news of an arrest. He took a moment to consider, then turned to the adjoining bay. "Yo, Ike, I'm taking my break."

I led him toward my pickup. I said, "I suppose the police have been to see you."

"Yeah, Chuck Scully showed up to bawl me out for hassling that fat cop the day Cassie was killed. Walter. Then he grilled me on what I knew about, you know, the situation. I didn't know a damn thing except that Sharanov had the hots for Cassie."

"Is that a guess or did she tell you something?"

"She didn't have to. I'd see him sometimes when I came to pick her up. It was all over his face."

"That's it?"

"He gave her presents. A sweater, a box—must have been a good five pounds—of candy. Other stuff. What the hell else was all that about?"

We were climbing into my pickup. "Was Cassie bothered by the attention?"

"No. And that ticked me off even more. She said he didn't

mean anything by it, it was just kind of a father thing. Yeah,
like ugh.''

It was hard to believe that Paulie was well into his twenties. His emotions were writ as plainly on that handsome face
as they must have been when he was fourteen. I said, ''Paulie, were you and Cassie lovers?''

He reared like a spooked horse. ''Were you?''

''Absolutely not.'' As I said it, my heart tapped lightly
against my chest. Once.

''I know that,'' he said disdainfully. ''And neither was I.
So where'd you get the idea?''

''It seemed logical. Almost inevitable.'' Like water running downhill. He was more than likely lying to protect her
good name.

Stubbornly he said, ''She was my girl, that's all. Beautiful,
inside and out. Every day she's gone I miss her more. But if
you mean were we doing it, no way.'' He seemed to be
challenging me to prove him a liar.

''Because she was too young?''

''Hell, no. I've been with girls younger than sixteen. Anyway, Cassie was no special age, you know what I mean?''

''So, what then?''

''She promised her mother, can you believe it? Swore to
her. And swore if she was ever thinking of changing her mind
she'd come and speak to her first.''

''That's a hard promise to keep.'' Water saying, I promise
not to run downhill. ''Very hard.''

He said, ''Not when you've got a mother like Cassie's
putting the fear of God in you. The woman's something.''

''Is that why I didn't see you at the wake? Mrs. Brennan
doesn't approve of you?''

''Approve of me? I've been in this town almost a year.
Mrs. Brennan doesn't even know I'm alive. I was never allowed to meet the lady. Can you figure that?''

''So you and Cassie had a secret romance. How did you
manage it?''

Tight-lipped, he said, ''We managed.'' But he knew that
wouldn't satisfy me. ''Sometimes she'd come over to my

place. I have a room in a house owned by this old couple? They wouldn't let Cassie go upstairs, but we'd hang out in the parlor.''

"Where did Mrs. Brennan think she was those times?"

"Working. Cassie had a lot of part-time jobs. Even if she didn't trust her daughter—and Cassie said she did—there was no way the old lady could keep tabs on her. Mrs. Brennan puts in a long day, but Cassie's were longer. She was out of the house before her mother woke up. Anyways, four days a week.''

"Doing what?"

"The breakfast shift at Mel's—six to ten a.m. Monday through Thursday. That's where we met. Sundays her mother got her up for early mass. Fridays and Saturdays were the only days she got to sleep in a couple of extra hours.''

It was beginning to dawn on Paulie that he was doing most of the talking, and that any information that passed between us had been from him to me and was likely to continue that way. He glanced at his watch. "Why did you look me up? What did you want to see me about?"

It was a moment of truth. I spoke slowly. "The day Cassie was murdered, Paulie..."

He shifted uneasily. "Jeez, don't remind me of that day."

"You showed up at the Sharanov house in a Huggins tow truck. The bad news had spread. It must have gone through the village in ten seconds flat and you had jumped in the truck and driven hell for leather to the Sharanov house. You were in pain, keyed up, emotional. Understandably. And you fought with the cop out front. Walter.''

"I didn't know what I was doing. I was out of my head. I already apologized for that."

"I'm not laying blame on you, Paulie. I'm trying to explain where I'm coming from. After you took care of Walter, you went for me. Remember?"

"You were in my way. I'm sorry. I wanted to get in that house—to see Cassie one more time. And to beat the living shit out of Sharanov.''

"So you tried to shove me aside. You put your hands flat on my chest and you pushed."

"Yeah. So...?" He didn't have the least idea where I was headed.

I said, "I don't get to the Laundromat that often. If a shirt's clean enough I'll wear it a couple or three times."

He rolled his eyes impatiently. "Hey, I'm only allowed ten minutes on a break. Okay?"

"I'm almost finished. Couple of days ago I reached for the shirt I wore last Friday. To check it for a second wearing. You know what? No grease stains. Not a speck."

As if by reflex, Paulie shoved his hands in his coverall pockets. And waited.

I said, "You had come directly from work. Paulie, there's no way you can work on cars and keep your hands clean. You hadn't been working that morning. What were you doing?"

He stared at me stupidly. If he had been prepared for the question he could have given any of a number of reasonable answers. But he didn't have one ready. His dark face flushed darker. Like a kid hauled into the principal's office, he sounded wounded and defensive.

"I was working. Check the time sheet. I don't know if my hands were dirty. Maybe they were, and your shirt was just plain lucky to stay clean."

When he fell back on the time sheet for his alibi I figured he had been at Huggins's. But that didn't mean he was working. "Okay, Paulie, maybe you were *at* the job. But did you pick up a tool? Or were you too troubled, too bothered by something, to do any work?"

"You report in, Huggins gives you a car. That's how it's done here. Labor's billed by the half hour."

"And you had a car that morning? I can check the billings."

"Huggins's bills? Who says you can?"

"Okay, then Chuck Scully can."

That gave him pause. "That morning?" He reached for the door handle. "I reported in, like I said. But I had a lousy stomach. Something I ate the night before was giving me the runs. I was mostly in the john. Huggins took the car from me, and I got half a day's pay. But I was here. Ask Huggins. Ask anyone. You satisfied?''

It was total bullshit. He couldn't even say it with real conviction. ''Paulie, you sure as hell weren't sick when you showed up at the Sharanov house and took on everyone who stood in your way.''

''You forget about sick when your girl's been murdered.'' The wounded voice rose an octave. ''When she's raped and killed by some Brooklyn gangster. The only girl you ever loved. What's my hands being dirty got to do with that? How come that butcher is still walking around while Cassie's planted six feet under? Why don't you go after the killer, mister hotshot New York detective, instead of my dirty hands? Why don't you nail the bastard?''

He had made his point and he knew when to quit. He flung open the cab door. His voice calmer now, he said, ''I can't afford to be docked again. I've got rent to pay. I'm going back to work.'' And he shot out of the cab and ran back into the garage.

EIGHTEEN

I DIDN'T FIGURE Nora Brennan to be back at work this soon after her daughter's death, but I had to pass the village hall on my way to her house, so I stopped by there to make sure. No, I was told, Mrs. Brennan wasn't expected in until Monday. Even that seemed soon to me.

"Nora's a strong woman," the village manager said and shook his head in wonder. "There aren't many like her."

As I left the building Chuck Scully was going in. His eyes widened when he saw me. "What are you doing here?" he said. "Did you come to see me?"

"No, I've got a tax problem," I said; I saw no reason to share my investigative agenda with him. "How's the case going?"

"Ask Docherty," he said, his tone turning sour. "I'm full-time on the bicycle thief."

I had forgotten that the county had shut him out of the murder. I offered what comfort I could. "Looks like the trail's gone cold. You may be better off."

"You're right, I may be. You don't have television. The local stations ask the same question every night: Why hasn't there been any action on the Cassie Brennan murder? What do they expect? Where there's no leads, there's no action. It's all Docherty's headache now."

"You know I've been subpoenaed."

"Yeah, well…" He looked sheepish.

"Well what?"

"You can't blame them for riding that horse." He had ridden it himself. "Though I don't know what it'll get them."

I said, "Do I have to tell you? The next time someone sticks a camera in Docherty's face he can say, 'The grand jury is talking to a key witness. I can't reveal any more at this point in time.' " I chalked up one more good reason for not owning a TV. "In the end he'll look like a horse's ass."

He said, "I guess." But his heart wasn't in it.

A PICKUP WAS PARKED in the Brennan driveway. I pulled mine up next to it and hopped out just as Jack Beltrano came out of the house. We were equally surprised to run into each other.

"What are you doing here?" he said, before I could.

"Same as you, I suppose. Paying my respects."

He looked as if he doubted that; my last visit hadn't brought the grieving family much comfort.

He said, "I've got my mother next door with her arthritis, so it's no big deal for me to drop in on Nora. I can kill the two birds with one stone. What else have I got to do, construction's still so slow?"

Who cared how he spent his days? He was telling me more than I needed to know. Something made me say, "Are both the Brennans at home?"

"Nora's in. A couple of neighbor women were visiting till a few minutes ago. You just missed them. Jim?" His eyes slid off me. "You'll have to ask Nora. If he's on a toot, can you blame him?"

He headed for his car, and now he was talking with his back to me. "Sorry to cut out, Sid, I'm expecting a prospect. A long shot, but that's the business today. You can walk right in, the front door's open. So long, see you around."

At his car door he turned to face me once more. "Say, maybe you'll give us another drawing for the volunteers' auction this year. Think about that. The guys would sure appreciate it, Sid. Okay, 'bye now."

I'd never heard him so mindlessly chatty, or seen him so herky-jerky. He hopped in his car and seemed to wait for my permission. Not until I waved did he back up and take off.

The Brennan front door was closed but unlocked. I opened it, rang the bell, and called, "Mrs. Brennan?"

Her voice came strong and clear. "In the kitchen."

SHE WAS SITTING at the kitchen table, starchily erect, dressed in black pants and a high-necked magenta blouse. A good-looking woman about to slide into middle age. Her color was ghastly. A long thin hand lay on a household ledger open in front of her, and the light through the kitchen window flooded one side of her face. She could have been sitting for a Flemish genre painter; all that was missing was a pitcher and a bowl of fruit. She looked at me expectantly with her daughter's eyes. Her mouth was a shut purse.

"The door was open," I said.

The purse opened briefly. "I know." This was not going to be easy.

She didn't invite me to sit. I stood in the kitchen doorway and said, "I'm used to that—an unlocked door where there's a death in the family. I'm a Jew. During the mourning period—seven days—nobody's supposed to ring your doorbell. I forget why. Maybe I never knew."

She said nothing and I pushed on. "After my father died— he was murdered, shot to death in the taxi he drove—a neighbor thought to tie the front door open. The cabdrivers who came to pay their respects—more than fifty of them—included Moslems, Hindus, Buddhists, and Christians, and they mightn't have known not to ring."

Still no reaction. But she hadn't stopped me, so I kept going. "It takes an outsider to think of the practical things when the death is sudden. And my mother was grateful for the company. She appreciated the respect it showed, even when it looked like the walls were bending out from the crowding." I was running off at the mouth, waiting for some give from the other side.

Nora Brennan's mouth softened slightly. "The door's open because I didn't want to keep jumping up. I'm trying to get my accounts straight. Among the unexpected consequences of sudden death is the expense of the burial."

She blinked, possibly shortcutting a tear. She said, "Why did you come here? You said your piece at the wake. You did your duty by my daughter."

"I owe your husband an apology. He was grieving and I

made things worse. Back there in your yard. I'm sure you heard. Is he at home?''

''No.'' She wasn't exactly adversarial, but it still looked as if I was going to have to do most of this by myself.

I had drifted into the room. Still uninvited, I pulled out the kitchen chair opposite her at the table. When she didn't object I sat down. ''When do you expect him?''

''I don't.'' Her fingers stroked the open page, then lay still. Waiting for more, I found myself looking at the table, grainy hardwood, tightly joined, probably made by the carpenter Jim Brennan in happier times.

And then the logjam broke.

''You'd find out anyway,'' she said, ''because I want everyone to know, but you happen to be here, so you're among the first. Brennan and I are separating. Not that we haven't been, for many years, mostly separated. But I am more or less formalizing the situation.''

I was less surprised than she expected. ''With a divorce?''

She made a face. ''No divorce. Not even a legal separation. But Jim Brennan is no longer welcome here. Not even on those infrequent occasions when he has been accustomed to showing up. I want as many people as possible to know that, to avoid any misunderstanding. This has been a long time coming. So if you're looking for him, you'll have no help from me.''

I had zero interest in finding Jim Brennan; he was my excuse for getting my foot in the door here in hope of stirring something up. This news was better leverage than I had any right to expect. I said, ''You say it's been 'a long time coming.' Why is it happening now? Because Cassie is gone?''

''That didn't take much insight, did it?'' she snapped. She had pulled back into her shell.

I proceeded with caution. ''That's true, but maybe this does. What I'm about to tell you. You'd know if I've guessed right, because you told me—and so did your daughter—that she shared everything with you. All her thoughts.'' Not quite, but what the hell, I was treading on delicate ground.

Nora eyed me warily, her long hands now pressing the edge of the table.

I said, "When I did those nude drawings of Cassie—"

She thrust her body forward across the table and bit out the words. "I don't want to talk about that."

"There's nothing to tell. It was a job, and she did it well. Professionally. She wanted to do it, she told me, because she was trying to wipe out an unpleasant memory. Exorcise it."

I waited a moment to see if Nora would throw up more flak. But she said nothing; she was curious to hear where I was going with this.

I said, "Cassie told me that once before a man had seen her without her clothes on. You must know about that, it had been an unpleasant experience. Deeply disturbing, by the look of her when she told me."

Nora didn't have to say anything; I could read on her face that this was not news to her. But eventually she said, "Yes, I know about that."

"That man was her father, wasn't it?"

The hands gripping the table retreated to her lap. "It was a year ago," she said. "He was drunk. He didn't touch her. But his look—the look on his face—she didn't like it one bit. She couldn't forget it."

"If you were going to cut relations with Jim, why didn't you do it then?"

"I wanted to. I would have that day, the day she told me. But Cassie said no, she would be more careful in the house from then on."

"She didn't want to lose him? Because she loved him?"

"She despised him. But she said please, he was the only father she had."

"And now..."

"Cassie is gone." Her voice grew stronger. "I wasted no time doing what I had intended all those years. This was not the first time Jim inflicted pain on his daughter."

"I know that he left her in charge of your younger daughter the day she was run over."

"Will God ever let me forget my Cassie, dissolved in tears

at her loss, this ten-year-old child, overcome with shame at having failed her sister?'' The words rose from someplace deep in her being. ''And her father shaking her in anger because she hadn't seen the accident and therefore couldn't help the police find the driver. Retribution was what was on Jim Brennan's mind, showing his he-man muscle, never mind the support and love his surviving daughter needed.''

I said, ''It sounds to me as though you've made a wise decision. But you'll be all right without Mr. Brennan? I mean, financially?'' I knew where I was headed. ''It's none of my business, but when I came in you were expressing concern about money. Will you be able to manage?''

''Jim was never a pillar of strength when it came to money. However I managed before, I'll manage now. Better. Cassie saved whatever she'd earned.'' She fought back another tear. ''Toward her liberation, she called it, from small-town life.''

''And emotionally?'' I was really pushing hard, but if my hunch was right I wanted to shake loose the truth. ''You have people you can lean on? Relatives? Friends?''

She took a while before she spoke the single sentence, ''I'll get by.''

She wasn't responding to my game plan, so I moved cautiously to the hardest part. ''Jack Beltrano appears to be a loyal friend.''

She answered almost too quickly. ''His mother lives next door. She's on a walker. Jack's around a good deal. Yes, that helps.'' The paragraph came out in a block, as though she had pressed a single key on her office computer.

''And his wife? I met her once. I didn't see her at the wake.''

Still quickly, ''They're living separately. Have been for a long time. Months.''

''I wondered.'' I took a long step on the tightrope. ''I had a brief talk with Jack outside just now. I hadn't realized how close you two had become.''

Her jaw dropped, and her dead white face was suddenly suffused with color. It didn't matter what she came up with;

she had given herself away. But she said, "What did Jack
say?"

"About what you'd expect. There's an empty place in both
your lives. It's only natural that you give each other support."

Her back had stiffened. "If by that you mean . . ." She
let the sentence die.

"I mean what I said, Mrs. Brennan. No more."

She could find no way to respond to that, no way to argue
with it. But muscles worked in her face.

I let a moment go by and then I said softly, my voice, I
hoped, neutral, nonjudgmental. "Was Cassie aware of your
close friendship?"

And now the stiff back bent, the shoulders shook, and she
began to weep uncontrollably. "I don't know," she sobbed,
"I don't *know*." Through the tears she looked up at me,
haunted, guilt-wracked.

My throat tightened; I wanted to reach out to her. Instead
I said, "Either way, it's all right. I'm sure she would have
approved."

Would she? Or would she have felt betrayed? But it was
the kindest thing I could think of to say. And that tortured
woman needed to find peace.

WHEN I GOT HOME there was a message on my machine.
"It's Tess. *Turkinton*." Pause for effect. "Or is it a clever
imitation of that wicked woman's seductive Texas drawl?"
She giggled an acknowledgment of her own wit before she
went on.

"Hello, Sid. Can you possibly guess? Daddy and I have
been invited out to Sharanov's beach place for the weekend.
Can you believe the man, with that poor girl's body barely
removed from his bedroom floor? A most peculiar individual.
He must have that Russian soup in his veins—borscht?—
where there ought to be blood. But Daddy insists on accept-
ing because they are about to wrap up their ongoing business
deal. Ongoing and ongoing *forever*. God, will I be glad when
this is over.

"So here is what I am going to do, as I cannot bear another unrelieved forty-eight hours with that mad Cossack. On Saturday night I shall slip away from the house of horrors and take you out to dinner. My treat, my choice of restaurant.

"I know precisely where your odd little house is and I will pick you up at a quarter to eight. That will give me a chance to browse through your work in the very place where it is created, and maybe you and I can hammer out a deal for one of your paintings. If we cut your gallery out of the transaction, we may do ourselves a hefty financial favor, don't you agree? That Morgenstern woman is a terror. Save me, please, from your aggressive New York women. Stand aside and let the steamrollers through! See you Saturday, Sid."

Talk about your steamrollers, she had allowed me no options in this deal. I was being flattened for delivery on Saturday night to a restaurant of Big D's choice. I would have called back to tell her what to do with her plan, except for that tiny sweetener—the sliver of a chance that I could sell a canvas. From my prayer to God's ear.

NINETEEN

GAYLE'S PRESEASON SALE seemed to be going well; I counted two customers in Gayle's Provocativo when I walked in, twice as many as I had seen in the shop at any one time since the previous fall, and an impressive number for any Wednesday. Gayle was handling both women smoothly; she dangled a smashing Gayle Hennessy cover-up from each hand as she winked a greeting to me and mouthed, "Five minutes."

I went to the window and turned to face the village traffic; otherwise I would have had to watch what was going on in the shop. Why is it that women who are embarrassed by a vagrant shoulder strap at a cocktail party will fling off their clothes with reckless abandon in a boutique? Gayle had a curtained area in the back for changing, but it was honored mostly in the breach.

Ten minutes later, after one sale and one "Let me think about it" we were alone. Gayle offered me a cup of coffee and a "To what do I owe the honor of this visit?" and we settled with our cups in the only two chairs in the shop.

"Just between us," I began, "I'm nosing around trying to get a fix on who might have done Cassie."

"I figured you were up to no good when I saw that you weren't wearing your painting clothes. Sid, you're retired. Get back to that jumbo canvas. You think you owe the girl? How well did you know her?"

"Well enough. If I was a cabinetmaker and she'd needed a coffin, I'd have been there for her. What she needs is justice, vengeance, closure. The whole package. She needs a gumshoe."

"Very pretty." Gayle was looking at me skeptically. "But

it's not like when you were there for me. You can't change anything for Cassie."

"True. But the living need closure too." Reluctantly, "I've got a grand jury breathing down my neck."

Now she understood. "Oh, boy." She gave me a Why didn't you say so in the first place? look. "Sid, that's got to be a crock. What possible reason would they have to come after you?"

"There's a theory floating around that I was hung up on Cassie. Obsessed. They can go miles on that before it runs out of gas. Their miles and my dollars."

"Uh-uh." She shook her head. "I teased you about that once or twice, but I never thought for a minute there was anything to it. Sid, I've got enough ego to believe that if you had an itch for adolescents you'd have hit on me when you busted me all those years ago. I was a real tasty dish at seventeen."

"To this very day."

She was eyeing me. "Is that why you're here? To get me to stand up for you, swear in court that you don't jump little girls?"

"I hope it never gets to that. No, I'm just poking around, dick style. To see who might know something about Cassie that could help."

"In my case, I don't see what." She sprang to her feet and began refolding a pile of tops on a counter. "Cassie got along better with men than with women. If she was going to share secrets with either of us, it would have been with you." She was faced away from me. "Did she?"

"One. She told me she was a virgin."

She looked back over her shoulder with a ghost of a smile. "No fooling? If she ever said anything like that to me I'd have washed out her mouth with soap."

"She started working for you months after she stopped sitting for me. Her status may have changed."

She thought about that. "I dearly hope so."

"So what about it, Gayle? You two spent hours together

in the shop—sometimes, I would guess, without interruption from a single customer.''

''Thanks, Sid.''

''There had to be some girl talk. If only to pass the time. Confessional stuff.''

''We weren't together that much. The point was for Cassie to watch the shop while I was up in the workroom.'' She had run out of merchandise to fuss with and she returned reluctantly to her chair. She pretended to be thinking about my question.

''Let's see. She was a fan of yours, Sid. She thought you were really something. But you must know that.''

''I didn't take it personally. She liked older men, period. They all looked good next to her father. I fell into the category.'' We weren't getting anywhere. ''Did she talk about her boyfriend? Paulie?''

''Is that his name? Didn't I say you knew more than me? I knew she was seeing someone, but she never talked about him. What's he like?''

I was here to get information, not to give it. ''He seems okay. You never tried to find out?''

Her answer was slow coming. ''Once.'' It was almost as though she was being painted into a corner.

''Yes...?''

Forlornly, ''To my regret.''

She waited till she was fully charged, then slammed her coffee cup on the counter and jumped to her feet. ''I *knew* it would come to this if we kept jabbering this way. I *hate* having to talk about this.'' Her face was knotted with anger. Or was it embarrassment?

''Calm down, Gayle. You're among friends.''

She looked at me, rode the emotion, and decided maybe it wasn't such a big deal. She took a couple of deep breaths and slid reluctantly back down into her chair and began to fiddle with her cup.

Finally she said, ''One day a few weeks ago she came to work looking too miserable to hide it. After an hour of stomping and fretting I figured it for a love life problem and maybe she could use some advice from a woman who'd been around the track in fair weather and foul. So I asked. 'Cassie, you got boyfriend trouble?' The kid shook her head no, but the tears flowed like I couldn't believe.

"It didn't take long to worm it out of her. She had seen something—she couldn't bring herself to say exactly what—that had knocked her flat. About her mother."

"She was having an affair."

She gasped, "You knew?"

"Not absolutely."

"Good for you." She looked at me with new respect. Then, "Anyway, Cassie was having a hard time dealing with the concept. It was just about blowing her away. I did what I could to give her support. I reminded her that she had never held her old man up as a pillar of the family. Tops, the guy's a bum. I said she had to remember that mothers are also people, they need love same as all of us. Of course, my own mother carried that to an extreme, but I managed to survive it."

I wasn't sure how much comfort this last would have been to Cassie but I said, "Did that help?"

"She wouldn't hear any of it. She felt as if she'd been let down, tricked, cheated. She was miserable all week. And I never did learn a damn thing about the boyfriend." That last sounded as if she had said all she wanted to on the subject.

"That's it?" I said. "The whole story? So why were you reluctant to talk about it?"

She slid her butt from side to side in the chair. She wished I had quit pressing, and I could see another major eruption coming. She looked out the window at the Covenant Street traffic and then back at me.

"Because"—this time when she slammed the cup down she broke it—"I was having kind of a thing with the same man. At the same time."

The words tumbled out of me. "You were having an affair with Jack Beltrano?"

She was on her feet again, wide-eyed. "You knew about that? About Jack?"

"Not about you and Jack, no. But about Nora and Jack, that they were close. Lovers? I couldn't be sure."

"Then you don't know Jack. If they were close," she exploded, "they were lovers. Beltrano comes on like a locomotive." Some of her anger was to cover her embarrassment.

I wanted her to tell it all, but calmly. Over my coffee cup, pleasantly, like a neighbor who'd dropped by to swap gossip, I said, "So how did you and Jack happen to link up?"

Satisfied that I was not being judgmental, only curious, she calmed down some. "It's a small town, Sid. How many choices are there for a woman alone and horny, and the wrong color for most of the locals? Beltrano is an equal-opportunity fornicator."

So was I, but I had dodged the opportunity with Gayle. I said, "You had a fire upstairs a few months back. Was that it?"

"You remember, very good. It wasn't much. I left the iron on in the workroom one morning. There was more smoke than fire, but it looked impressive as hell, and Jack and a couple of his volunteer guys showed up with boots, hatchets, and foam extinguishers. They didn't bring the truck. They didn't need the truck." She was starting to erupt again. "Beltrano is a one-man fire truck all by himself."

"You just called him a locomotive."

"Did I? That too." She made a try at a laugh, and failed; it still hurt. "Anyway, he came back the next evening, without the boys, 'to double-check the wiring.' He happened to mention that he and his wife were separated, and then he checked everything carefully. Very carefully." She took a beat and added with a regretful smile, "And, I must admit, very skillfully."

I wanted to be supportive. "About his separation," I said. "That could be true."

"Chalk one up for Beltrano. Sid, don't feel sorry for me, I went in with my eyes open. But I was stupid enough to believe after a while that we were beginning to have something. You know? He does have a way."

For a moment she looked almost wistful. She shook it off

and said, "Anyway, when Cassie told me about her mom, I broke it off with Jack. Fast. Back on Adam Clayton Powell Boulevard I'd have broken off his weenie is what I'd have done."

Poor Gayle. She'd come out to the east end at least in part to establish her independence from men, and she'd been badly used by still another man. I said, "You didn't tell Cassie about you and Beltrano, did you?"

She looked at me as if to say, Are you out of your skull?

I STAYED a few minutes more to shake Gayle out of the mild funk I had put her in, then I kissed her on her handsome forehead and left the shop to retrieve my pickup. The chief's car was pulled up next to it.

Chuck Scully stuck his head out the window as I approached. "I thought this looked like your heap," he said. "I've got a message for you."

"If it came through your office it can't be good."

"Relax, it's a civil matter. A lawyer called from the New York city attorney's office. He couldn't find you at home and he wondered whether we had you in custody. Not a bad guess, with the badmouthing you're getting these days."

"What did he want?"

"His number is on your answering machine. It's about that pending police brutality case. He wants you in the city tomorrow to be deposed by the lawyer for the plaintiff."

I was looking at, probably, a three-hour drive to the Wall Street district, more money to park than the damn Chevy was worth, and three hours of insults from a personal injury lawyer whose wife needed a new spring wardrobe.

"Shit," I muttered.

"Yeah, I thought you might see it that way."

He was about to drive off. I held up a hand. I don't know why the question popped into my head. "Tell me, Chuck, are Jack Beltrano and his wife separated?"

"What makes you ask?"

"Curiosity. And I'm confused. I've heard it both ways," I lied.

"Both ways is correct. Sometimes they are, sometimes they're not. A scorecard helps."

"How about these days?"

He shrugged. "They were together Monday night. Unless they just happened to fall into adjoining seats at the Sag Harbor movie house."

Gayle deserved better. So did Nora Brennan.

On another front, so did I. I deserved better than to be dragged into court by the man who put a bullet in my father's brain.

TWENTY

TWO TRIPS TO the city in less than a week constituted cruel and unusual punishment. But with no radio in the Chevy to distract me—it had been stolen on a previous trip to New York—I had the entire journey free to review my concerns. These did not include Ray Drummit and his miserable lawsuit; I would hold off on that nasty item until I saw how the deposition went. For the time being I was free-associating the open window in Sharanov's bedroom, his wrongo bed, and the little I knew about the people who touched Cassie's life, one of whom may have brought it to an end. In the course of nearly a hundred miles I had no luck locking any of these pieces together.

A small distraction kept getting in the way of my efforts. When I came out of the shower this morning—my appointment with the lawyers was for noon—there was a phone message from Tom Ohlmayer at his Manhattan squad room:

"Sid, you can't be happy with the way they're dumping on you out your way, so would you please call me? I've got a news flash that's sure to pick you up."

Dripping wet, I called. Tom's partner told me he was on another phone and would have to get back to me. I dressed, slowly, in my all-purpose city clothes, and waited. By the time I absolutely had to leave for the city I still hadn't heard from him. That put one more thing on my mind, but at least this one promised to be a plus. Tess Turkinton's fingerprints must have found a match in the FBI's national file.

RAY DRUMMIT'S LAWYER had agreed to take my deposition at the office of the city attorney who was handling the case for the NYPD. I found it, exactly on time, on a high floor of the ponderous Municipal Building in lower Manhattan. They weren't ready for me. No surprise. I was deposited on a bench in the corridor, probably to make sure I understood the pecking order.

I had never been on this floor of the building. The work here was mostly about defending the city's money against all comers, and there was a hushed air of serious purpose. Anyway, that's the way it looked today. After fifteen minutes the bench, designed no doubt by some malevolent civil servant, was digging seriously into my back. If I had brought a pencil and sketch pad I might not have noticed.

Eventually a wan, youngish lawyer with a thin mustache and wearing a blindingly white shirt and busy necktie burst through an office door, arms extended to grasp my hand, face filled with concern. If he had left his jacket on, the padding would have given the impression that he had shoulders. He introduced himself as Joe Pomphrey, or Humphrey; I hadn't gotten it on the phone message yesterday and I still didn't get it. He offered his ritual caring apology for keeping me waiting and ushered me into his office.

Inside he closed the door, waved me to a chair, went behind his desk to shuffle some papers and rearrange some others; he handled them as though they were not sterile. He looked up and remembered that I was there and asked if I'd like coffee or a soft drink.

I said no, and was this where I was going to be deposed? Because where was the lawyer from the other side, and didn't they need a stenographer or at least a recording device? And could we get on with it, because this business was costing me a day I could ill afford.

He looked mildly surprised. "Aren't you retired?"

"Not from life."

Pomphrey/Humphrey cleared his throat. This was a moment of truth.

"Okay. There isn't going to be a deposition," he said. "I called your home an hour ago to tell you not to come in, but apparently you had already left." He sounded injured, as if I had somehow let the side down.

"As you know," I said, "I live on the east end of Long

Island. If I had been home an hour ago to take your call I wouldn't have made it here for a noon meeting.''

He plucked a couple of the possibly germ-laden papers off his desk and said impatiently, ''Of course.'' Having lost the point, he was moving on. ''I have some news that should please you, Mr. Shale.''

Two pieces of good news today; my cup ranneth over and into my shoes. ''Tell me,'' I said. ''I could use some good news.''

''There isn't going to be a deposition,'' he said.

''You already told me that.''

''I mean ever. The complainant is dead.''

He was right; this was good news. ''Drummit? Why wasn't I told? When did he die?''

''At three o'clock this morning.''

''What was it, a heart attack? I hope he lived long enough to suffer.''

''He was shot to death in a cab he was attempting to rob at the point of a gun. The cabdriver was an undercover police officer.''

Relief coursed through me, followed by elation. I said, ''So maybe there is a God.''

Humphrey/Pomphrey wasn't listening. Sulkily, he said. ''This litigation has been a headache and a half to this office. Counsel for the late Mr. Drummit has just informed me that he is withdrawing from the case. For all practical purposes the case is dead.''

He was looking at my hand. ''Is that the ring that got you in all the trouble?''

''My father's,'' I said. ''And my grandfather's.''

He was staring at it. ''Mmm,'' he said, and I detected a faint sneer. If he had said any more I'd have floored him. On general principles. And let the lawsuit fall where it might.

''SID-NEY, *FOR LUNCH?*'' Enzo, polishing glasses behind the bar, could not have been more surprised when I walked into Muccio's. ''And on a Thursday? Your gang won't be in for another, let's see, thirty hours.''

"Yeah, I'm a little early."

I owed myself a celebration, and no way was I going to turn right around and make that drive back to the beach. There were things I could do in town, and I had maneuverability. Having failed to extract my car from an extortionist garage during its first hour of bondage, I was stuck with a minimum charge of ten hours.

I had made some phone calls and filled my dance card. The earliest meeting I could set up was for three-thirty, so I tried to grab a cop friend for lunch; I was hoping for a briefing on the taxi sting that killed Ray Drummit. All three of the old gang I called were out chasing lawbreakers. My taxpayer dollars were at work, which is why I was here alone.

Why Muccio's? Habit, the mighty force that keeps Eskimos living in the frostbite zone. And Muccio's wasn't that far from the Municipal Building.

With Enzo's voice carrying from the bar, "Two weeks in a row, Sid-ney? The kitchen will be pleased," I went into the backroom and seated myself at a table for two, a first for me. I surveyed the room while a waiter slammed down bread and water and scaled a menu my way. A red sauce thumbprint in a corner told me this was the one I had been given the previous Friday.

The Muccio customer mix was a little different during the day. Today it featured two large tables of nattily dressed gents who spoke in low voices and plowed through meals that called for several large dishes to be set before each of them at the same time. I recognized two or three of these serious diners. They could well afford more expensive restaurants, but Muccio's had a floor of bare tiles, and mob guys disdain "rug joints." One or two of them probably recognized me, but I doubted that my presence made them uncomfortable; cops and crooks often move in the same small world.

While I waited for my lunch ("Please be patient," Muccio's menu should have noted, "all dishes are reheated to order") I reviewed my schedule. Kitty Sharanov was my three-thirty, and I was meeting Alan for dinner. The period between Kitty and Alan would not be dead air. I had called Lonnie at the gallery for help in tracking down Alan, and she told me that he was at home studying for an exam. It was good that I was in the city, she added; she had just received something she knew I would want to see. I agreed to drop by the gallery at about five. My cup was now overflowing my shoes.

Because of the above productive schedule I attacked my eggplant parmigiana with a clear conscience. While I ate I amused myself by trying to guess what forms of felony were under discussion nearby. Soon after my double espresso and rum cake arrived (this was a day for reckless splurging) a very large shadow fell across the table.

Behind me a bass voice said, "Hey, Lieutenant, how're they hanging?" and Bobby "Wee Willy" Sonnino came around the table and put a foot on the chair opposite me, like a dog registering his claim on a tree. Wee Willy had been arrested twice on union racketeering charges and once for murder (that's how we first met), but he had never been indicted. His street name, inevitably, had been inspired by his size, six three in every direction.

"Hello, Bobby," I said, "I didn't see you."

"If I'd been here you'd have seen me," he said confidently; of course, he was right. "I just come in. Okay if I sit?"

I said what I'd have said to the eight-hundred-pound gorilla. "Help yourself."

He dropped into the chair. It held. He looked at my dessert and said, "How's their rum cake here?"

I pushed the leaden dish across the table and said, "Why don't you finish it? I have to go swimming in half an hour."

"Yeah?" He had already picked up the sodden cake between two meaty fingers and was shoveling it into his mouth. "Too sweet," he said. But down it went. "I hear you put in your papers, got yourself a place out there at the beach."

"That's right. I wore out young, Bobby, keeping my eye on guys like you."

"Sorry about that. You anywhere near Misha Sharanov? That Russian who a girl was killed in his house?"

"He's my neighbor. Was that a shot in the dark?"

"Not exactly. His people are saying there's heat on you for that dead girl."

"They're saying that because Sharanov is taking some heat himself. Bobby, where is it you run across his people?" Wee Willy was a sometime extortionist, Sharanov had once been in the shakedown racket, and they could very well have locked horns in the past. But now?

"Here and there sometimes." Wee Willy smiled and wiped rum cake from the corners of his mouth. "It happens I took a Jewish broad out to the Tumbra—Tundra?—couple of nights ago. She'd heard about it and she made a stink that's where she had to go. It was a first date, so could I whack her in the chops and drag her by the hair to one of my joints? I went. You ever eat that Russian shit? Garbage. I got to tell you, what these foreigners put in their mouth..."

He shifted gears. "Anyway, that's where I heard you trashed. From one of his people. You worried?"

"No. But thanks for asking."

Wee Willy's gaze was fixed covetously on an invisible prize in the middle distance. "That's a real money machine, that Tumbra. You know they don't take plastic."

"Neither does this place."

He hadn't thought of that. "Yeah, but this place..." He looked for a way out. "This place is nickel and dime. The Tumba's bigger than the Garden. And can those Russkys knock back the sauce." His eyes shone with envy. "Sharanov has to be stuffing mattresses with the skim."

"Is that a guess, Bobby, or do you know something?"

He shrugged. "Does a bear shit in the woods?"

"How well do you know the man?"

"We would run across each other. Years ago."

"You ever run across him with a woman?"

"Not his wife, if that's what you're asking. But he did like the broads."

"How young?"

"How young? Young. I don't think he knows from 'too young.' You expect any different from these animals?"

He heaved himself out of the chair. "I'm meeting some people." He pointed at the plate that had held the rum cake. "Not that bad. I might order me a couple of those."

KITTY SHARANOV had put me off till three-thirty because when I called she was on her way out to the hairdresser. It was a new Kitty Sharanov who opened the door to me now, with a new, younger hairstyle and a tailored suit that made much of her long legs and flat hips. And she was sober. Either the visit to the hairdresser had imposed a few hours of abstinence, or this really was a new Kitty Sharanov. Whichever, I saw for the first time what Sharanov might have seen when he married her—a young Katharine Hepburn, the pluckily independent, unattainable WASP. Just about the opposite, I would have guessed, of Misha's Russian wives.

She didn't offer me a drink. The only theme that carried over from my previous visit was a renewed hint of come-hither in her eyes. She may have had me marked as a possible target for her first postmarital adventure. Brother Roy, she told me almost before I stepped over her threshold, was out for the afternoon.

"Is that what you wanted to see me about?" she said. "Roy's behavior?" She had settled on a short couch, and she indicated I was to sit next to her. "He told me you two had some sort of misunderstanding at the beach house."

"What we had was a knockdown fight. I thought he was a burglar. He was skulking around like one."

"I'm sorry," she murmured. "If you think you've seen messy divorces, this one will top your list. I'm trying to find out what Misha's assets are."

"And *where* they are?"

She looked away. "He keeps his books in his armpit. My lawyer throws up his hands in despair."

"You must be entitled to a healthy settlement. How long were you married?"

"Thirteen years. And we were seeing each other for two

before that. While he untangled from that awful Russian. His second wife. Misha is a slow learner.''

"You must have been in high school when you met."

"Not quite nineteen, thank you, and a year out of Miss Porter's. If you're counting on your toes, I'm thirty-four.''

"No kidding? I'd never have guessed.''

"Whatever that means.''

I opened my mouth to lay on some additional flattery, but she held up a hand. "Please, don't spoil it.''

I managed to get in a plug anyway. "So where does an eighteen-year-old debutante of the year meet—what?—a close-to-forty-year-old Brooklyn hood?''

She neither confirmed nor denied the debutante accolade, but her tone softened. "I didn't know he was a hood. He had a box at Belmont next to my grandparents'. It was the last year they had it. It was the last year,'' she added bitterly, "they had *anything*. Misha knew how to bet. He was good-looking, well dressed, almost courtly. With just enough of a foreign accent to be interesting.''

And probably flashing a roll of bills that would choke the winner of the feature race. I said, "Thirteen years seems a long time to be married to a Mikhael Sharanov.''

"Especially when there are no children. Misha already had a couple he didn't much like by his dreary first wife. He didn't want any more.''

"Where are those kids?''

"One is a lawyer who works on environmental issues, the other is in graduate school, studying, I think, astrophysics, whatever that is. They are Misha's despair.''

She'd had enough of that subject. She leaned toward me and touched my knee lightly with two fingers. She said, "Is this a social call or are you playing detective again?''

I said, "Your lawyer will tell you it's too soon for you to receive gentleman callers.'' I hoped I sounded regretful, but she withdrew the fingers. I added, "Yes, I'm still on Cassie's death. You told me you cared about her, too.''

Impatiently, "I did. I do.''

"Last time I saw you I said I thought Misha may have

slept at the beach house the night before Cassie died. Do you remember my asking if you could guess who was with him? Because his bed was made and you agreed he'd never have made it himself?''

She took some time weighing how to answer this. Finally she said, ''Are you trying to pin Cassie's death on Misha?''

''Would that worry you?''

''Plenty. Because whatever the bastard's assets, they do me no good if they go to a clutch of lawyers defending him on a murder charge.''

I said, ''No, I don't think Misha did it. I'm just trying to sort out what was going on in the beach house around the time of the murder.'' She didn't respond to that and I had to prompt. ''As I remember, your first choice, and your brother's, for a sleeping companion for Misha, was Olivia Cooper.''

''I believe it was. So?''

''I spent a couple of hours with Cooper later that evening. And what troubles me is, she didn't seem anything like the bimbo you and Roy described.''

''I don't care what she *seemed*. I know what I know.''

''Which is?''

''What is this about, Mr. Shale?'' She had pulled the chain on her flirty look. ''I'll grant Olivia this much—she knows how to manipulate men. Don't tell me she's worked her magic on you.''

The best I could do was, ''I'm puzzled, that's all.''

''Okay, you asked, so here's what I know.'' She was simmering, and the story came pouring out. ''Misha and I were at the house one weekend late last summer. We were having our usual marital ups and downs and this was during a rare up. On Sunday we were supposed to have lunch with a girlhood friend of mine who had taken a rental in Amagansett. At the last minute Misha complained that his arthritis was kicking up and the long drive would just about kill him. Since Midge was my friend, why didn't I go on alone? So I did.

''About fifteen minutes east I discovered I had left Midge's address at home, and I had to turn around and drive back. I went into the house, and down that goddam ramp. I headed for our bedroom, where I'd left the note with Midge's address and phone number. Still with me, Mr. Shale?''

"I may be ahead of you."

"Passing the main guest room I heard sounds. The door was open a crack, and I pushed it wide. Misha and Cooper were locked so tight you couldn't tell where he ended and she began, except that I don't think the hand on her ass was her own. She couldn't have been there more than a few minutes. He must have called the instant I was out of the house, and she came running like a bitch in heat. They hadn't even heard my car. Maybe the heavy breathing drowned it out. Bimbo enough for you, Mr. Shale?''

She seemed to take pleasure in watching my face. The air of hospitality in the room had dissolved and there wasn't much more I was going to learn from Kitty. In point of fact, I had learned everything I came for. As soon as I could do it gracefully I thanked her for her time, asked to be remembered to her brother, and made my exit.

At the door I turned with a final thought. "If Misha was such a bastard—and I bet that wasn't the first time you caught him—how *did* you stick it out for thirteen years?"

"After I taught him he couldn't knock me around the way he had his Russian wives, he was very much the husband I wanted. I was used to having good things and he gave me good things. Many. And, oh yes." She smiled sweetly. "When he put his mind to it, he was a hell of a lover."

TWENTY-ONE

MS. MORGENSTERN is engaged,'' Jackie informed me triumphantly, and I felt a split second of alarm until I saw through the open office door that what she was engaged in was a hard sell to a brace of clients. Funny how I didn't want Lonnie for myself, but neither did I want her to want someone else badly enough to become engaged to him. I wasn't sure why; maybe it had to do with how much less time she would have left for selling my work.

Jackie suggested that since I had to wait, mightn't I profit from a serious look at the gallery's new show that opened this week? I had already taken a quick glance and I said, no thanks, but I might take a stroll up their alley for a serious look at the neighbors' garbage.

Jackie favored me with a venomous smile and, ''As you wish, Officer Shale. To each his own.''

We were saved from a continuing duel of wits by the break-up of the meeting in the office. The client couple left, a bit dazed-looking, and Lonnie came to greet me wearing her victory smile: There had been a sale, probably after some heavy arm-twisting. Whether the sale was the reason or not, she was radiant—confident and startlingly attractive. She locked an arm in mine and pulled me back toward the office.

I said, ''You're a great-looking woman, Lonnie, but you always have a special glow after sex or when you've made a good sale. Can I take a guess?''

I'm not sure my compliment, if that's what it was, registered. She closed the door and said, ''I just sold two paintings. I wish one of them was yours.''

''So would that bursar in Vermont.'' Every time she told me she had sold someone else's work I felt cuckolded. ''Better luck next time," I said gamely and moved on to business. "You said you had something to show me."

"Yes, but you'd better call your son first. He phoned twice looking for you. He seemed anxious."

"That sounds like a cancellation. Have I done something to turn him off?"

"Absolutely not. He adores you. Why do you think he paints? He can't wait for the end of school, so he can go out to the beach for as long as you'll have him. He'll clean brushes till the bristles fall out."

I phoned, and my hunch was right. Alan was sorry, but he had this heavy math exam tomorrow and he hadn't nearly finished reviewing for it. I said, evenly, I thought he had stayed home from school today to do exactly that.

"Take it easy, Dad, I did. But then I got this call from the principal's office and I had to go in. Coming and going and everything killed a good two hours. And it was weird. I wanted to tell you about it."

I was disappointed and a little pissed. "So tell me."

"A guy from the Treasury Department had come in to school to see me."

"The Treasury Department? To see you?" I spelled it out. "The United States Treasury Department?"

"He showed me ID. It looked good to me. And to the assistant principal, I guess, or he wouldn't have called me at home and scared the shit out of me. Oh, yeah, I had faked being home with a bad cold. So I had that to deal with too. Man."

"Okay, what did this Treasury agent want?"

"He wanted you, Dad. But he said he couldn't find you. He said he had some questions he needed answered in a hurry and if I could help him he wouldn't need to track you down. I must have looked funny because he said not to worry, they weren't looking into your taxes—'there's no IRS audit,' he said; they didn't do things that way.

"I said, so what was it about? He said it was a complicated interstate matter he couldn't explain because of, he said, 'confidentiality rules,' but that you weren't in any kind of trouble. He gave me some bullshit I couldn't follow, and then he started asking questions.''

"Like what?''

"Like, did I know who my father sold paintings to, and I said I had no idea. And were my parents still legally married. That one I answered, because it's a public record, right? And then he wanted to know whether my father still received paychecks from the New York Police Department, and *that* sounded to me like a tax question and I told him I wasn't going to answer any more questions because I had to go study for an exam. I gave him your number at the beach and told him to talk to you. And I got out of there.''

"Good for you, Alan. You did fine.''

"What's it about, Dad? Should you be worried?''

"About the IRS? Forget it. I've never earned enough to cheat on my taxes. I think I know what this is about, and it's not important.''

What it was about, I had decided, was the impending action against me and the city that had blown up this morning with the claimant's death. Ray Drummit's lawyer must have set an investigator snooping to find out if I had assets worth pursuing, and he hadn't had time to call the man off. I told Alan I was sorry I wouldn't be seeing him tonight and I was looking forward to our spending at least some of the summer together.

"Me too, Dad. And I'm sorry to leave you stranded for dinner.'' He took a beat. "Hey, why don't you ask Mom? I know she's not doing anything special.''

"Uh-huh. Thanks, I'll see.'' The little matchmaker.

When I got off, Lonnie looked up from searching for a piece of paper on her desk. "Everything okay?'' she said.

"Fine. He's just got too much work to go out.''

"That's a shame.'' She held up a fax. "This is what I wanted you to see. You know how I hate to lose a client. When I blew the deal with the Turkintons on *Seated Girl* I wanted to find out if they might be serious collectors.''

"Translation: Do they have enough money to make them worth chasing?''

"Have it your way. I'm sure you're aware that Dallas is fertile soil for an art dealer. I've said it before: There's more oil on the walls than in the ground. *And paintings don't deplete.*" Her blue eyes were shining with the rightness of it.

She said, "I have this contact in the Dallas—Fort Worth area I occasionally ask to look into prospects for me."

"Lonnie, a PI?"

She didn't like being confronted with the term. "I suppose that's what he is."

I thought, You've come a long way, Baby, from apprentice sleepwear buyer. I said, "You put him on the Turkintons?"

"That's exactly what I did." She handed me the fax:

Hi there, Leona,

Well, Honey, I'm afraid there's damn little I can give you on this one. Yes, there's an account under that name in the bank you gave me, and it'd cover the check you faxed. But I can't find a home address for a Ben Turkinton, and he doesn't vote here. I did find a business address for a Ben Turkinton. That turns out to be a Mexican restaurant downtown. Three partners, none named Ben Turkinton, none, for that matter, an Anglo. Try as I might, I couldn't find out where his mail gets forwarded—if he gets any. No trace of any Tess Turkinton. I don't have to tell you, this pair smells like last week's fish. Sorry, better luck next time.

Cal.

I said, "I hope you didn't pay a bundle for this information. Because I could have told you that those two were probably pulling a con."

"Probably, but not definitely. What in the world are they after?"

"A few hundred thousand off Mikhael Sharanov for a restaurant that will never happen."

"They didn't ring true, but they didn't seem *crooked.*"

"They may think they're not. They may think they're performing a public service by fleecing Sharanov."

"Here's the only part that interests me, Sid. I believe in the end we're going to sell *Seated Girl* to the Turkintons."

"What gives you that idea?"

"We know they set aside the money for it, and it's exactly what they need to firm up their swindle. When their deal ripens in a week or two, they'll be back to me."

"Maybe, but the painting won't be here."

"What do you mean?"

The idea hadn't formed till I voiced it. "I'm taking it off the market. For the time being at least. It's going into my ever-expanding personal collection."

"Sid, don't be foolish. You need this sale."

"Tell me. But I just decided I can't bring myself to exploit this dead girl. Or let the Turkintons do it. Specifically, the idea of her hanging on Sharanov's wall makes my flesh crawl. You'll sell someone else another one of my paintings."

"Not tomorrow, I can promise you that much."

"Sooner or later. I have faith. Right now here's what I'm going to do." It was hurting but I had to say it before I changed my mind. "My pickup's in a garage not far from here. I'm going to ransom it and bring it around. Would you have *Seated Girl* wrapped for me?"

And then I said something else that came out before I had given it any conscious thought. "Before I take her home, how about you and I go out for a bite to eat? I mean, if you're free."

Lonnie, who was almost never at a loss for words, took some time to find a few. "That sounds do-able. Let me see if Jackie will hold the fort. And then, I insist, dinner's on me. I can charge it to the business."

She had almost spoiled it. I said, "No, this isn't business. I came out on top in a legal action today. I was going to celebrate with Alan but now you're the lucky winner."

I was damned if I would let her floor me with her economic muscle. That had been a principal cause of our breakup the first time around.

I caught myself. What the hell did I mean by the first time around?

BEFORE I KNEW IT we had slipped under the East River and were on our way to Brighton Beach. I don't know why, except that we weren't that far from the Brooklyn-Battery Tunnel and I knew we wouldn't need a reservation at the Tundra on a weekday, especially at this early hour.

We didn't. When we arrived, fewer than two hundred diners were at work downing the Slavic noshes that sat on thousands of small plates. Gallons of vodka speeded their passage. There were still enough unoccupied tables in the hangar-size room to cause snow blindness—a problem, come to think of it, not that unusual on the tundra. I had figured Lonnie would be amused by the place, and she was. And incredulous.

"Does this go on every night?" she asked.

"This is nothing. You can't get in on a weekend."

We had kept the talk general and bland on the drive out: how well the kids were doing, the current state of the art market, how much SoHo had changed and how little Quincacogue had. It didn't come easily; we had trouble getting a handle on a dialogue different from our usual one—Lonnie nagging me about my work and me needling her about her commercial bent.

But after a few minutes at our corner table we had smoothed out the social kinks with vodka. The several shots it took to wash down the plates of herrings, smoked fish, and God knew what soon had us swapping reminiscences about our early years together. Before we knew it we were out on the floor dancing to the mammoth retro orchestra that came on duty at eight-thirty.

Motor memory is forever: Once you learn to ride a bike you can go thirty years without, then take off on one with never a wobble. Lonnie and I hadn't danced since well before the divorce, but we fell in with each other as easily as though it was yesterday. We had been pretty good and we were still pretty good, especially with the joints nicely oiled. And Lonnie's supple back and still slim waist felt not much different than they ever had. Better than good enough.

I would never have shown my face at the Tundra if I thought Sharanov might be on hand. But I knew he had still been out at the beach this morning supervising the redecorating of his bedroom, and he was likely to have stayed out, since he was expecting the Turkintons for the weekend. I did glimpse the faithful Nikki at the far end of the room sheepherding the staff in his tux. He glanced in our direction and then quickly away. He must have been keeping tabs on us, but he seemed no more interested in a confrontation than I was.

The dinner passed in a rose-tinted glow. I was, arguably, with the best-looking woman in the room, and we were having a mellow good time. We ate, we drank, we danced; eventually we even sang, if softly. It was only when the check came and I pulled it to me and took a quick peek that I was struck with a dampening thought: The Tundra didn't take plastic.

Not remotely did I have enough cash on me to cover this tab, and I would rather have hung by my thumbs than ask Lonnie for help. I slid the check into a pocket and left the table, supposedly in search of the john.

Instead I found our waiter and drew him behind a potted palm, out of Lonnie's line of sight. "Okay if I give you a personal check?" I said.

He looked me up and down. "Is possible. I must ask the manager." There was a note of doubt in his voice like a winter wind off the steppes.

I said I'd wait for him not at the table but *right here,* and he took off.

Terrific. I had this flash image. The waiter comes back with Nikki, who says, We do usually take personal checks but in your case we will make an exception. In your case we will beat the shit out of you and throw you into the alley.

I waited behind the potted palm like a hotel detective. A minute or two later I could see Nikki approaching from the entrance foyer, the waiter trailing. Sure enough, the giant was fuming, his face the color of beets. This seemed an excessive reaction to my modest request. When he got close he sent the waiter packing in Russian.

I said, "Hey, Nikki, how you doing?"

His return greeting was "Come wid me," spat through clenched teeth. Without waiting for a reply he turned and marched back the way he had come.

I followed, but at a less purposeful pace. For a lousy $112 he was definitely overreacting.

He led me through a narrow side door in the foyer into the coatroom, where he ordered the frightened elderly attendant to get lost. She did. This was the coatroom, I recalled, where a body had been found three years ago with two slugs in its chest. Nikki was rummaging around behind some coats. He came out with *Seated Girl*. Part of the brown paper wrapping had been ripped away from the front, revealing most of the two faces, the one looking up and the one looking down.

"What is dis?" Nikki demanded. "What de hell is dis?"

What had happened was that when Lonnie and I parked in the Tundra's lot I realized I couldn't leave the painting unattended in the open flatbed of the pickup, so I had brought it in to the restaurant and checked it. It was tightly wrapped and I can't even guess what instinct had made Nikki rip away the wrapping.

I answered his question. "It's a painting," I said reasonably. "I'm taking it out to the beach."

"It is de dead girl," Nikki said, and his carved yam of a face actually trembled. "Why? Why you bring dat here?"

"Easy does it, Nikki." He was looking at the portrait hypnotically, almost in awe; I thought of Russian peasants in attendance on an icon reputed to have mystical powers. "It's just a picture I painted."

"You bring it here to show Mr. Sharanov. To make him feel bad. Get it out of here."

"I intend to. Just as soon as I pay this bill." I was holding it out.

He snatched it out of my hand and crushed it; he would

brook no delays. "Get out! You hear me? Take dat picture out of here *now*."

"Sure. Absolutely. I'll get my lady and pick up the painting on our way out."

"Do it."

I went back to the table and threw a couple of tens down for the waiter. "Come on," I said to Lonnie. "We're leaving."

She said, "Now? Don't you have to pay the bill?"

"No," I said, and flashed her a confident smile. "We've been comped."

FIVE MINUTES INTO the drive back to Manhattan Lonnie was fast asleep, a casualty of the vodka. As she nodded off her body movements told me she was wrestling with a decision: Should she slump down with her head resting on my shoulder, or in the other direction? The latter choice offered the hard and probably cold surface of the door and window, and she began sliding toward me. But not far. She soon checked herself. And tilted the other way, settling firmly against the doorpost.

I made sure her door was locked.

AT WEST ELEVENTH street she stirred as I eased the Chevy to a stop in front of her brownstone. She forced her eyes open. Not many women look good when they first wake up. Lonnie always had, and she still did. I would have invited myself in with the excuse of needing a cup of coffee against the long drive on the expressway, but what would have been the point, with Alan up there, asleep or studying? And even without Alan, was anything likely to develop that would be of interest to my libido?

While I weighed this useless question Lonnie pecked me on the cheek and opened her door. "Don't bother getting out," she murmured. "It's late and I can manage. Nice evening." She was cold sober.

As she climbed down, the brisk night breeze seemed to

give her a jolt of energy. She said, "Sid, not to nag—that's the last thing I want to do—but would you please at least think about doing some work with sales potential? If you'd take on portrait work I could land you a commission in five minutes. How painful would it be to paint the teenage daughter of a stock broker or Wall Street lawyer sitting on her favorite jumper or cuddling the family dog? How about it? Sid, would you at least consider what I'm suggesting?"

The air had definitely gone out of my balloon. I said, "I can't paint animals. I never know what they're thinking. Find me a teenager I can paint cuddling the family fortune." And I slammed the door.

She shot me a What's the use? look and turned to march up her stairs.

And with Cassie Brennan lying in the flatbed behind me for company, I began the long drive home.

TWENTY-TWO

IN THE MORNING I bowed to the inevitable and called the only lawyer in the area I knew, Tony Travis, a man about my age who had an office over the hardware store in the village. The word was that Travis had been eased out of a Wall Street firm when a drinking problem kept him from making partner, and after his wife dumped him he retreated here to do a little lawyering and a lot more drinking.

I first met him at the bar at Pulver's, and we would run into each other there once in a while, but nowhere else. I don't think I had ever seen him when he wasn't drinking. I had no idea how good a lawyer he was, but I suspected he came cheap, because how heavy a hitter can you be in an office over a hardware store? Cheap was what I needed.

I called him at his office, and he said he could see me at eleven. His voice sounded different—crisper and firmer. This would be the sober, prelunch Tony Travis. Good; my grand jury appearance on Monday was scheduled for 11 a.m.

The call to Travis forced me to face up to another I had to make. But rather than phone Lonnie at home and get into a dialogue that could end in a blowup, I called the not yet open Leona Morgenstern Gallery. After taking a few deep breaths to steady myself I left a message on the machine:

"It's Sid. I've been thinking about the sensible suggestion you made last night. You're right, I can do portraits. Alan has told me the one of you I did when you were pregnant with him is hanging over your working, if smoky, fireplace. Not a great spot for it, and I hope you're not making a statement. Anyway, as you know, I am facile, and can work in many styles. It's a curse.

"Here's what I'm getting at. Besides Sarah's school fees, I'm going to have a lawyer's bill before long that I don't think I can get comped. So, yes, if you can find me a portrait commission I'll take it. No animal companions, if possible, but I'll happily take on a composition with two human heads. Two heads pay better than one, right? As you can tell from my choked voice, I am calling with a mouth full of humble pie.''

I HAD LOADED my drawing gear in the pickup, and after the session with Travis I drove up to the bay and parked at a dead end on the water where I had never sketched. I put in a couple of therapeutic hours on half a dozen drawings, not all of them good. I had gone several days without drawing, and it took a while for my fingers to get a fix on the dense vegetation at the front of the rocky bay, so different from the spare seascapes I more often drew these days.

As usual, my eye was on the scene I was drawing, but my mind was somewhere else—in this case back at Travis's office. Our meeting had gone about as I had expected. Travis was familiar with the Brennan murder from the heavy media coverage and from village gossip, and it was his opinion that I had nothing to worry about from the grand jury—even though, he wanted to make sure I clearly understood, his practice was almost entirely in real estate and his opinion might not be much better than mine.

The meeting lasted no more than twenty minutes, including the times we had to stop talking because of the piercing sound from the key-making machine in the hardware store directly under the office. I was pretty sure Travis would not deduct those nonproductive periods from his billing time. The prelunch Tony Travis was all-business.

When we finished our meeting—neither of us having brought up the subject of a fee schedule—Travis walked me through his secretary's room and down the stairs to the street, chatting amiably all the way. I figured he had turned the billing meter off when he left his desk (would he have the nerve to charge me portal to portal?), so I stood with him outside the front door and let him ramble. Half a dozen years on the east end had just about rubbed prep school out of his voice.

Eventually he looked across the street to the municipal building and pointed out Nora Brennan's window on the second floor. He said, "She hasn't been in since her daughter's death. It's strange to glance up there and not see Nora behind her window, bent over her desk. Talk about your workaholics, she's in five mornings a week, winter and summer, well before eight."

He could see the question I was forming. He said, "Of course *I'm* not around before eight, but that's what they tell me. Nora opens that office and she closes it." He shook his head in wonder at the sheer energy that took.

I said, "That schedule didn't give her much time for the family, did it?"

"The husband's basically out of the picture. And the girl was an independent soul. But close to her mother. I'd see them together over a quick lunch at Mel's, two busy working gals, Nora dispensing wise advice, the daughter listening, taking it all in. Do your kids take advice from you? Mine tell me to go sell it."

I hoped in my case he wasn't putting too high a price on it.

I TOOK ANOTHER look at my drawings of the bay when I got home and decided I didn't like a single one of them. Something had to be bothering me for the work to have gone that badly, and I supposed it was my cash flow situation. I would have to put that out of my mind. Sure.

There were two phone messages. Olivia Cooper reported that she was about to leave the city, and she was reminding me that I was expected for dinner at her beach place tonight. She spoke her Southampton address slowly into the machine.

If I had been able to come up with an excuse at this late hour that didn't make me look like a jerk I would have canceled Cooper. Kitty Sharanov's graphic description of her with Sharanov in a tangle of steaming bodies had robbed me of my taste for the evening.

The other call was from Tom Ohlmayer. He was sorry he had missed me when I was in town. What he wanted to tell me yesterday I probably knew by now: The punk who was pursuing me on assault charges had been shot dead during a taxi robbery. But now Tom had a piece of news on another subject. I would like this, but I would absolutely have to keep it under my hat.

I expected item two to be a report from Washington on Tess Turkinton's fingerprints. Not a word on that. What I got was a vague rumor from "somebody" in the department: Mikhael Sharanov was about to be placed under arrest. Tom assumed that if the rumor was true Misha was being tagged for Cassie Brennan's murder. And wouldn't I be relieved to hear that?

I would. If the County Crime Scene Unit had come up with some hard evidence against Sharanov I would take back every ugly thought I had entertained about Detective John Docherty. With Sharanov under arrest I would be able to cut off Tony Travis before the billable hours started ticking me toward insolvency.

But the rumor was vague and shaky; it sounded more wish than fact. I got little nourishment from it.

I was in a lousy mood. This was not a good time to make a critical judgment, but I took another hard look at those sketches I did at the bay and tore them up.

I was entitled to at least one positive act today. I could still put in a few hours on *Large* before I had to start getting social with Cooper. I climbed the scaffold and dove in.

I was reckless with the vermilion.

TWENTY-THREE

THERE WERE RENEWED signs of life in the refurbished Sharanov house. Driving slowly by early in the evening on my way to Southampton, I saw lights both upstairs and down, and bodies moving from one level to the other. The red Cadillac was once again parked out front, along with other cars; it had apparently been furloughed for the week in favor of the black Volvo that delivered me to the Gulliver. Had Sharanov also shown respect for the deceased by drinking vodka martinis with black olives?

I had no idea what to expect at the address Olivia Cooper gave me. The odds favored a trendy beach house, a bitterly contested prize in an ugly divorce settlement.

What I got was a traditional brick and stone two-story, a small gem set back on mature landscaping on a street of similarly traditional houses halfway between the beach and downtown Southampton, and a stroll to either. True, it was the smallest house on the block, but Cooper was a woman alone. If she got this place in a divorce she must have given up a lot elsewhere.

My next thought was that my previous assessment had been knee-jerk sexist. It was as likely that Cooper had earned the house through the sweat of her brow. In our previous meeting, what she did for a living had never come up.

My tired pickup looked as if it had been dumped on this solidly middle-class street by a hurricane. I drove it as deep into Cooper's driveway as I could; a high privet hedge and a two-door Mercedes would hide it from all but the most prying eyes. There was no need to stir up neighborhood gossip. Or had Cooper already given these solid burghers plenty to gossip about?

After her sledgehammer come-on when she invited me to

dinner I half expected her to greet me in an at-home outfit out of a Victoria's Secret Valentine's Day ad. But she came to the door in the clothes she must have worn to work in the city that day—a suit the color of dark chocolate and totally unadorned. Its boxy jacket said, Don't you dare shut me out of the Big Meeting; its pencil skirt was cut high enough above the knees to add, But don't you ever forget that I'm a woman.

While she led me into the house she told me that every time her visit to Muccio's came to mind this week she had been unable to control her giggling. In meetings, elevators, wherever. And then we were in her living room, where the furnishings went perfectly with the house—tasteful and safe. I could see where Muccio's must have seemed on a planet in another solar system.

After more small talk while she fixed me a drink, she said, "I didn't leave the city as early as I expected, and then— would you believe it?—the Friday afternoon summer traffic is starting to build. We're not even seriously into May! Couple of more weeks and forget it. Anyway, I haven't had a chance to slip out of these damn work clothes, so would you excuse me? I promise, I'll be no more than five minutes." And she retreated to her bedroom.

Had I gotten everything right but her timing? Was the sinuous at-home outfit lying fetchingly across her bed waiting to be wriggled into? Would she reappear in it soon enough, pausing in the doorway long enough to say, "This feels so much more comfortable?" Could she be that obvious? I pushed aside the image and studied the walls.

They weren't that bad. In front of me were a couple of splashy outdoor scenes by pseudo-Impressionists—school of Renoir, school of Monet. Logical choices for a weekend retreat, they said Let's get out of the house and enjoy nature. But they were so safe. Instead of springing for the Mercedes sitting out front she should have hung that money on her walls; she could have done a lot better for herself.

Directly behind me was a school of Dufy. No, that *was* a Dufy. She *had* done better. So she wasn't afraid to spend.

And since she could spend she could do better still, move the room forward to the millennium. With, for instance, something like *Seated Girl*. The Cassie painting would make the room jump, take twenty years off it. When I was ready to sell.

And then my hostess reappeared in her at-home outfit—a baggy Irish cable knit sweater and a pair of jeans she didn't have to wriggle to get into. Either she was secure enough as a seductress to believe she didn't need tarting up to work her magic, or I had totally misread the tone of her invitation. Maybe the wish had been father to the thought.

She watched me watch her make herself a drink—ice cubes, scotch, water, all three too quickly juggled into the glass. Something had her nervous. She may not have even noticed that she had filled a brandy snifter. She said, "How hungry are you?"

"Anytime you're ready. Soon, if you'd like." With luck, I could make this a short evening. Even putting aside what I had heard about her since last Friday, I had liked her better that evening, when she had been loose and easy.

She may have caught a hint of impatience in my voice. She said, "Don't worry, this won't be one of those dinners where you're on your fifth drink and chewing the carpet before the hostess remembers to start cooking. I made a casserole in the city last night. It'll take ten minutes to heat, so you just holler ten minutes before you want to eat. I think I can approach"—she smiled impishly if a bit nervously—"and possibly even match, the kitchen at Muccio's." It was the second time she had made that weak joke.

"So you're able to go home and cook after a hard day at the office." I cut to the chase. "Or aren't your days at the office that hard?"

"I'm not in the office that much. But yes, my days are sometimes intense."

She wasn't giving me what I wanted. "I forget. Did you tell me what you do?"

"Did I? I don't remember." She took a slug of her Scotch.

Would I have to prod her with still another question? And then she said it. "I sell insurance."

So was this what her heavy come-on had been about? A chance for a one-on-one to explain a sensible low-cost policy that would protect my loved ones in case "something" happened to me? Something, in this connection, meaning death, a word that insurance people find drains the fun from their pitch.

I said, "Uh-oh."

She laughed nervously and said, "Don't worry, you're safe. I don't deal in personal policies."

"Then...?"

"I do commercial work."

I had a blinding flash of what could have been understanding. I made sure she was looking full at me and I said, "Do you insure Misha Sharanov's business?"

Her ears reddened. "What makes you ask that?"

I wasn't ready to tell her. Instead I said, "You're friends and neighbors, and from the way you live you're too good at what you do to let a juicy prospect like Sharanov go somewhere else for his peace of mind."

She took a moment. "Yes, I insure the Tundra." She let it all out. "Fire, theft, liability."

"A healthy account."

She looked deep into her snifter; she may have been double-checking that it had really been hand-blown in Czechoslovakia. Then she looked up at me. "Actually, it's because I insure Misha that I invited you here tonight. Can I freshen that drink?"

I held it up; I had barely touched it. "I don't see how." I wasn't going to let her slide off the main topic that easily. Not while I was beginning to understand what was going on.

I said, "Tell me if I have this right. To make sure I accepted your invitation, you hinted that dinner might not be the only pleasure of the evening."

She winced. "Did I really come on that strong? God, I'm really sorry." She smiled a quick dutiful smile and went back to looking uncomfortable. "I didn't mean to...to..."

She couldn't decide what it was she hadn't meant. This definitely wasn't the easygoing Cooper I had admired at Muccio's. But she rallied. "I didn't expect to say what I have to say until I'd softened you up with my never-fail shrimp casserole. You're lousing up my program. Is this a sample of your grilling technique from your years as a cop?"

"As close as I can get to it without my nightstick. Why don't we talk first, eat later? Better for the digestion. What did you want to tell me?"

She got up and began a measured pacing. Neither the floppy sweater nor the easy-fitting jeans succeeded totally in hiding her trim figure. Hell of a good-looking woman.

She said, "This has been bothering me for a week. Do you remember my telling you that Cassie Brennan had come here to work for me?"

"Once, you said. She cleaned your house." I thought I knew where she was going. "But you said you couldn't tell me anything helpful about her because you two hadn't really talked."

"That part wasn't true. We did talk. Cassie poured herself out to me."

"About Sharanov?"

She nodded.

I said, "Something ugly, right? And you were reluctant to tell me because if it got back to Sharanov he might figure you for the source and start looking for an insurance broker who knew how to demonstrate loyalty."

"Very good, Sid. You should never have quit the police." She stopped pacing. The worst appeared to be over; some of the tension went out of her body and she sat down.

"I've been wrestling with my conscience and I lost," she said. "I'll feel better when I get this off my chest." She sighed mournfully. "Cassie was an awfully nice kid."

I waited.

She said, "She had just mopped the bathroom floor when she came to me. She had been waiting for me to take a break from some work I had brought out with me. I was putting away the files. She wanted to know, Could we talk?

"It came out in a torrent. She had seen me around Sharanov, I seemed to know him—how to handle him—and maybe I could help her. Because she didn't want to lose her job with the Sharanovs. They paid her generously—*very*—there were little gifts, Kitty had been good to her, and so on.

"But Misha had been coming on to her, and it was getting worse. He could be thoughtful in little ways, but he could be nasty, especially when he was drinking. And what had started out as flattery and teasing and then casual flirtation had built into crude pressure. He told her exactly what he expected of her, spelled it out in words of one syllable."

I said, "Where could he do this around a house that was usually full of people?"

"Anywhere. The basement, the grounds, the house itself. He would corner her in a room when there were people in the next. He didn't seem to give a damn. One time, when she had left the house for the day, he forced her bike off the road with his Cadillac, so they could 'talk.'"

"Were his threats all talk or did he put his hands on her?"

"He wasn't physical in a sexual way. But he would grab her by the wrists to hold her attention. Sometimes it hurt. When she threatened to tell Kitty he laughed and said it wouldn't be news to her. Once he drove out from the city by himself when she was alone in the house doing the week's cleaning. For the first time it was just the two of them and she was scared."

"How did she handle that one?"

"She ran. Literally. She said she needed to buy some cleaning supplies and she jumped on her bike and beat it the hell out of there. And she made sure to keep off the road for the first mile. That's where things were between those two when she came to me."

"This happened last season," I said. "And Cassie was still working at the house when she died. So whatever advice you gave her, it must have worked."

"I hope so."

"You mean, either it worked, or Misha won the argument. Which do you think?"

"Next time I saw her she thanked me, but who knows? She wasn't likely to tell me she had gone to bed with her tormentor, was she?"

"So tell me. What was the advice you gave her that may or may not have worked?"

"I told her to do what I had done. Because it worked for me."

Did it? My doubts may have shown, because she hesitated. I said, "Go on."

"Misha started hitting on me as soon as the ink dried on the first policy I wrote on the Tundra. For a time I was able to keep him at arm's length with the standard tricks women learn in the business world. I acted dumb, as if I didn't know what he was getting at, then I pretended he wasn't serious, then I spoke of my heavy 'commitment' somewhere else.

"Misha is not easily discouraged. One weekend when we were both out here he phoned me to come right over to his place, he had a serious problem involving his insurance. I canceled my tennis game and hurried over. It turned out the problem wasn't that serious, but Kitty was out of the house and we were alone. That was serious.

"And so was Misha. He'd been drinking, and for the first time he put his hands on me. We got into some serious wrestling. He's a strong son of a bitch."

"Did that surprise you? Didn't you know he used to do strong for a living?"

"I'd heard the rumors," she admitted. "But that had been business, this was personal. Very. Things weren't going well for me in that bedroom when Kitty showed up. She had come back to the house for something she'd forgotten and she walked in on us. She took one look, turned around, and walked out. It was ghastly. But she had succeeded in breaking Misha's concentration, and he backed off.

"That little drama was a turning point for me. I had felt like a piece of dirt. Worse. I waited a day to calm down and then I told Misha if he ever tried anything like that again he would damn well have to take his insurance business somewhere else. And the important thing is that I meant it.

"And you know what? It worked. He decided he preferred having me around than not, and for that to continue he would have to behave on my terms. And that was the advice I gave Cassie. I told her that no way should she have to deal with Misha's Neanderthal courtship ritual, that she should tell him if he didn't lay off she'd quit. But she would have to *mean it.*

"And then I assured her that he did want her around, absolutely, and he'd accept her conditions. I reminded her that any number of gumdrops he could hit on were drawn to his house, that women are attracted to a man who is already surrounded by good-looking woman; they're like a seal of approval, a sign that he's been pretested. I said he would come to think of Cassie and me as bait. And that's the whole of it. All I can tell you is that Cassie listened to every word I said."

Cooper was finished, and she didn't even wait for a reaction from me. She said, "What do you say to my putting the casserole in the oven while you finish that drink?"

"Not yet," I said; I was no longer interested in rushing things. I said, "You must know that what Cassie told you would be of interest to the police. Have you spoken to them about it?"

"No, I haven't."

"Telling me doesn't get you off the hook. You have to put yourself on the record with this. If Sharanov finally did strong-arm her into going to bed with him, he becomes a likely suspect in her death."

"That would be true. Except that I know he didn't kill her."

"How?"

"Because he spent last Thursday night—the night you thought he might have slept in his bed at the beach house— at my apartment in the city."

I had a flash recall of what Sharanov told me at the Gulliver: He had spent that night with a woman he declined to name. So here was that woman. Or was providing an alibi, along with a wall calendar at Christmas, a thank-you for

Misha's insurance business? My take on Cooper's character and motives had gone back and forth these past few minutes like windshield wipers in a snowstorm.

"If he got to spend that night with you," I said slowly, "there must be a flaw somewhere in your 'touch me at your peril' strategy."

She didn't take offense; she was amused. "I didn't say he spent the night with me. He spent the night *in my apartment*. On the couch."

"Because...," I prompted.

"Because otherwise he'd have been in my bed. I wouldn't have liked that one bit."

I said, "I meant, how come he was spending the night in your apartment at all? On whatever piece of furniture?"

"It was an act of charity on my part. Misha and Kitty had been fighting, he was staying in a hotel, and he was so drunk he couldn't remember which one. It was after one in the morning and the doorman's buzz on the intercom had yanked me from a deep sleep. Misha had been asked to leave a bar, and everybody else he could think of to crash with lived in Brooklyn.

"Anyway, that was his story. By the time the doorman got him upstairs he was practically out on his feet. And too drunk to be a threat. I set him up on the couch and went back to sleep."

"You don't think he was carrying out a clever plan to get in your bed?"

"Of course that occurred to me. He may have thought that since he and Kitty were separated I might change my mind about an involvement with him. I never gave him a chance to test the possibility. I threw him a pillow and blanket and closed my bedroom door."

"He stayed the night?"

"Yes. And pretty well ruined mine. Around dawn I heard him bumping around the living room. He knocked on my door, and when I didn't answer he tried the knob. I had locked myself in and after a few seconds he called, 'Thank you, Olivia, for your hospitality. Good-bye.'

"A minute later I heard him on the phone ordering Nikki to pick him up. Can you imagine, at six-thirty in the morning? I know that's what he was doing because the address was in English. Ten minutes later the front door opened and closed and I finally got some sleep." Abruptly she said, "I'm suddenly very hungry. Okay if I turn on the oven?"

I discovered I was hungry too. I said, "Do it."

It was late when I started for home.

Painting rechannels much of my sexual energy toward the work at hand. *Large* was a voraciously demanding canvas, and Olivia Cooper was the first person with whom I cheated on it. She was well worth the wait.

Or was she faking it? I hadn't even been able to tell whether all, some, or none of what she told me about Cassie, Sharanov, and herself was true or merely self-serving. It sounded right and I didn't stop to analyze it. She caught me on an uptick in my constantly changing feelings toward her and we went from her shrimp casserole to her bed as naturally and inevitably as a barrel rolling over Niagara Falls.

I would have stayed the night—sweet night!—but Cooper explained regretfully and with many apologies that if her neighbors saw a rusting pickup on her property at the crack of dawn she would have to pack up then and there and move. She walked me to the door, naked under an open robe.

I resolved to draw her that way, her gently curved hip gleaming against the dark flannel. The image was vivid enough so that I might be able to do it from memory. I kept it firmly fixed in my mind as I eased the Chevy out of the driveway and began the trip home under a heavily overcast sky.

When I passed the Sharanov house I made out the red Cadillac still in the driveway. In the starless night I couldn't tell if there were other cars on the property, but the house was dark. Admittedly it was late, but not for Sharanov. Misha seemed to be spending an out-of-character quiet Friday night. Out of respect for the dead, no doubt.

Halfway between his place and mine I dimly spotted a car pulled up in the underbrush, its lights out. High school kids, I figured, making out. It had happened before, as this was a relatively untraveled stretch of Beach Drive. But my tires on the gravel may have panicked them into abstinence. Even before I drew abreast their headlights sprang on and off, possibly in the scramble of untangling bodies. Or not.

My eyes went not to the car but to my house. I had seen a flashlight bob, then wink off—echoes of Kitty's brother Roy skulking around in the Sharanov house. Damn.

I gunned the motor, roared to the front entrance, and stopped on a dime. I raced to the door; it was closed but unlocked. I dove through and flicked on the overhead light.

There was no movement, nobody in sight. But the door to the beach was wide open.

My burglar—Roy Chalmers, whoever—had a good head start on me. I ran out onto the beach and turned west. He would be running that way, toward whoever had signaled from the parked car. In the distance I thought I saw a rustling of dune grass, beach to road. I turned and ran back through the house and out the front.

Up the road the waiting car had emerged from the underbrush and turned to face west. A door was wide and a figure plunged through it to the interior. Even before the door had closed the car was racing into the dark, its lights still out.

By the time I took off in pursuit it would have vanished up any of the many side roads that led away from the beach. Hopeless. I went back in the house.

I couldn't believe this. Déjà vu with a vengeance. The desk drawers were open, their contents scattered. This time papers and drawings covered the floor, paint tubes were scattered, cans of brushes overturned. So far as I could tell from an eyeball survey, nothing was missing. *Seated Girl*, wrapped in a tarp now, sat on its side against the wall where I had placed it.

What the hell could the thief have wanted? I didn't have

anything of value but my art, and the jerk didn't seem interested in any of that, so he was probably a local.

I didn't even make a try at straightening up the place. I went straight to sleep.

3

...AND A WEEKEND

TWENTY-FOUR

IT WAS AFTER ten when I opened my eyes on Saturday morning, and I quickly closed them. I had forgotten that the room was a holy mess. The room was always a mess, but I was used to my mess. This one was alien, an affront. That bastard.

Eventually I forced myself out of bed and set to work bringing the place back to a logical disorder. None of the paintings or drawings had been damaged, and my first priority was to get those safely back where they belonged. I picked up the drawings first.

One of them surprised me. I had forgotten that I drew it.

It was the sketch of the tall, skinny, Don Quixote—like fisherman in a floppy hat, T-shirt, and baggy pants I saw on the beach early on the morning of the murder, the sketch I drew at the police station on the back of a calendar for Chuck Scully, who identified it at once as Harry Gregg.

But now this reminder of Gregg popped a thought into my head that should have occurred to Chuck or me when we spoke to Gregg the other day; that it hadn't bordered on stupidity. There was still a way Gregg might be helpful.

I remembered that his shift at the Gulliver didn't begin until two in the afternoon (did he work at all on Saturday?) and even if he went fishing this morning he would be home by now. There was a good chance I could catch him there.

I TOOK the long way around, through the village. Covenant Street was enjoying its liveliest Saturday since fall. Cooper was right; the infiltration of summer people was beginning to build toward the late May invasion. The new arrivals hadn't yet settled into the rhythm of village traffic flow. Cars backed and filled in frustration, especially around the hardware store, where homeowners with winter damage would be loading up on repair supplies. I also noted shoppers peering in the window of Gayle's Provocativo—a harbinger, I hoped, of a good season for Gayle.

I don't know what made me glance at the village hall as I passed it, up toward the window that Tony Travis had pointed out as Nora Brennan's; I certainly didn't expect to see her at work on a Saturday. But there she was, in sharp profile, still as a cameo, eyes on her computer screen. At this distance the lines of care and aging washed out and she looked almost as young and pretty as her daughter.

I supposed she was making up for the week of work she had missed. She would have no distractions on a Saturday, and for a workaholic like Nora the office was preferable to sitting at home and brooding.

I wondered whether it was gazing at Nora from the firehouse across the street that had given Jack Beltrano the itch for her. The firehouse doors were closed this morning. Beltrano would be busy receiving inquiries at his contracting office outside of town; the sap would be rising this weekend in more than a few owners of undeveloped land who half believed the time might finally be right to put up a couple or three spec houses.

ON HARRY GREGG'S haphazard street on the outer rim of the village his nearest neighbor was in the front yard finishing his spring cleanup. He stared at me with naked curiosity as I climbed onto Gregg's porch; I had the feeling a visitor was a rare event in Harry's life.

So was a spring cleanup; his yard looked as if he had missed the last few. Distributing his overflow fishing catch among the neighbors might have been his way of keeping their good will in the face of the affront his house and grounds were to the neighborhood.

It took a long while for my insistent knocks to be answered, and then the door was opened only a couple of inches. Gregg was visible in the crack, dressed in wrinkled pants and a denim work shirt. His long face was set in what I suspected was its most natural expression, deep suspicion.

He said, "Yeah?"

I said, "Hello, Harry, remember me? I dropped by with Chuck Scully the other day."

He looked over my shoulder to see if Scully was with me now. He said, "Yeah, I remember. Was that you the other night at the Gulliver called my name?"

"Right. You were carrying an air conditioner."

"Could have been. Those window units they got there are more trouble than the damn things are worth, especially after the salt air's had a few years to get at them. Are you a cop?"

"No, but I used to be. Chuck's swamped, and I'm sort of helping him out on that case he was here about." What the hell, it was a small lie. "There's something maybe you can help with. Okay if I come in?"

I knew he'd say no. "If you want, you can sit out here for a minute." He slipped out and closed the door behind him. "You wouldn't like it in there, it's a mess." He tested for a strong part of the porch railing and sat on it.

"I know what you mean," I said, "I don't like visitors in my house either. Without a woman in charge it looks like the village dump."

He looked at me appraisingly and the suspicion eased slightly: Maybe he had found a kindred soul. He said, "My mother knew how to take care of the place. Even my wife, some. They're both gone, one way or another."

"Thinking about another wife?" We were cozying up.

"Nope," he said, and allowed himself the shadow of a smile. "I do better with fish than women."

"It's about the same with me. Substitute painting for fishing. That's what I do. Paint."

He couldn't have cared less, but I figured we had established a bond. I didn't know how long an attention span he had, so I went for the meat.

"When we were here the other day," I said, "Chuck asked you whether you saw any cars at that big white house on your way to the beach the morning Cassie Brennan was murdered. The one with the spiral ramp. Do you remember that?"

"Of course. The Russian's. Where the girl was killed. I'd have remembered a car anywhere along that stretch of road. But there wasn't none. I told Scully that."

"You did. You had passed me on the beach at around seven a.m. or a little after, and Chuck was trying to find out if anyone had been staying overnight in that house. What he forgot to ask—and that's why I came back to see you—was whether you saw any cars there on your way *back* from fishing. Someone who might have shown up between your going out and coming home."

"On my way back? Yeah, sure, there was a vehicle then."

Bingo. Gently, I said, "Don't you think you should have mentioned that to Scully?"

"Why?" Gently or not, he knew when he was being criticized. "The paper said the girl was killed after nine o'clock, when she came in to work. I was back home from fishing way before nine. Couldn't have been as late as eight-thirty when I walked past that house. And the vehicle I saw had already pulled out of the driveway, heading toward the village."

"How can you be sure all of this didn't happen after nine?"

"Because on my way home I dropped off a bluefish—I only caught the one—next door at Al Bolger's. He was still home and he leaves for work the very latest a quarter to nine."

"Still, Harry," I said, "didn't you think it worth mentioning that you saw a car at the Sharanov house the morning of the murder?"

"Not a car, a truck. Hell, no. I figured it was out on a service call and the driver had been given the wrong address."

"A service call?"

"That's right. I only caught a glimpse of it as I cut across the dunes. It was already well down the road, but I'm pretty sure it was a tow truck out of Huggins Service Station."

I PULLED UP at a rambling frame house, probably built in the twenties, that sat on a wide street with shade trees of the same vintage. I had wangled the address from one of Paulie Malatesta's co-workers at the Huggins Service Station. It turned out that Paulie didn't work on Saturdays.

The bony man putting down mulch in his foundation planting was sixty-something, his children probably grown and out, so renting a room to a bachelor made sense. He greeted me pleasantly, said no, Paulie wasn't at home. He didn't hang around on his day off, and who should he say had been asking for him?

I gave my name and said I knew Paulie mainly through his girlfriend—the teenager who was murdered last week?—and that I'd come around to express my condolences.

"A terrible, terrible thing," the man said, and laid his rake aside. "The boy's been a wreck all week. We're the Hamiltons, by the way." His ruddy complexion flushed a deeper red when he volunteered his name; he didn't want to seem forward.

I acknowledged the introduction and said, "Paulie's been living with you for some time?"

"Since he moved to the village. Eight or nine months. The irony is, he came out here to get away from big-city violence. He'd seen enough, he said, to last a lifetime. And yes, he'd found himself a lovely girl. Full of life. Sixteen? I was surprised when I read that. She seemed older."

"You knew Cassie?"

"Met her briefly, two or three times. We'd vanish, leave them alone, the wife and I." So there'd be no misunderstanding he added, "In the front room, downstairs. They were entitled to their privacy. I learned that much raising boys of my own."

"I was very fond of Cassie. Do you think he loved her?"

"I do. I really do. Oh, they fought, sometimes like tigers, but people in love fight, don't they? It shows they care."

"I didn't know they fought. What about?"

"I wouldn't know that. It's true, sounds do carry in this house. If my wife sneezes in the attic I'll say 'Bless you' in the basement. But you can't make out words. All I got from those two was the tone when their voices rose. Angry. Does it matter? They cared for each other.''

"I'm glad to hear that. It helps. Do you have any idea where Paulie went today, or what time he might be back? Did he maybe go into the city to see his family?''

"I don't believe he's got any kind of family. He never spoke of one. And no, I wouldn't know where he's gone. Not far, because what he drives is a Huggins tow truck.''

"He keeps it here?''

"He's on call, that's the deal. He's got a car phone. And they'll phone him here at night if there's an emergency, and he'll go right to it. It's a gypsy life. Sad, but I don't think the boy's ever known any other kind.''

TWENTY-FIVE

WHENEVER SARAH CALLED—and she didn't call often—it was always on a weekend, when the phone rates dropped. She had left a message on my machine:

"Dad, hi. I'm sorry I missed you. Listen, I know you're having trouble meeting the tuition, and this is getting silly. I don't have to go to Bennington next year, I really don't. I'd probably be just as happy at a state school, maybe happier. Can we talk about this? I love you."

And that was it, short and sweet.

I called her back; naturally she wasn't in. I hated myself for failing her. Bennington was the only thing Sarah had ever in her life asked of me. She was pitching in with two part-time jobs that paid slave wages, she had a full-time job with Gayle lined up for the summer, and her mother was coming up with her half of the tuition. (Lonnie would have lent me my half in a minute; I'd sooner choke.)

If I could sell even a small painting and put off paying Tony Travis until sometime early in the next century I might be able to lift my end of the load. It would help even more if I nailed Paulie Malatesta for Cassie's murder before the weekend was up. That would allow me to achieve one of my current life ambitions—firing Travis by Monday morning.

My unassailable integrity, my pose as an artist whose personal vision made no allowance for the marketplace, had once again gotten me in trouble. The hubris had piled up like horseshit. I would have to make good on my promise to Lonnie to grow up and do some work I could *sell.* Pretty beach scenes, charming village landscapes, portrait commissions.

Something perverse had been at work in me. I had even destroyed the marketability of my one sure-fire salable painting—my sexy portrait of Gayle, *Green and Brown Morning.* On impulse one afternoon I had aged Gayle forty years on the canvas and turned the work into a statement on the vanity of youth.

I was too old to be a free spirit, I had too many responsibilities. I looked up at *Large,* and at that moment I hated it. I saw a self-indulgent, show-off acre of canvas and pigment. The cost of the paint alone would have covered a measurable portion of my children's education.

I needed to find Paulie Malatesta. If he was in the area, that tow truck would stick up like a schoolboy's cowlick. I went out looking for him.

IT DIDN'T TAKE long to find him. The village cemetery, where the jumble of graves went back to the seventeenth century and some stones were as thin as shirt cardboards, had gone standing room only decades ago. The annex across the road was larger, brighter, more in touch with the living; flowers, real and artificial, nestled at the base of some of the newer stones. I spotted the Huggins tow truck parked at the curb from two blocks away.

The cemetery's Catholic section was toward the rear of the annex, half a football field away. As I approached it along the narrow path that ran down the center I made out Paulie sitting cross-legged in front of the still raw earth that covered Cassie's grave. His back was to me, and he was so deep in thought he never heard my footsteps.

I stopped a couple of paces away. Rather than intrude on his somber meditation I waited for him to become aware that he wasn't alone.

After a long minute he sensed my presence and turned. I didn't know whether I had expected him to register guilt, embarrassment, surprise, or what. He was perfectly calm, as if our meeting here was the most natural thing in the world. He acknowledged me with a nod and a small sad smile. This was a subdued, contemplative Paulie I hadn't seen before; maybe it was the Paulie that had attracted Cassie.

"Oh, hi," he said.

"Hello, Paulie."

"So you came to see her too," he said mournfully. "It helps, doesn't it?"

So that was why he had accepted my presence so readily. "I hope it will," I said. "Have you been here long?"

"Have I? I don't know." He looked at his watch. "Wow. Yeah, I didn't realize."

I sat down next to him on the cold earth. I said, "I'll bet that after you've been here a while you start telling her the things you never got a chance to say when she was alive. Things you were saving for just the right moment."

Warily, "Something like that."

He fell into a reverential silence, and I followed his lead. Or pretended to. Grave sites don't especially stir me to thoughts of the deceased; those are as likely to sneak into my head while I'm brushing my teeth or crossing a street. I had been thinking of Cassie off and on all week; what I was thinking of at this moment was that opening up Paulie Malatesta in this place wasn't going to be easy. He would probably talk more readily somewhere else, away from that ton of fresh-turned earth pressing on his sweetheart's casket.

While he meditated I stole glances at him. Nice profile, well-defined chin. He was good-looking, all right, well fed and well fleshed. But there was an underlying tone of want around the mouth and in the eyes, as though he had been brought up on junk food and cold love, both doled out in small portions.

Cassie had looked for father substitutes. (Me? Sharanov?) In a boyfriend she may have wanted someone she could take charge of. And Paulie was a grown-up waif, still needy, still short of nourishment. Had he been angered to murder when Cassie began to withdraw her support?

After we sat quietly for a while I could see that the mourner was restless. He was becoming self-conscious about sharing this private time with me. Finally he murmured, "I have to go" and scrambled to his feet.

I quickly followed. "I'll walk out with you," I said.

After one last hungry look at the grave, he turned and we

started back toward the gate. I felt I ought to fill the silence. "She'll be missed," I said.

"She'd have *been* something," he said savagely.

"I agree. She was well on her way. You should have heard the praise from people at the wake. I'm sorry you weren't there. You really think you'd have upset her mother?"

"The boyfriend who was nine years older? And Italian? Are you kidding?" He kicked at a pebble. "The sad part…" And he stopped.

"Yes?"

He had to say it; it was a matter of pride. "The sad part, Cassie *did* finally agree to bring me home. After all those months of no way, she was going to introduce me to her old lady."

"What made her promise that?"

"I don't know. She was mad at her mother, had been for weeks. She wouldn't say what it was about, but it was a first; she worshipped that woman. And that's when she said she would take me to see her. She insisted. We were going to do it that weekend. She was looking forward to it."

"Out of spite, you think?"

"Tell me. She was like spitting in her old lady's eye and I was the spit, right?"

"That sounds about right. I'm sorry, Paulie. It must have hurt."

"What do you think?"

"Did it make you angry at Cassie?"

"No. No way could I get sore at Cassie."

"Really? How come some of the Hamiltons' neighbors"—why finger poor Hamilton himself?—"say they could sometimes hear you arguing in the front room?"

He stopped walking, his face suddenly flushed. "They did? Somebody said that?"

"Yes. What was that about?"

His jaw tightened as he realized where this was heading. He faced me angrily. "You still on that kick? You and Chuck Scully can't find a way to arrest that creep Sharanov, so you're looking to lay Cassie's death on me? You think I cut the throat of the only person in my whole life I ever cared about?''

He started walking again, more quickly now. I stayed with him, and took his arm. I shook it reassuringly.

"Easy does it, Paulie. Nobody's accusing you of anything. What're you steamed about? That people heard you and your girlfriend arguing? That true love didn't run absolutely smooth? It hardly ever does. Join the club.''

"We didn't argue. We had nothing to argue about," he said grimly. His truck was now just a few yards ahead and he was trying to pull away from me.

I dropped his arm and let him distance himself while I delivered a measured shot across his bow. "I thought maybe you'd had a fight with her the night before the murder and were looking to make up. And that's why you drove over to Sharanov's house Friday morning.''

He had one foot in the truck, but he took it back out and turned to me, startled. "Who said I was there that morning?'' His voice was tight.

"A fisherman who was cutting across the dunes from the beach saw your truck pulling out of the driveway.'' I tried a strategic lie. "At nine-something a.m.''

That roused him to action. "No! It was nothing like nine. More like eight-thirty. Maybe earlier. I have to punch in at work by eight forty-five. Huggins docks you when you're late." He was so indignant about what time he was at Sharanov's that he hadn't wasted time denying he was there.

I said, "What were you doing at the Sharanov house at all?''

Now he was rattled, and he took a moment. "What do you think? I was looking for Cassie. I thought I might catch her for a couple or three minutes. Because I wouldn't see her all day. I rang the bell, knocked on the door, but she wasn't there. So I left. That was it.''

"Of course she wasn't there. She wasn't due at work until nine. You know that. Why would she come in earlier?''

"How do I know? She might have, this once. I took a chance.''

I was leaning on him, and he didn't like it. But I had to follow this line to the end. "Why didn't you try her at home? She'd have been alone there. Surely you know her mother is at work by eight."

"Damn right I knew that. Did I ever think about going to her house? You bet I did. So what? If I ever pulled up at Cassie's house in a tow truck at eight-thirty in the morning her mother would hear about it in ten minutes from the neighbors."

He had me there. I switched tracks. "You didn't think it important at least to mention to Chuck Scully that you had been to Sharanov's house the morning of the murder?"

"Why should I? So he could dump on me? Screw that. I've been dumped on enough for a lifetime."

And he hopped into the driver's seat and took off, leaving me with a thin coating of road dust and a thick layer of doubt.

THERE WAS A MESSAGE on the phone machine from Tom Ohlmayer: "Call me. I've finally got what you've been waiting for."

Naturally, he wasn't in. His partner said, "He's on his way home. Try him in ten minutes." In ten minutes there was no answer at Ohlmayer's home; no Tom, no wife, no kids. They had probably gone to her mother's, or shopping. I had waited this long, I could wait a while longer. I had changed into painting clothes and I climbed onto the scaffold.

TESS TURKINTON CALLED at six. I let the machine take it. I was still up near the ceiling trying to deal with a section of canvas I had meant to suggest was bathed in moonlight. It still looked to me like the beach at high noon, and I had my work cut out.

"Sid?...Sid, it's me," she began. Apparently in the Turkintons' world people were supposed to know who "me" was. Only after she waited without success for me to pick up did she grudgingly reveal herself. "Tess."

Another interval. "I suppose you're in the shower. I *hope*

you're in the shower. We've got a date at eight. Remember, it's my invitation, I'm the host, but could I ask one bitty favor? Would you pick me up here at Misha's? I hate driving at night, just hate it. We'll spin back to your place for a quick look-see at your oeuvre—don't you just love the word?—and then I've reserved for nine o'clock at a new place in Water Mill they say does something totally outrageous with swordfish and Grand Marnier. You call me right back if you have a problem with any of this, you hear?'' She rang off.

I didn't think Tess wanted to hear about a problem I might have. Ever. And I was in terror that the next bitty favor would call for me to pick up the restaurant tab because she'd left her credit card in her other purse. Not to mention that I don't want anything ''outrageous'' done to swordfish; I find it just about perfect as is.

But I decided to go with the flow. I shut down my painting for the day and climbed down from the platform.

I hadn't yet reached Tom Ohlmayer. I tried him now at home. He was there.

TWENTY-SIX

THE FRONT DOOR at Sharanov's was opened by Dimitri, the second banana on Misha's muscle squad who had helped Nikki escort me to the Gulliver the other evening. As this was Saturday night I supposed Nikki was in Brooklyn keeping an eye on the till at the Tundra. Rather than risk his limited English, Dimitri confined his welcome to a spastic backward jerk of his head toward the unoccupied living room. Then he waddled off to the kitchen. His jacket strained against his beefy back, and I could see that he was packing.

The first thing I noticed in the living room was that my drawing no longer hung on the wall. And then my eye shifted to Sharanov, rising on the ramp from the bedroom level like Venus on the half shell, resplendent in an electric blue sports jacket some salesman had earned a double commission unloading on him. But the statement told me he was on his way out for the evening.

"Ah, Shale. Thank you for taking my advice to heart," he said with a broad smile. *Advice* came out almost *adwice,* a rare indication of Misha's first language. "I have had no further attention from the police."

I smiled back; we were going to be social. I said, "Never give up hope, Misha." I indicated the blank wall. "I see I'm no longer on exhibition."

"Your drawing? I still own it. I've done some redecorating this week. Why do you ask? Are you looking to buy it back?"

"I wish I could afford it."

"I may donate it to the next volunteer firemen's auction. It brought a good price last time."

"Thanks to Cassie."

"Yes…" His eyes narrowed appraisingly. "She was a diligent promoter. A loyal fan of yours."

I said, "You may have made a mistake when you thought that by appearing to share her enthusiasm for my work you could also make her a fan of Mikhael Sharanov."

"She was already that."

And then, more in the way of seeking information than giving it, he added with an insinuating purr, "But possibly not yet as big a fan as she had been of yours…?" The prurient son of a bitch.

I said, "You thought you were almost there. Wrong, Misha. She came on to you for the same reason she had to me. She was looking for a daddy to replace the one she'd been dealt."

He didn't respond to my pop psychologizing, but his usually impassive face showed that he recognized at least a germ of truth in it. And then he looked relieved—possibly because the prize he had failed to win had escaped my grasp as well. He was also a competitive son of a bitch.

And that was the end of that subject, because Ben Turkinton was coming up the ramp, wearing the same hint-of-rancher suit I had seen him in the other day, and his booming voice took over the air space.

"Okay, Misha, let's do it," he said. "I can eat a horse, but I'll settle for cow. So don't lead me to no damn lobster. If I'm obliged to wrestle my dinner off its carcass, give me a T-bone steak every time. Evening, Sid."

He struck me exactly as he had the first time we met, as a Texan out of central casting. His overplaying didn't register on Sharanov's ear; Misha was swallowing the performance whole. His face didn't show it, but his barrel chest shook with silent laughter.

Turkinton let me know that the two men were going out to dinner, to talk "bidness." Tess would be up soon—"don't ask me when, you know women"—so would I please "hold my horses." That last conjured up stallions in the driveway rearing, whinnying, and pawing the gravel.

Tess didn't show until Sharanov's Cadillac sounded its

motor. Applause was in order. She was wearing an emerald green Chinese-y sheath she may have sprayed onto her figure. Try as it did, it failed to expose any figure flaws.

Instead of a hello she greeted me with "I don't have a clue how people dress in these parts on a Saturday night. Tell me this is wrong and I'll go right back down and change."

"Don't you dare," I said. If I had criticized the outfit she'd have belted me.

She hadn't listened anyway. She was peering out the window, watching the Cadillac disappear. She said, "No way was I going to climb up that boat launch until those two were gone. Honestly, that Russky!"

"You having problems with him?"

"He's all *over* me. Has been from day one. He doesn't even care if Daddy's right *there*. So Daddy gets embarrassed, then I get embarrassed. The man's a Slavic cave creature. Right out of Siberia, I wouldn't be surprised."

"What do you say, shall we go?" I said. I was suddenly tired of this charade and ready to bring it to an end.

She must have caught something in my tone. "Is something wrong?" she said.

I rallied. "When I'm with a vision in green and the evening stretches before us?" I said. "What could be wrong?" I pushed the front door open.

She picked a shawl off the back of a couch but hesitated before she wrapped it protectively around her shoulders and walked out into the night. She looked troubled.

Good.

HER SUSPICIONS HAD pretty much dissolved by the time we reached my place. I had put her in an easier frame of mind by passing on some gossip about local people who had nothing to do with either of us. She had begun to smile, and once she even came close to outright laughter. I wanted her loose, with her guard down, when I delivered my one-two punch.

She walked into my single room and said, almost before she'd looked, "Great studio, Sid. I love it." She looked up at *Large* and announced, "Work in progress." Since there were still countless yards of raw canvas, she wasn't going out on a limb with that observation.

But it was the closest she came to a critique. Her eye moved on quickly to finish its inspection of the room. "Terrific work space. Is this the whole house?"

Her dismissal of *Large* had pissed me off and I was even more impatient now to get this business over with. "Yes, except for the bathroom," I said, and indicated the closed door of the closet.

For a fleeting instant she looked confused. "How"—she hesitated—"compact."

I said, "Don't you mean, how stupid of me? Because you know it's the *other* door that leads to the bathroom."

"How in the world would I know that?" But she was beginning to suspect that her cover was unraveling.

"Because you must have found out last night."

"Last night?"

"When you were here snooping around." I waited the full count. "Ms. Julie Klampf."

The color drained from her face, then came back with more intensity.

"How long have you known?" she said. Her voice had dropped half an octave and the twang had gone flatline.

"About an hour. Remember the wine I bought you at Muccio's? I gave the glass to a cop friend to check for latent prints. I thought you and Daddy might have a history in New York. The pair of you gave off an aroma. If you weren't bit players in a community theater production of *The Best Little Whorehouse in Texas* you had to be con artists. Okay, I was only partly right."

"Latent prints," she murmured. She had sunk into my one chair like a deflating balloon. "Damn it, so you *are* still with the NYPD."

"No. Absolutely no connection. I wasn't put on your tail. I would never even have known of your existence if I didn't happen to be the guy who painted the picture you thought would help soften Sharanov for the kill. You okay with that?"

She made a sour face and opened her mouth to speak.

I said, "Let me finish. Turned out you had no record in New York and I stopped thinking about you. But meanwhile my cop friend was trying the national print file at the FBI in Washington. Lo and behold, you turned out to be a U.S. Treasury agent name of Julie Klampf. By the way, I much prefer that handle to Tess Turkinton. You work out of Washington, but are you originally from Texas?"

"What the fuck's the difference?" she hissed.

"You're right, none. I was trying to be sociable. You and 'Daddy' are not related, are you?"

"God, no."

"You guys sure worked up a lather over this case. Misha must owe Internal Revenue a bundle."

"What makes you think he owes anything?"

"The Tundra is a cash-only operation with God knows how many hundred seats and an average tab per cover of what, sixty, seventy dollars? You tell me how much he's been skimming with creative bookkeeping these past half dozen years. Not to mention what he picks up from his other shadier dealings. His wife knows. She sent her brother out here sniffing for hidden sacks of cash. Come on, Julie, what's his federal bill?"

Reluctantly, "With penalties? Three million. Close to."

"So you and 'Daddy' are the bait to make him a secret partner in a Dallas restaurant that will never happen. Flushing out what, half a million or more in undeclared income? Prima facie evidence for an indictment. Correct me if I've got it wrong." I waited for an answer.

"That's the plan in its broadest, crudest outline." She sounded weary.

So far, so good. I said, "Let me come at you from a new angle and make an informed guess. This isn't the first time the IRS has tried to nail Sharanov."

"So…?"

"You got burned. Someone in the NYPD is on Misha's payroll and tipped him off to your operation."

"You knew that?"

"I told you, it's an informed guess. The detectives trying to make a local case against Sharanov were shut down recently by the top brass, no explanation. To forestall a possible leak, I assume. So when I came on the scene and you heard I was an ex-cop you must have shit a brick. There was a good chance the "ex" part was phony. And whether it was or wasn't, I could blow your scam. So you've tried everything short of hypnotizing me to find out where I stand in this. Jesus, you even went after my son."

The spoiled Texas princess had vanished. She was looking more and more like a lost little girl playing grown-up in her momma's Chinese-y sheath, especially when she tried, pathetically, to tug the hip-high slit closed over her thigh. It was almost sweet.

She said, "Okay, Sid, so where *do* you stand?"

"Absolutely nowhere. I'm not going to talk to anyone about what I know. You and 'Daddy' get to finish your amateur theatrical, drop the curtain, and make your collar."

She brightened some. "We do?"

I crouched to put us eye to eye. "Provided you do one small thing for me."

"And what's that?" She braced for the blow.

"It'll be practically a steal at the moment. There's no gallery commission, because it's back in my hands."

"I don't know what in hell you're talking about."

"*Seated Girl*. You're going to buy her."

She rose out of the chair. "Are you out of your mind? With what? Government money?"

"Damn straight. You were prepared to spend government money on her last week. There's government money available in situations like this. You'd have paid an informant ten percent of what you extract from Sharanov. Two, three hundred thousand dollars. I'm asking less than ten percent of that."

"This is not an informant situation. You're not an informant."

"Not for the IRS, no," I said darkly.

Her jaw tightened. And then she decided to ignore the

implicit threat. She said, "The department would have mad the gallery buy back your painting once we had Sharano under indictment."

"Good luck. You'd have had a fat chance of getting Leon to agree to that. But *I'll* buy it back. In a year or two."

"Then why even—"

"At the moment I've got a serious cash flow problem."

"And if we don't solve it for you?"

"I'll be nervous, depressed. Most of my friends are cop and in my addled state I don't know what I might acciden tally blurt out over dinner with them at Muccio's—as earl as tomorrow night. Or where what I say at that dinner tabl might go. Or to whom."

She said, "You are a goddam bastard." But her face tol me I had won.

"Hang her opposite your desk. In a good light," I sai "She'll give you a great deal of pleasure. She has me."

TWENTY-SEVEN

JULIE KLAMPF AND I never did get out to that dinner she had promised to spring for. My ultimatum had taken the fun out of the evening, and Klampf had gone back to Sharanov's house alone (''I'll walk, thank you''), with her dignity shredded.

What had been my hurry? I could have waited to blow her scheme until after the lobster, the good bottle of wine, and the associated flirting I could expect from Julie—her all-out effort to pry loose my secret plan, if I had one, to tip her hand to Sharanov. In connection with the flirting I would now never know how far Agent Klampf had been prepared to go to honor her responsibilities to the U.S. Treasury Department.

With my deficit problem solved, I had my best night's sleep of the season. I awoke Sunday morning clearheaded, and ideas surged through my brain like bubbles in a newly opened bottle of seltzer. But when the effervescence ebbed I was left roughly where I had begun a week ago, with that badly made bed in Sharanov's house. And that brought me back to Paulie Malatesta.

Most murders are about money or sex. Cassie had no money, but she was well-supplied with the other. I lay in bed for a time and contemplated Paulie.

I would have to do something about that kid. I had avoided leaning on him for his quirky behavior the day of the murder. Much of it could be excused because he had lost his girl, the rest because Paulie was something of a loser anyway, and he had behaved like a loser. I felt sorry for him, I almost liked him, and he didn't need my hassling.

On the other hand I didn't need the grand jury tomorrow and all that went with that. I climbed out of bed, took a long depressing look at *Large,* and got in the shower.

WHEN I DROVE UP, Mr. Hamilton, Paulie's landlord, was trimming deadwood from the evergreens at the side of his property. He looked at me guiltily as we exchanged greetings and then he explained that he and the missus were skipping church this morning, as she was "helping her sister, who's not all that well."

I don't know why he felt compelled to seek my approval for playing hooky from church, since I was dressed, at best, for bowling. But I gave it to him anyway.

"Heaven will appreciate your making the world a little tidier this morning," I beamed, indicating his work on the evergreens. Then I downshifted to business. "Is Paulie in?"

"At this hour on a Sunday? He's likely still asleep. Why don't you just go on up and knock on his door?" When I hesitated he added, "It's all right, there's no one else in the house. Top of the stairs, end of the hall to your left." We were not in New York; it never occurred to him that I might be here to lift the silver.

The stairs were at the back of a small unadorned entrance hall. They were covered with a worn runner and they climbed straight and steep. The several doors on the second floor were all shut but I could hear movement behind the one Hamilton had indicated was Paulie's. I went to it and knocked my commanding cop's knock.

"Huh? Yeah?" came Paulie's puzzled voice. He was not used to visitors. Not at this hour, anyway. "Mr. Hamilton? Come on in, okay?"

I opened the door and walked in. I don't know what I had expected, but Paulie was on his feet, dressed in denim pants and a flannel shirt, and he held a dumbbell in each hand. Naturally he was surprised to see me. He said, "Yeah, hi. What's up? You have some news?"

The room contained a single bed, unmade, a kitchen chair, a footlocker, and a dresser that held a clock radio and a telephone. Nothing on the walls, nothing to personalize the tenant's abode. I suspected that Paulie didn't have a clue how to make a room his own.

I said, "No news. I came to talk. I wanted to catch you

before you went out for the day. Mr. Hamilton thought you might still be asleep.''

''Fat chance.''

''Yeah, your bed looks as if you've been wrestling in it. I guess you haven't slept that well since Cassie's death.''

''What do you think?''

''That you haven't slept well.'' Uninvited, I sat in the chair.

Paulie's shoulders sagged; he realized he wasn't going to get rid of me in a hurry. He tossed the metal dumbbells on the bed and that sagged too.

''This is my day off,'' he said. ''Do me and you still have something left to talk about? I don't know what, but how about if it waits till tomorrow, when I'll be on Huggins's time.''

''I wish. I'm going before the grand jury in Riverhead tomorrow,'' I said. ''And I want to get straight in my head what I'm going to tell them.''

''The grand jury? What's any of that got to do with me?'' His chin was thrust forward defiantly, but his voice wasn't nearly as sure.

I said, ''That's what I came to find out. But first, I don't like having to look up at you when we talk. Either you sit down or I stand up.'' He stared dumbly and didn't move a muscle and I said, ''Which'll it be?''

He flopped back onto the tortured bedclothes and put a hand on each dumbbell, as though to steady himself. His dark face registered sulky.

I said, ''I guess you haven't had a chance to make your bed this morning.''

''Make it for who? I didn't invite nobody for Sunday brunch.''

I nodded sympathetically. ''I know. I sometimes let my bed go all day. Then I'll crawl into the same wrinkled sheets I left in the morning. It's a guy thing. Women make beds, men make fires. Do you *ever* make your bed?''

''Do I? What the hell kind of question is that? I never thought about it.'' He thought now, and said, ''I grew up thinking about the kitchen table—what there'd be on it for supper. *If* there'd be anything on it for supper. Not the frigging bed and whether I made it.''

I said, "And now, comes Sunday morning and you've got the whole day free, you get out of bed, you get dressed, and you reach for the dumbbells."

His eyes narrowed. He said, "You're leading up to something. Why don't you spit out what the hell it is?"

I took the plunge. "The morning of Cassie's murder the bed in Sharanov's room was made. Badly. Either by a woman in a hurry or by a man who didn't know much about bed making. I've decided you're the likeliest candidate for the second theory. How about it?"

His hands were gripping and ungripping the dumbbells. They looked like five pounders. He said, "Why would I make that bastard's bed?"

"How about this?" I took a breath and let it roll; it was at least worth the shot. "You and Cassie made love in that bed. Afterward you had a fight. You had been fighting for weeks. One of you got a knife from the kitchen and somehow it was Cassie who ended up dead. And then you made the bed. Out of guilt. A muddled attempt to hide what you had been doing in that bed. I don't imagine you were thinking too logically. Not after killing your lover."

"You shit!" he exploded. He sprang off the bed, a lethal dumbbell cocked at his ear, the other half-raised.

I had expected a reaction, but not one this big, and I knocked over the chair in my haste to back off to the door. Meanwhile I pulled my .38 from where I had tucked it under my sweater at the rear of my belt before leaving the house. If I had known that ten pounds of dead metal would be part of this equation I'd have spent even more time trying to find the ammo before I came out.

"Calm down, Paulie," I said.

Paulie hesitated, the dumbbell still raised, his eyes on the piece. Then he said with quiet intensity, "Do you really think I killed Cassie? That I *could* kill her?"

I took a moment. "Probably not," I said. "Not on purpose. If you were mad enough to stab her there'd be one or two random wounds. Whoever cut Cassie's throat did it deliberately. He—or she—wanted to make sure she was dead.''

Paulie was slowly lowering the dumbbell. His mouth made a couple of false starts and then he said, ''Then what—?''

''I said *I* believe you didn't do it. Who knows which way a grand jury will go? You were weird that day. Off the wall. There are witnesses. Including your boss.'' I tucked the piece back in my belt.

''You talked to Huggins?''

''Half an hour ago. All the police asked him was whether you came in on time that morning. I wanted to know how you were acting that day. Huggins thought about it and said what I'd have said. 'Not like himself.' Even before anyone knew Cassie was dead.''

''I already told you I—''

I waved him silent. ''Don't give me that bull about being sick. Huggins said he learned long ago the difference between sick employees and bullshit sick employees. Now he's concerned that he should have told that to the police, even though you were at work at the time of the murder. If they don't come back to him he's going to call Chuck Scully.''

I had made this up out of whole cloth and a gut feeling, to move us off dead center. Huggins had told me he'd taken Paulie's story of being sick that morning as the truth. Why not? The kid had always been straight with him.

Paulie took a long moment before he said, ''What the hell do you want out of me?''

''I want you to tell me what happened that morning. Step by step.''

''Why? What difference will it make? I didn't kill Cassie.'' His voice was dead flat.

''Because when I know what you know, maybe I can help you. When that detective from County starts asking you questions it won't be to help you but to charge you. Same for Chuck Scully.''

''Scully would love to see me arrested. Scully had eyes for Cassie.''

Cassie was dead but she could still spark jealousy. "S⟨
wouldn't it be better to talk to me?"

"Would it? I don't know."

In a deep sulk now, he sank back on the bed and bega⟨
clunking one dumbbell against the other. He was working u⟨
the courage to talk.

I figured a nudge might help. "I can set it up for you t⟨
talk to Scully if you think he'd be a better listener."

That did it. He dropped the dumbbells on his blanket, ⟨
sign of final surrender. He said angrily, "Mr. Hamilton tol⟨
you someone heard us arguing? He'd have been deaf not to
We fought off and on for a good month. Hot and heavy. Bu⟨
it stopped way before Cassie was killed."

"What were you fighting about?"

"Can't you guess? Look, Cassie and I were in love, reall⟨
in love. You have to understand that." His eyes met mine t⟨
make sure I did understand before he went on. "It got to b⟨
way past time we were, you know, going to bed together
But Cassie wouldn't."

He shook his head; her attitude remained beyond his com⟨
prehension. "She'd made that dumb promise to her mothe⟨
and she wouldn't break it, wouldn't lie to her old lady."

"But she did break it, didn't she?"

He couldn't say it but he nodded.

"When?"

"Not that long before she died."

I had to press; this was like pulling teeth. "What made he⟨
change her mind?"

"Her mother got knocked off her pedestal. Flat on her fac⟨
in the mud." He bit out the words. "Cassie caught her wit⟨
a guy. Saw them through a window. It blew her mind. Sh⟨
shook when she told me."

"So all bets were off. And you two had sex."

"Not right away, no. She was coming around to the idea
but she took her time. She hated the kids in high school wh⟨
were screwing in cars, under the grandstand, on the gol⟨
course, in the woods. Like animals, she said. Worse, becaus⟨
the woods is where animals live, it's their home." His eye⟨

were misting. "That's the way Cassie talked, the way she was."

"I know."

"We couldn't go to my place, we couldn't go to hers, and she said flat-out no when I offered to spring for a motel, like on a Sunday afternoon. She wanted it to be right."

"And what was right?"

"That we'd be together all night. That's when we came up with the plan."

I thought I was beginning to get it. "The plan was to use the Sharanov house to make love?"

"Cassie had a dozen part-time jobs." His voice was strained but full of pride. "Some days she worked ten, twelve, fourteen hours. But she was at Sharanov's every Friday. She even managed it last fall, when she was still in school. She did a half-day gig cleaning his house, nine to two."

Maybe I didn't get it, after all. "Those were hours you were at work at the garage."

"Not the night before, I wasn't. On Thursday night Cassie would wait for her mother to go to sleep, then she'd close her own bedroom door and bike over to Sharanov's. Sharanov didn't come out until Friday around noon, so she had her own key. I'd meet her at the house, we'd spend the night together, and then I'd leave to change for work. Cassie was already *at* work. It was pretty neat."

"And Cassie's mother…?"

"She left for work every morning by seven-thirty. She'd never disturb Cassie at that hour."

"You couldn't be sure."

"Pretty much. Cassie was busing tables at Mel's, six a.m. to ten, Monday to Thursday. Friday morning was her chance to sleep in some, and her mother let her. If she ever did open Cassie's door and found her missing, Cassie would have made up some excuse for why she went out early. But it never happened."

"How many Thursday nights did you have together?"

My devout wish was that there had been many; I hoped

Cassie had more than a glimpse of this particular glory of the world before she left it.

His voice was sepulchral. "The last was our third."

"And all was well when you left her in the morning?"

"Couldn't have been better."

"What time was that?"

"Close to seven. I went home to shower and get ready for work. I needed air in my tires, and gas."

"Paulie, your truck was seen leaving the Sharanov house at around eight-thirty."

"Yes." He had been waiting for this and his jaw trembled; this was going to be the hard part.

He said, "While I was home I got a road call. Woman with a flat, around a quarter to eight. When I got to her a neighbor had already changed her tire. But I was out, and I had a few minutes of slack, so I headed back to the Sharanov house. It wasn't that far, and it would be my last chance to see Cassie all day. I wanted"—he swallowed hard—"I wanted to hold her, tell her again how much I loved her. Needed her."

He stopped and I waited.

"God, it was awful. The blood . . ." He stopped again.

"Was she still alive?"

"No, I could see right away she was dead. I was sick. I wanted to throw up. My Cassie . . ." He rubbed the heel of his hand against his eyes. "And then I was scared. There was no way I could help her and I wanted to get out of there…"

"Because someone who showed up might think you were responsible…?" He nodded quickly and I added, "But you didn't leave right away. You made the bed."

"You knew?" He looked frightened.

"Don't worry, there's no physical evidence, it was just a guess. Why did you do that, Paulie?"

"Because the bed…the unmade bed . . ." It was an uphill fight. "The police might guess Cassie had slept in it. If she did, she probably wasn't alone. I didn't want that idea out there—her name dirtied up with scandal. I wanted the police to believe she'd come in to work as she always did, at nine in the morning.''

Especially if the person she had slept with in that bed was most logically her boyfriend. But I didn't say that. I said, "Paulie, it was a *made* bed that looked all wrong. Nobody would have noticed an unmade one. Sharanov's was probably that way every time Cassie came to work."

"What do you mean? It was always made when I met her there on Thursday night."

"Because Cassie made it for you. Clean sheets, a nicely made bed, a proper place to make love. She wanted everything to be right for the two of you."

He thought about that. "I didn't know... She never said..."

I waited while he blinked back welling tears before I asked a final question. "When the police came, the windows were all shut tight. But there'd been one open earlier. I sketched it that way. Did you open it the night before?''

"When we went to bed. The room was airless. Stifling."

"And then you closed it when you came back after eight?"

He nodded. "I thought I was making the room look the way it usually did when she came to work." He took another beat. "I wiped anyplace I might have left fingerprints—that window, doorknobs, wherever."

"Congratulations, Paulie. You may have wiped away the killer's prints."

Paulie's hands were clinging to the dumbbells as though he believed they had the power to restore some stability to his life. He knew that Cassie Brennan had been the best thing that was ever likely to happen to him, and he was just beginning to come to terms with his loss. He looked shattered.

I left a minute or two later. I would have liked to stay for a while and keep him company, but I had business elsewhere.

TWENTY-EIGHT

PROPELLED BY WHAT Paulie had told me, I went home and for the second time that week laid out the sketch I drew for Chuck Scully on the back of a wall calendar a few days after the murder. Another hard look confirmed what memory had told me, and I rolled the sketch into a tube and slipped a rubber band over it.

After that I spent a good ten minutes looking still again for the ammo for my Smith & Wesson five-shot, with no more luck than I'd had before. I ended up putting the piece back where I kept it hidden. I wasn't about to violate for a second time that day the basic rule about carrying a weapon: don't, unless you're prepared to use it.

I called the police station and the duty officer answered. Helen, who usually handled the switchboard, was off on Sundays. So, it turned out, was the chief; at least, he wasn't in today. I asked if he could be reached.

"The wife's taken him to church," the sergeant said. "I don't like to page him there, it pisses the priest. Mass should be over in a few minutes. I'll try him in half an hour. They'll be on their way to his sister-in-law's in Riverhead."

I gave him a message for Scully and I carried the rolled-up sketch out to the Chevy and took off.

AT THE GREGG place I parked at the curb behind Harry's heap. Harry was sitting in the middle of his disorderly front yard on an Adirondack chair with a missing arm. He was wearing a faded checked shirt and frayed jeans and he was untangling a spool of fishing line, a Sunday chore he obviously preferred to cleaning the yard.

He didn't glance up until I had walked to within a yard of him. "Hold this," he said by way of greeting.

I shifted the rolled-up sketch to my left hand and took the section of line he held out to me in the other. He was so concentrated on the knot he was undoing that I kept my mouth shut until he'd licked it. Then I said, "How many man-hours do you figure you put in per bluefish caught?"

"I never figured."

"Because on my list of the ten tastiest fish I'd rank the bluefish number fourteen."

"It's better when it's smoked," he said. He had found another, less challenging knot, and was picking at it. "Anyways, I'm in it for the sport, not the taste. I can tell you're no fisherman."

"Nope." I let it go at that.

He finished his knot and glanced at the tube of paper in my left hand. "You got something there for me?" he said.

"Yes," I said. "Okay if we go in the house?"

"You can give it to me here."

"I think it would be better if we went in the house."

He thought about that. "Maybe you're right." He got up and placed the fishing line on the chair's good arm. "I'm in no hurry for this. It's a backup."

Neither of us said anything as we picked our way across the junk-strewn yard and up onto the porch. As he opened the door he said, "It's kind of messy inside."

I feigned surprise. "Is it? That won't bother me."

The kitchen was to one side of a narrow entrance hall. He steered me the other way, to a corner front room that should have been bright with sunlight but was dimmed down by musty drapes that tinted the room a dull crimson. The two walls that were without windows each sported a large fish that had been mounted too many years ago. Open French doors led to an adjoining back parlor that looked even darker.

The unifying theme of the furniture here was shabby genteel, heavy on the shabby. The beer cans of the last three days hadn't been collected, and the ashtrays were spilling the butts of the last six. The place looked like a college fraternity house the morning after a pledge party—anyway, like the one at Columbia where I once sorted out the aftermath of a fight.

Gregg waved me to a stuffed chair, but I chose to sit on the expiring couch; I needed the coffee table that fronted it. I put the tube of paper on the cigarette-scarred table. Gregg got the idea. He came around and sat down next to me, his hands on his knees.

"So what is it you got there?" he said. He didn't seem that eager to find out.

I slipped the rubber band off the tube and laid it out flat, with an ashtray holding down each side. I said, "Recognize this picture?"

"Could be me," he said slowly, and then, "yeah, that's me. That's good. You did that?"

I nodded.

"How come? You looking to sell it, or what?"

"Not right at the moment. I drew it because I'd told Chuck Scully that I'd seen a man on the beach a couple of hours before Cassie Brennan was murdered and I thought maybe Chuck could identify him."

"That was me you saw."

"Right. Chuck and I were wondering if Sharanov had slept in his house that night. Someone passing the house early in the morning would have seen a car out front. And you did."

"On my way back from fishing. The tow truck that was pulling away. So what? That was way before the girl was killed."

"Apparently not."

"I read the papers. They said the girl was killed after nine o'clock."

"They were wrong. By the time the police brought in the medical examiner from a fishing trip, he couldn't pin it down any closer than a two-or three-hour span. The police said "after nine" because nine was when the girl was supposed to come in to work. Why would she come in earlier? She had to stay till two o'clock anyway. But it turns out she *was* there earlier. She'd been there all night."

"That a fact?" His hands hadn't moved from his knees; he was rock steady. "I see. You think whoever was leaving in that tow truck could have done her. Sorry, I wasn't close enough to see who that was. I already told you it was a Huggins truck. Is that what you're looking for?''

"Thanks, Harry, we found who was in the truck. He has an alibi.'' The sketch had begun to curl at the edges and I put my hands on it to flatten it. I said, "Does anything in this drawing strike you as peculiar?''

He looked at me, not sure what I was getting at, and then at the drawing. "Is it my face?'' He was genuinely puzzled. "Is my chin as long as that?''

"Not really,'' I assured him. "I exaggerated it. Why don't you take a look at how you're dressed?''

His eyes narrowed. He was examining the sketch stroke by stroke, but he said nothing.

"It's the way I remembered you,'' I said. "When we met on the beach that morning.''

"Okay. So?'' If he got it, he wasn't letting on.

I said, "The boots with the pants tucked in? The hat? The T-shirt? Your rod in one hand, the creel hanging from your shoulder?''

"What is this, some kind of fucking game?'' He hadn't raised his voice. "You got something to say, say it.''

"Harry, it was seven o'clock in the morning, with a stiff breeze off the water. I was wearing a shirt and windbreaker. And you were going surf casting in a cotton T-shirt?''

"Maybe I was, maybe I wasn't. Who the hell remembers?''

"I do. That's how you were dressed. But I don't think you left your house that way.''

I waited for a reaction, but I didn't get one. He just sat there, hands on knees, eyes on the sketch.

I said, "I think when you set out for the beach you were wearing a sweater or a windbreaker, something over that T-shirt. By the time I saw you it was probably stuffed in your creel. I doubt it left much room for fish.''

"You don't know what the fuck you're talking about.''

I said, "You weren't dressed for the beach any longer but you couldn't go home. Because some neighbor might wonder why you came back so soon, why you weren't following your

usual routine. So you had to push on down the beach in your
T-shirt and spend an hour or more in the surf pretending to
fish. How'd that feel, Harry—wave after wave rolling up
your legs and whispering God knows what?''

"That's the biggest load of bullshit I ever heard in my life.
I go fishing wearing any damn thing I please.''

"Sure you do. And you did that day. So why don't you
ask me, Harry?''

"Ask you what?''

"How come I think you had a jacket, a sweater, whatever,
in that creel?''

He wasn't quite dumb enough to ask, so I volunteered.
"When you cut her throat, you cut an artery, maybe both.
The blood was jet-propelled. It couldn't miss you. Not to-
tally.''

He didn't shout but his voice grew strong with indignation.
"You're crazy. I didn't kill that girl.''

"Maybe not,'' I said. Could I be wrong? "I think you did.
I think you're a sneak thief. Your basement is probably
loaded with those bicycles that are missing all over town.
The Sharanov house was a target of opportunity. This was
the first time you'd walked by it out of season and seen a
window open. Before seven o'clock on a Friday morning.
You figured the owner forgot to lock it when he left for the
city on Sunday. An open window at ground level, no climbing required. Practically a gift.''

"You're crazy.''

"Over and in you went without a moment's hesitation,
except maybe to put on your fishing gloves. And then what?
The girl came in from the hall, or maybe the bathroom where
she'd just gotten dressed to start work, and she caught you
flatfooted, up to no good. She may have thought you'd been
watching her get dressed. Maybe she thought you'd been
spying for hours. She wouldn't have liked that. Harry, she'd
have hated that. I'll bet she screamed. And kept screaming.
And you stopped her screams with your knife.''

Almost quietly, he said, "That didn't happen. It couldn't.
I read in the paper she was killed with a bread knife.''

"The murder weapon had a jagged edge. So does a fisherman's knife."

"So what?"

"If the police had considered that a fisherman's knife might be the murder weapon you could have popped into their heads. But you shortstopped that speculation by lifting a bread knife from the Sharanov kitchen on your way out the front door. I wish you hadn't dumped that knife at my place, Harry, but all in all I give you a lot of credit for the knife."

"Except it wasn't me. If Chuck Scully thinks he can lay this murder in my lap because I'm a little bit of a loner in this town, uh-uh, it's no go."

"I've got it all wrong?"

"Damn right you do. Everything you said is just talk. That's all it is. Talk and more talk."

"That's true. It's just talk until it's supported by hard evidence. The police will ask you to show them your creel. If they find so much as a trace of Cassie Brennan's blood on it you're in deep shit. No matter how well you think you cleaned that creel, her blood will have soaked into the wicker."

"If that's what they're after, I'm in the clear," he said and jumped to his feet. "There's no blood on that creel, not even fish blood. I'll show you. Take it outside, look it over in the daylight."

Before I could stop him he had charged angrily into the adjoining back room.

I couldn't possibly be that wrong. And still . . .

I called after him, "Harry, you're wasting your time. It's not up to me. Chuck Scully will send that creel to the county crime lab."

By then an alarm had gone off in my head. How could I have been so dumb? But it was too late. Gregg was back in the doorway, and instead of the creel, I was looking into the black eyes of an ancient double-barreled shotgun he was holding at shoulder level. As calm as he had been before, that's how agitated he was now.

"Get up," he said, and then, "I said get up."

I didn't get up; I wasn't going to compound my stupidity. I said, "Why don't you sit down, so the two of us can talk about this."

He said, "We're not going to talk. You're going to get up." He groped for a reason. "I want to show you something."

His feet were doing a fidgety dance, his cheek was pressed against the gun stock. "We have to go to the cellar." His voice had grown tight.

My stomach dropped to my knees. The cellar was bad news; what he wanted to show me down there was the business end of his double load.

I said, "Harry, don't make it worse for yourself. They're not going to throw the book at you. You didn't plan to kill the girl." Even if he hadn't, it was a felony murder, but maybe he didn't know that. I said, "Don't pile on more charges."

I doubt he heard me. He was in a state, his mouth twitching, his shoulders working.

He said, "All I went looking for was loose cash. That's all I wanted, you understand?" He was looking to make sure I did understand. "The money weekend people leave around when they go home. I never would have climbed through that window if I thought she was there. If I'd seen her first I'd have turned around and dived back out that window. I was never going to touch her."

"The girl wasn't raped, Harry. We know that. And I know you wouldn't do anything along those lines."

"Damn right," he said.

He was in a state, but he felt compelled to unburden himself, maybe to justify himself. He moved his cheek off the gun but he didn't lower it. "She was coming out of the bathroom pulling on her shirt and she stopped dead when she saw me. She stared and her eyes bugged out. And I knew it then. That she *knew*."

"Knew what?" I was beginning to think he was losing it.

"So much time had gone by I thought I was safe. Sure, she'd seen me that day years ago, but she didn't see, you know? She'd looked at me when I stuck my head out the window to check what I'd hit and she saw me drive away. The papers said she told the police she didn't see the accident, didn't see anything, but I knew she did.''

Now I understood; I felt a wave of nausea. ''Why didn't you turn yourself in?'' I said.

''I'd been drinking. I looked it up. 'Vehicular homicide.' They can hit you real heavy for that. At first I was scared out of my head. I couldn't even sell the truck, I was never sure I'd got all the blood off it. But after a while I began to figure I was safe. I'd spot her somewhere in the village every few months and I'd look away or cross the street. It didn't matter, because I knew she didn't know. But then in that bedroom, just the two of us in that room, she all of a sudden knew. She started screaming how I'd killed her sister, murdered her baby sister, stuff like that. The words came pouring out. So I knew I had to do her. Right then. If she hadn't remembered I wouldn't have had to, you know? I'd have just beat it out of there. I'll never understand how she all of a sudden remembered like that.''

This wasn't the time to explain repressed memory and its cause, or what had kicked loose that memory in Cassie when she came face-to-face with her sister's hit-and-run killer. My immediate concern was the rusty shotgun pointed at my chest. It held steady no matter how much Gregg twitched and fidgeted. I began to think he might be too keyed up to make it to the cellar; he looked ready to blow me then and there through the parlor wall.

I said, ''Things went wrong. It happens. Not your fault.''

He wasn't interested in my opinion. ''That's enough,'' he said. ''We're going.'' His long explanation had satisfied him; he wanted to get this over with.

I said, ''Don't make things worse for yourself. There's ways out of this. Things the right lawyer can do…''

''Get up,'' he said. ''Now.''

''Harry, my pickup's standing at your curb. There's no way you can get rid of that, no way you can explain it. People will come looking for me.''

"I can't think about that now. I'll take care of it. Get up, you hear?" And when I still didn't move he shouted, "Damn it, stand up." The gun went back to his cheek. His face darkened with anger.

I stood up slowly. Once I had the coffee table out from between us I would have to make some kind of move. I saw no way it could succeed, but no way would I go to slaughter like a Christmas goose.

I edged around the table. Gregg backed off to a wall and waved the gun for me to move on out to the entrance hall. He was wild-eyed but not stupid; he kept enough air between us so that he could blast me before I reached him. The gun loomed like a cannon. This was unreal but it was happening. Sarah and Alan suddenly crowded my thoughts. I wasn't going to spend the summer with them, I wasn't going to see them ever.

I had stopped walking and Gregg began stabbing the air with his gun. His face was flushed, his mouth a slash. "Move it, move it," he said.

What were the odds on going for the gun as against making a low dive for his legs? Astronomical either way, but it was now or never. I took a small positioning step.

And was spared the decision. A rap on the front door sharp enough to carry through the entrance hall froze us both. Then Gregg poked the gun toward me and mouthed for me to keep shut.

The rap was repeated, louder and firmer. More a pounding. Followed a moment later by a familiar voice. "Open up, Harry."

And then, "For Chrissakes, I know you're in there. It's Chuck Scully. Open up."

"What's he doing here?" Gregg whispered fiercely. His eyes were wide and crazy.

"I called him," I whispered back, flooding with relief. "He knows I'm here."

"Damn it, open up," Scully shouted. I was liking that kid more by the second. "Open the damn door."

Gregg seemed paralyzed. Nothing moved but the eyes. He

was gripping the gun so tightly his knuckles went white. And then I could see him considering an option—blast me, shoot Scully through the door.

I shouted, "He's got a gun!"

Gregg hissed, "Shut up, shut up,"

"Okay, Harry, you want me to shoot out the lock?" Scully called. "Because that's what I'll do."

Gregg unfroze. He had made his choice. Still pointing the gun, he backed swiftly into the entrance hall, past Scully's insistent banging, and vanished toward the kitchen. I could hear his retreating footsteps.

I ran into the hall and unlocked the front door. Scully rushed in, gung ho, his .45 held high in both hands, and swept his eyes around.

I said, "He went that way. Into the kitchen."

He started to move and I grabbed his arm. "Easy, Chuck. He confessed to the murder. But he's got a shotgun and I think he's coming apart."

"Let go," he said. "He has to be stopped."

"Not this minute. He's got nothing to lose. You get in a gunfight now and there's a good chance you'll get hurt. Call for backup."

"There's no time for that." He pulled loose.

A distant shot, muffled but unmistakable, stopped him in his tracks. He breathed, "Shit, what's he done now, gone and shot somebody?"

The echo-y sound had come from the cellar. "Just himself," I said.

The poor bastard, it was probably for the best.

EPILOGUE

THREE MINUTES AFTER hanging up on County Detective John Docherty I called Tony Travis and fired him. Travis took Docherty's news well—better than Docherty had taken it. The ADA on the case had delegated the detective to tell me never mind, I wouldn't have to present myself to the grand jury in Riverhead after all.

Docherty was less than gracious about the disinvitation. With good reasons. He had failed in his ambition to nail an ex-NYPD cop for Cassie Brennan's murder; even worse, his name never came up in media stories on the crime's solution.

The credit for that went entirely to Quincacogue's Acting Police Chief, Chuck Scully. Chuck had offered to share his triumph with me, but I declined. I already had my pension, I explained; a feather in my cap would carry no financial benefits, whereas a solo spotlight could have positive career consequences for Chuck.

So the accepted wisdom had it that Harry Gregg committed suicide when he learned that Chuck Scully's investigation was narrowing on him relentlessly. Not that far from the truth, come to think of it.

Rummaging around in Gregg's cellar after his death Scully found a wool cardigan in an old steamer trunk; it was smeared with what proved to be Cassie Brennan's blood. The serrated fisherman's knife that had slashed her throat was hidden at the back of a shelf in a bedroom closet.

"We had our eye on Gregg from day one," Chuck explained to the assembled media, "even though he tried to throw us off by planting a bread knife stained with the victim's blood. We always figured the murder weapon to be a fisherman's knife and Gregg had been fishing in the area the morning of the murder."

Chuck proved to be a nimble embroiderer of the truth and I predicted he would go far in law enforcement.

Sure enough, a month later he was offered the chief's job at a north fork town twice the size of ours, at a substantial advance in salary. He left Quincacogue on cordial terms; the locals were grateful for the return of six missing bicycles plus assorted household goods that turned up in Gregg's basement.

The stolen items may have been the guilty reason Gregg had been reluctant to ask Chuck and me into his house. In a rambling interview for a local weekly, one of the two thousand psychiatrists (my estimate) with summer homes in East Hampton hypothesized that Harry Gregg, who had a good job, stole for no better reason than to compensate for the love that was absent from his life. Did I say hypothesized? Make that pontificated.

I added my own take to the hypothesis: Cassie's guilt over her failure to protect her little sister from harm had caused her to block out all memory of the fatal accident until her traumatic encounter with Gregg in Sharanov's bedroom.

Before Scully left for his new job I asked him why he hadn't looked for a thread that might connect the deaths of the two Brennan sisters.

"I did," he said. "I couldn't find one. How about you?"

I hated to admit it. "It never occurred to me."

My main reaction to the crime's solution and the suicide of its perpetrator was one of relief. Cassie's troubled spirit—*my* spirit, weighed down by her unresolved death—could now find honorable rest, and Cassie's mother decent closure. Nora Brennan would never learn, thank God, that her secret affair with Jack Beltrano had propelled Cassie to the love-making sessions in the Sharanov house that led to her death.

Two weeks after Harry Gregg's suicide, "Ben Turkinton" brought his restaurant sting to a satisfactory conclusion. He coaxed six hundred thousand dollars out of Mikhael Sharanov, the source for which Misha had no reasonable explanation when Treasury agents arrested him. After prolonged negotiations Sharanov managed to escape jail time, but his back taxes and punitive penalties—to say nothing of his legal fees—came to nearly four million dollars.

The Tundra went into bankruptcy and was bought on the cheap by a national restaurant company that specializes in fake ethnic restaurants. The Tundra was soon as fake as any of them, and its Russian clientele abandoned it to thrill seekers from Great Neck and Short Hills who thought they were rubbing shoulders with the Russian mafia when they were merely mingling with each other. As a by-blow of the turnover, Olivia Cooper lost her underwriting deal to the new owners' insurance broker.

Sharanov's economic bind forced him to sell his East End house at a steep loss. The sleeping jungle beast was so panicked by his monetary situation—he no longer had a permanent roof over his head—that he scrambled to patch things up with his estranged wife. Oddly enough, Kitty readily accepted his solemn promise to end his philandering. She kicked out brother Roy, and the declawed tiger moved back in with her. Kitty was confident that her husband would somehow find a way to maintain her standard of living. He would think of something.

The Treasury Department had kept its word: It bought my painting *Seated Girl*. But later there was an unexpected development. Once I was in a position to buy back the painting, the Treasury Department refused to sell. A high-level IRS career civil servant had taken a fancy to the work and hung it in his Washington office. He wouldn't give it up.

Julie Klampf was in town around that time and she bought me lunch, in part to break this news. Julie said the aide, whom she refused to name, thought the dismembered figure in the painting eloquently conveyed the spirit of the average taxpayer on April sixteenth.

Whatever. I have always said the viewer has to bring his own baggage to my work. And it was probably best that *Seated Girl* hang where people were unaware of its subject's tragic end. My principal regret was that Cassie had fancied her portrait displayed at the very least in a shop window, and it had ended up in a location a good cut below even that.

Julie Klampf, by the way, is a totally different woman when she is not playing Tess Turkinton. At my suggestion, because I couldn't think of anyplace else, our lunch was at Muccio's. It ran so long, thanks to Enzo's industrial-strength drinks, that by the time we left Mona had come on duty. For some reason she sent us out the door with a head-pounding "Havanagila." That almost spoiled a hell of a good afternoon, but not quite. I like Julie. We have been keeping in touch.

It turned out to be a fine summer. Both Alan and Sarah were out at the beach for all of it. I didn't have room to put them both up, so Sarah bunked in with Gayle Hennessy in her apartment over Gayle's Provocativo, where Sarah worked as a sales clerk all through the busy season. Gayle charged her up to the point where Sarah is considering going into fashion design. Gayle says she has a definite flair.

Alan I put to work beside me on *Large*. Was I founding a painting dynasty, like the Wyeths? The jury is still out on Alan's talent, but his pick and shovel contribution to the work (no greater than that of Rembrandt's disciples on many of his paintings) helped move the project along. I didn't tell him, but I had already decided to give Alan his great-grandfather's ring when he graduated high school; I had been waiting to make sure it wouldn't slip off his finger.

We finished the painting by Labor Day. By then I hated it, really hated the overheated monster. But in October, miracle of miracles, Lonnie managed to sell it to a department store conglomerate with headquarters in, I think, Waukegan, Illinois. Anyway, somewhere beyond the zone of influence of New York art critics. The chain's CEO was caught by Lonnie's title for the work, *Man's Eternal Striving*. Life began at the water's edge, she reminded him, and humankind crawled up from the beach to challenge nature and conquer it.

Again, whatever. The CEO planned to hang the behemoth in the conference room as an inspiration to his management team. I could have kissed Lonnie for *her* inspiration when she phoned with the news.

I did kiss her a couple of weeks later, at the end of a celebration of the sale that went late into the evening. Kissed her and a great deal more. Our relationship is undergoing changes. In exactly which direction and how far it is still too early to say, because I see Olivia Cooper fairly often, and Julie Klampf when she gets to New York. After a long drought, my cup really doth runneth over.

That's good and it's bad. Bad because the sexual energy I had redirected into my work I was now directing back into sex. I was drawing less, painting hardly at all. I needed a major project to help me sharpen my focus, and I am beginning to form an idea for a really big painting, a *Large III* that calls for more wall space than I've got. There may be a way to extend my shack a few feet to the west.

I am working on that.

Take 2 books and a surprise gift FREE!

SPECIAL LIMITED-TIME OFFER

Mail to: The Mystery Library™
3010 Walden Ave.
P.O. Box 1867
Buffalo, N.Y. 14240-1867

YES! Please send me **2 free books** from the Mystery Library™ and my free surprise gift. Then send me 3 mystery books, first time in paperback, every month. Bill me only $4.19 per book plus 25¢ delivery and applicable sales tax, if any*. There is no minimum number of books I must purchase. I can always return a shipment at your expense and cancel my subscription. Even if I never buy another book from the Mystery Library™, **the 2 free books and surprise gift are mine to keep forever.**

415 WEN CJQN

Name _____ (PLEASE PRINT) _____

Address _____ Apt. No. _____

City _____ State _____ Zip _____

* Terms and prices subject to change without notice. N.Y. residents add
  applicable sales tax. This offer is limited to one order per household and not
  valid to present subscribers.

© 1990 Worldwide Library.

MYS98

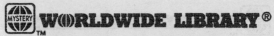

DEATH

IN GOOD COMPANY
EDGAR AWARD WINNER

GRETCHEN SPRAGUE
A MARTHA PATTERSON MYSTERY

Frustrated by retirement, Martha Patterson is now a pro bono attorney, working for West Brooklyn Legal Services, a poverty-law firm. But she's getting more human reality than she ever bargained for.

It begins with the visit of client Wilma Oberfell, whose words "I don't know whom I can trust" echo long after Martha discovers her strangled body. Unable to dismiss the murder as simply another casualty of poverty, Martha probes Wilma's complex and tragic life…and uncovers a shocking tale of greed, fraud and murder.

Available February 1999 at your favorite retail outlet.